D0181586

HER OWN VIETNAM

Also by Lynn Kanter

The Mayor of Heaven
On Lill Street

HER OWN VIETNAM

LYNN KANTER

Shade Mountain Press
Albany, New York

Shade Mountain Press
P.O. Box 11393
Albany, NY 12211
www.shademountainpress.com

Kanter, Lynn
Her own Vietnam / Lynn Kanter
ISBN 978-0-9913555-2-5 (pbk.: alk. paper)
1. Vietnam War, 1961–1975—Fiction. 2. Vietnam War,
1961–1975—Veterans—Fiction. 3. Women and war—Fiction.
4. Nurses—Fiction. 5. Women veterans—Fiction.

Also available as an eBook

Printed in the United States of America by
    McNaughton & Gunn
17 16 15   4 3 2

Excerpts from *Her Own Vietnam* have been published in *Verbsap*
(2005); and *Lost Orchard*, ed. Jo Pitkin (State University of New York
Press, 2014).

The author and publisher gratefully acknowledge these generous
donors for their major financial support of Shade Mountain Press:
Pedro Cabán, Heather Burns and Kathleen Maloy, Mary Hood,
Rubén and Moraima Morales, Paul Navarro, and Steve Calderwood.

Shade Mountain Press is committed to publishing literature by
women.

Cover photo: Janet Coleman. Author photo: Michelle Frankfurter.

FOR JANET

I don't speak about Vietnam, and most people in my world don't even know I'm a veteran. I prefer it that way.

—Mary "Chris" Banigan
Captain, U.S. Army Nurse Corps,
Vietnam 1969–1971

CHAPTER 1

DELLA BROWN pushed open her front door and stepped inside. The house felt clenched like a held breath, until she reminded herself that Abby was gone. Funny how the silence of a house where no one else lived felt different from the hush of a house where everyone was out.

But there were all kinds of silences.

When Abby was growing up, Della sometimes imagined the serenity of an empty nest. Now she had one, and it took some getting used to. No loud music, no dirty dishes in the sink. No one to talk to. Her knees creaked as she stooped to pick up the mail scattered across the dark linoleum floor.

In the kitchen, she watched blue flame bloom under the dented silver teakettle before she flicked on the light. The butter-colored walls and worn wooden table made the room feel cozy despite the afternoon chill. It was late February. Spring was weeks away from her corner of New York state. Della was wearing a blue short-sleeved scrub suit, and when she ran her hands down her arms, the skin felt pebbled.

She sorted through the mail. A bill. Another bill. Junk mail for recycling. *The Clinical Journal of Oncology Nursing.* A hot pink card inviting Abby to rant and rave at some club. She hesitated before sailing that one into the recycling pile. Abby wouldn't care about a club here; she was sharing a rundown apartment in Manhattan with six other girls, all trying to make it as actresses. Della slapped down another bill. Then she held up a slim white envelope.

It was a letter, an honest-to-God letter. She'd thought they were extinct. The handwriting was familiar, though she couldn't place it. The return address in Boston meant nothing to her. She raised the envelope to her nose, but all she found was the vanilla scent of her own hand lotion.

Della sat down at the table. The bentwood chair's gold corduroy cushion, which Abby had made in seventh grade, was worn to a velvety stubble like the miraculous new hair that emerges after chemo. The fabric prickled against the back of her legs as she slit the envelope and pulled out the single typed sheet.

Hello, Della.

Been a while, hasn't it? I tried to find you so many times, back in the day. Now here we are—well past fifty!—and thank goodness for the Internet.

Here's why I'm writing. My son Will is getting married this summer. Now, this isn't one of those June-moon-swoon kinds of wedding. Will is twenty-seven, and his bride is thirty-three. They're paying for the whole thing, and they don't want a big bash. My husband and I are only allowed to invite ten people. My son said, just invite the ten people who've meant the most to you.

There was something about the way he put it that really made me think. And what can I say, Della, you made the top ten.

Now I know that's kind of strange, since you and I haven't spoken since before Will was born. And I know that seeing each other again after all these years is more than a notion. So I'm not going to invite you to the wedding of a boy you've never met, but I am writing to ask if you will see me sometime. We can meet in your town, my town, or somewhere in between. You choose.

Don't worry, I'm not going to stalk you like that little corporal from Minnesota. Remember him? I bet you do. I bet you remember all of it, like I do. They say time heals all wounds. I don't know about you, but I'm still waiting.

Della, I hope this letter doesn't upset you. If it does, just remind yourself... it don't mean nothin'.

—Charlene (Johnson) Randall

Della's heart racketed around in her chest. She twisted off the flame beneath the shrieking kettle. She refolded the letter and held it flat between her palms like a prayer.

Charlene Johnson. Her closest friend, her comrade, the one person she had ever trusted with her life. No way was she going to call Charlene Johnson.

It didn't matter that she missed Charlene, missed her with a yearning that had grown fierce and lean from feeding on silence. What mattered was that Della had spent the past thirty years trying to erase the one thing she and Charlene had in common.

Della was twenty-two years old when she returned from Vietnam, twenty-two and broken already. It was only a year of her life that took place ages ago. But the experience still fluttered against her heart, like a moth tucked away in a box of sweaters. Years later you could reopen the box only to find that the moth had chewed the sweaters into shreds, then vanished in a smear of dust.

"But why did you have to go to Vietnam?" her daughter, Abby, had once asked, peering down from the heights of adolescence, from which she could see that everything Della had ever done was wrong. "Why did you even join the Army?"

Abby could not imagine how few options a working woman had in those days, when the women's movement was just a rumor to be ridiculed on the evening news. After high school, Della had known exactly what her choices were. She could spend her life in restaurants, as her mother had. She could learn to cut hair. She could be a secretary, or a teacher, or a nurse. But those careers would take years of schooling, and Della could barely afford a semester.

The bargain had seemed simple enough at the time. The Army paid for two years of nursing school. In return, they owned her for three years. And where did Abby think the military had sent its newly trained nurses in 1969—to Berkeley, perhaps, to care for the injured protesters?

No, ma'am. It was first stop, Long Binh; next stop, Cu Chi. Last stop, forget about humanity and hold on to your sanity. If you can.

Della knew her daughter never would have made such a bargain. She probably would have been an anti-war activist, flinging tear gas canisters back at the police. Abby had a life that allowed her to make choices, even mistakes, secure that there would be a margin of safety to protect her.

But no one could provide Della with that kind of life. So she began her adulthood sweating in a war zone, surrounded by carnage and courage and pure brutal stupidity. Even today, if she thought about it too long—if she thought about it at all—Vietnam could rise from the dead and blot out the sun with its powdery wings.

As she sat at the kitchen table, the letter began to rattle in her hands. It was only fear. Fear was an old companion, and she understood its many moods. This was not the spiky panic that followed a loud sound late at night. It was the deep cold dread that sometimes gripped Della when she began to realize exactly what she was in for. She had felt it after Abby was born, the first time she faced three a.m. with a screaming infant she could not comfort. She had felt it the day her husband moved out. And she felt it now as Charlene's letter threw its thin light on all Della had been refusing to see.

She recognized herself, a trim woman with hazel eyes and chestnut hair dusted with gray, finally ambushed by her own history. Her own anger. Her own nostalgia. Her own bloody shadow, and her nation's.

CHAPTER 2

IT WAS AN AUGUST morning in 1969, but it could have been any time. Every day was the same festival of hell in the intensive care unit of the Twelfth Evacuation Hospital in Cu Chi, South Vietnam. Soldiers screamed in pain. Delirious men cried out for their mothers in high, staccato bursts of anguish. Doctors and nurses conversed in brisk medical shorthand, voices calm but edged with urgency. Beneath it all, oxygen tanks and respirators cranked up their faithful racket.

After three months in Vietnam, Della was intimate with the frantic rhythm of a "mass-cal," a mass casualty situation. She pushed IV morphine into a post-op patient whose legs had been sheared off by flying shrapnel. His bare chest was pale and hairless against the green hospital sheets; his face and throat were deeply tanned. He had the slender neck of an adolescent.

As she cleaned his oozing stumps with antiseptic soap and packed the wounds with absorbent fluff dressings, Della wondered if he had reached his adult height. Well, he would never be tall now. He would spend his life in a wheelchair, eye-to-eye only with children. Della bundled the dressings with layers of padded gauze bandage that gave the stumps a pillowy look. She rolled elastic stockinettes over the bulky dressings and wrapped them with ace bandages, then hung a six-pound weight from each stump to keep the skin from retracting.

With the back of her wrist, Della swiped at the sweat crawling down her forehead. She looked across the ward, a long central aisle with a row of forty-five cots on either side. The men in these beds had been charred by flame, lacerated by gunfire, dismembered by explosions, mangled by shrapnel, ravaged in every conceivable way by the technologies of war. Some of the patients were recovering from surgery; others were marshalling the strength to survive an operation. Several were beyond the help of a surgeon's blade. Every few minutes she could hear the pounding heartbeat of the hospital: the *whup-whup-whup* of a helicopter delivering fresh casualties from the battlefield.

Della scanned the nearby cots and spotted a red stain blossoming on a white dressing. She grabbed the angled scissors from the sleeve pocket of her fatigues and cut the bandages from the soldier's thigh. A few small blood vessels had begun to leak underneath the dressings. Della smiled at the patient, a boy with honey-colored skin, curly black hair, and a shadow on his upper lip that was more bravado than mustache.

"Don't worry, this is no problem," she told him, and watched the pucker of anxiety disappear from between his heavy eyebrows. She touched each rupture with what looked like a matchstick, its head treated with silver nitrate. The nitrate cauterized the bleeders, turning the blood vessel gray at the point of contact. She had long ago learned to ignore the sickly sweet odor of the singed tissue. Swiftly she redressed his wounds and moved on to the next bed.

For twelve hours a day, six days a week, this I.C.U. and the doctors, nurses, and corpsmen who inhabited it were Della's universe. She knew them all so well—their moves, their skills, their talents, their breaking points, their steps in the risky ballet of combat medicine.

The patients she knew sometimes by name, and sometimes only by the roll call of their damage. With steady hands, Della received the wounded. With soothing voice she eased them into the primeval world of flesh and pain that would now be their home.

One of her patients today had been injured when a white phosphorus flare he was carrying went off accidentally. White phosphorus was perfect for marking targets because it ignited when exposed to air, releasing dense white smoke. Willy Pete, the guys called it, like a friend who demanded respect. But Della only saw Willy Pete after it had gone wrong. Once it touched flesh, the substance turned savage, penetrating layer after layer of tissue until it burned through to the bone. It was almost impossible to pick every fleck of Willy Pete out of a charred, raw wound.

When Della removed her patient's bandages to change the dressing, his burns began to smoke, the residual white phosphorus reignited by the fresh air. She rushed to neutralize it by pouring on a solution of diluted copper sulfate as the soldier tried to stifle his screams.

Morning stretched into afternoon. Della ran IVs, changed catheters, turned patients in their beds, monitored vital signs. Still the helicopters thundered in with new casualties. Hour after hour she replaced dressings saturated with pus and blood. She clamped chest tubes and emptied glass suction bottles that had filled, in ghastly shades of yellow, pink, and white, with fluid from men's lungs. There was no time to stop, to rest, to eat. The urgency of the work and Della's sizzling adrenaline kept her in motion. It was not until the sun faded and she began to click on the gooseneck lamps that she realized the choppers had stopped bombarding them with fresh bodies. For a moment, the war and the healers had reached a draw.

She hoisted herself up on a gurney and slumped there, elbows on knees, staring past her boots at the filthy concrete floor, awash in blood and gauze and the plastic wrappers from bandages. The other medical staff had taken similar postures of exhaustion, resembling casualties themselves in their bloodstained uniforms. It was like those moments in high school at the end of swim practice, Della thought, when she realized she had given everything to the water and had no strength to meet the gravity of the dry world.

In a few minutes, most of the nurses would begin to clean up and restock supplies to prepare for the next batch of casualties. They would mix IV bottles and do another round of wound care and monitoring. But Della would not join them. Tonight she had a different job. She had been assigned to body bag duty.

Together with a somber handful of other nurses and corpsmen, Della would unfold thick, green plastic bags to take care of the soldiers no one could save. They would not get to bathe the bodies or tidy the gory uniforms the soldiers had arrived in; they could not indulge in any of the small rituals that sought to sanctify death even here, in its hometown. This was strictly a bag-and-tag operation. They would go through each boy's pockets to itemize his possessions, and in the process collide with his vanished life—the photo of his girlfriend in her prom gown, the letter from his dad, the guitar pick he carried for luck.

Even worse were the leftover body parts, the severed legs and arms, now cold and doughy to the touch and shockingly heavy. They would strive to match all the pieces together so that each corpse could go home whole, but it could not always be done. Sometimes torsos had been blown into mush; hands or legs had been left on the battlefield. On days like that, body bag detail was nothing more than a grisly game of mix 'n match. Della had learned this early in her tour by trying to match a blown-off foot with the patient it came from. The task was not just to satisfy the Army's need for tidy accounting: the soldier's dog tags were stashed in his boot. He must have found that the jangling metal disks made too much noise when he wore them around his neck.

❧

THE SUN HAD disappeared by the time Della finally stepped through the swinging double doors of the hospital. The sodden heat of Cu Chi wrapped her in the mingled smells of mud, fuel, sewage, and rotting vegetation that she and her friends called *eau d' Nam.* Tonight Della noticed another, sharper scent—cigarette smoke. She did not have to see him to know who it was.

"Mac," she said quietly.

He was squatting against the corrugated metal wall of the Quonset hut that held the I.C.U., the sleeves of his faded fatigues rolled up to the elbow. His face was tipped down and covered in shadow, and the overhead light turned his tousled brown hair golden. Without haste, he rose to greet her.

She nodded at the cigarette. "Those things'll shorten your life, you know."

"Yeah, I've been meaning to quit." The joke was too familiar to bring a laugh—how long could a chopper pilot in Vietnam expect to live, anyway?—but they both paused to acknowledge the effort.

"What are you doing out here?" she asked.

"Waiting for you." He ground out the cigarette against the sole of his boot and slipped the butt into his shirt pocket. "Came to see if I could take you out to dinner."

"What time is it?" Her watch had stopped sometime in the early afternoon, and she'd had to borrow one from a corpsman to complete her shift. Now Della's surroundings gave no clue of the hour. At night the vast Army base was a mosaic of large circles of harsh yellow light, surrounded by craters of darkness. The sky was no help either; it was the rainy season, and even in daylight the sky looked as low and gray as the arched roof of the Quonset hut.

Mac ambled over to her, his boots announcing each step on the raised wooden walkway that traversed the red mud. "What does it matter what the clock says? It's time to relax, to lay back and let the night sky shine down on you."

"Oh, a poet." Della could hear her voice automatically fall into the joking cadence she used with all the guys.

"That's right. I'm the poet of the sky, here to wine and dine you in style. My chopper awaits." He inclined his head in the direction of the helipad.

These pilots—extravagant with words, but they didn't waste a gesture.

"You do know the mess hall is within walking distance," she said.

"No mess hall for you tonight. I'll take you to any officers' club you name."

"Honolulu."

He laughed. "Any O club within an hour's flying time."

Della ran her hands down the front of her uniform and felt the crusty stains, the ballpoint pens poking up from the chest pocket. "I'm dressed a little informally. I don't think blood and guts will do for evening wear."

"I'll wait if you want to clean up." Mac leaned in closer. She could see his long, thick lashes, the hollows of weariness under his heavy-lidded green eyes. "But you look beautiful to me, Della."

Back in the World, that line might have moved her. But here, surrounded by thousands of young men, she heard it a dozen times a day. "Beautiful" was just a synonym for "female" or, more likely, "available." And if there was anything Della was not, it was available.

She studied Mac. "Well, you look married to me."

He took a quick step backwards. "How does someone look married?"

"By rubbing his thumb across his ring finger, like you're doing now."

The pilot slid his hands into his pockets. "I'm not married." His grin revealed a slender gap between his two front teeth. "No one's married here."

"I've noticed that."

"C'mon, Della." Even with three feet of space between them, Mac had a way of crowding her. Maybe it was his voice, low and confident and sliding over her skin like suede. "Tonight will be something special. I'll take you to a place you've never been."

"Oh, really? And where might that be?"

He said it with reverence. "The sky."

In fact she had flown in a helicopter. She knew about the thrilling ascent, the shudder of the rotor lifting her far from the animal clash of war. She had seen a fresh green planet spread out beneath the dangling boots of soldiers who perched in the open doorways and trained their rifles on the ground.

It was the other journey Mac offered, the journey of skin and breath and heat, that Della had never taken. And now it was too late. She couldn't lose herself in a man's flesh after she'd seen so many butchered.

Footsteps clattered toward them on the wooden planks. Della recognized the rise and fall of women's voices—Charlene and Mary Grace, two of her roommates in the nurses' quarters. A rush of relief took her by surprise.

"Hi, guys," Charlene called out.

"Hey, Charlene," Mac replied, defeat already in his voice.

Mary Grace scooted past them, her hands clasped in front of her as if she had captured a small, wild creature between her palms. "I can't stop to chat," she said, her eyes fixed on her boots. "We've been doing lap tapes, and if I don't get in the shower within the next ten minutes I'll just have to kill myself, which shouldn't be too difficult considering where we are."

Mac turned to Della. "Music for lap dances?"

"Not even close. In the operating room they use lap tapes to soak up the blood. Usually they throw them out, but when we're short on supplies they have to reuse them. The O.R. nurses boil them in big tubs."

"Why would Mary Grace freak out about doing laundry?"

She left it to Charlene, an operating room nurse, to explain. "Have you ever seen your mother make chicken soup?" Charlene asked Mac. The brown skin of her throat glistened with sweat.

"Yeah, I think so."

"You know how she has to keep skimming off little pieces of fat and skin while the broth boils?"

"Got it." He whistled lightly through his teeth. "You nurses must have balls of brass."

"That must be it," Charlene said. "I'm heading home. It's been a rough day."

Mac nodded. "Roger that."

Charlene moved off. "Della, you coming?" she said over her shoulder. "Johnnie's waiting in the hooch."

"Be right there."

"Wait," said Mac. "How about dinner?"

Della thought of different answers. That she was twenty-one years old and still believed in the possibility of one true love. That she hoped to God the one for her was not as doomed and luckless as a soldier in Vietnam.

"Maybe another time, Mac. I'm beat."

"Della, who's this Johnnie guy?"

She smiled. Here, at last, was something she could give him. "It's not a guy. It's a bottle. Johnnie Walker."

Finally Della knew what time it was. Time to drink.

CHAPTER 3

IN THE KITCHEN, Della ran her thumbnail down the crease where Charlene had folded her letter. It made a noise like the sweep of a broom, and Della realized that Charlene must have heard the same sound just a few days ago. Charlene had handled this sheet of paper, she had flattened it into thirds, she had released it into a mailbox. She was real.

For so many years Charlene had been a confidante, someone who could hold Della's most searing thoughts and never get singed because she was only a memory. Now Charlene had touched her with this handful of words and Della didn't know what to feel. She might be lonely, once Charlene was no longer a presence she carried in her head, but a flesh and blood woman with demands of her own. And then Della might fail her once again.

She stuffed the letter into the envelope and pushed away from the table with a squeak of wood against linoleum. Her family would be over for dinner soon, and her mother would be staying over for a couple of nights while her own apartment got painted. Della was nowhere near ready. She hurried to the bedroom, shoved the letter in the back of her underwear drawer, and yanked off her scrubs.

She was standing under the shower, hot water beating against her back, when she felt it—the familiar ache somewhere beneath her bones, a hurt deep inside a hollow. An ominous thump of pain, like a chord played on the lowest keys of a piano. Della had never found a way to describe or explain this hurt, so she hadn't told anyone about it. It was like a phantom limb: you wanted to press the injured spot, soothe the damage with your hand, but there was nothing to hold. The bones of a phantom limb could never be set, its muscles never eased. Nothing could heal a part of you that was already lost.

❧

"ANY PLACE CAN be home to me," Anne Isaacs said as she speared a chunk of tofu with her fork. "I'm not that picky."

They dined together most Thursday nights—Della, her mother, Ruth, her sister, Rosalind, and Rosalind's partner, Anne. Della had organized the weekly dinners shortly after her divorce, so her daughter could feel part of a strong family structure. Abby, of course, had lost interest almost immediately. Now, seven years later, even Della could no longer tell if the ritual was a pleasure or a habit.

"If anyplace is home," said Rosalind, "I guess we can return that fancy new stove."

"That's not what I meant. I like living here, and I love cooking for our friends. But we can move to Denver if you want. It's not that important to me, because my home is in here." She tapped her chest. "And with you."

Della turned to her sister. "Now don't you feel small?"

"Tiny." Rosalind pressed her thumb and forefinger together.

"Girls, girls," their mother murmured, as if they were tussling over dolls. She sat on the edge of her chair, both feet flat on the floor, slicing her steak into stamp-sized pieces. Age had settled on her face like a veil. Her blue eyes were clear, but her eyebrows had turned as white as her hair. Della wondered when that had happened.

"Now what are you going on about?" Ruth asked Rosalind.

"I got a call from a company in Denver," said Rosalind. "They want to talk to me about a job."

"Oh, my word. Don't they have enough lawyers out there?"

"Apparently not."

The heavy smell of meat clung to every surface in Della's kitchen that night: the wide wooden table, the nubby cotton placemats, the flowered curtains that framed the black window above the sink, even her own clothes. When it was her turn to cook, Della took care to prepare varied, interesting vegetarian meals. Why her relatives sometimes felt the need to contribute their own carnage was a mystery to her.

"You know, Rosalind, you'd probably like tofu just as much as steak if you smothered it in ketchup like that."

"I doubt it. Anyway, I'm middle-aged. I don't need to learn to like any new foods."

"Yes," Anne said, "we wouldn't want to have any new experiences at our age. Now tell me again, honey, why do you want to move across the country?"

"Very funny. But doesn't it intrigue you at all? A whole different way of life, in a different landscape. Maybe we could get into snow sports."

"You mean like skiing? We live in the snow belt. How come we don't ski here?"

Rosalind exchanged a glance with her sister. "Because skiing is for rich people," she intoned.

"And golf is for Republicans," Della chanted in reply.

"What about tennis?" prompted Ruth.

"Tennis is for tourists!" they sang out in unison.

Their mother gave a delighted laugh. "I am so tickled you girls remember."

The gospel according to Ruth. How could they forget? "Anne," Della said, "what would you do in Denver?"

"First I would buy myself a big cowboy hat and some boots." She smiled. "Then I guess I would work in a flower shop."

"You wouldn't consider practicing law again?"

"Nope. Those days are over."

"But what about all your education?" Ruth said. "It's such a waste."

When Della had first met Anne, some fifteen years ago, she had thought this new girlfriend of Rosalind's was likable enough and pleasant looking. Now that she'd grown to love Anne, Della couldn't imagine how she had failed to notice her quiet beauty.

They made a striking couple—Anne and her wintry coloring, blue-gray eyes and black hair, next to tall, sunny Rosalind and her wild auburn curls. Rosalind and Della had the same square forehead with its off-center widow's peak, the same full lips bracketed by deep smile lines, the same strong, arched eyebrows. But Rosalind had lively brown eyes and a smooth, freckled face that made her look at least a decade younger than Della, instead of the five years that really separated them.

"The way I see it," said Anne, "a florist provides people with beauty and comfort. If you can do that and still draw a paycheck, why would you want to do anything else?"

Ruth nodded. "My work feeds the body, and yours feeds the soul. And there's not much of a paycheck either way."

"Whereas my work pays very well," Rosalind added cheerfully, "and feeds the corrupt egos of some rich white capitalists down in New York City."

Della felt as though she was watching it all from a distance, perhaps hovering somewhere near the ceiling. She wondered what Abby was doing right now, as their family played out patterns that had become so routine. It had seemed timeless and unchangeable, these women gathered around a table. Yet look how it had changed already.

Aunt Liz had been gone for three years, pulled under by ovarian cancer. The doctors told her she was imagining her symptoms. Della's mother always seemed invulnerable, but she tired easily these days and she was, incredibly, eighty years old. And here was Rosalind, talking about launching a new life far away and taking Anne with her.

For the moment, at least, they were still together—laughing, bickering, retelling threadbare stories, chafing under the well-worn habits of love and expectation. All of it cherished. All of it doomed.

"Besides," Anne said, "I love working with my hands. There's something so calming about it."

"I don't remember feeling all that calm," Ruth said, "when I had a knife in one hand and a spatula in the other, and a waiter behind me demanding his special order."

"No. But you worked with fire. Or patients," she said, nodding at Della. "I just work with flowers. Once you get the hang of it, it's almost Zen—mindful and mindless at the same time."

"I should try it," Della said.

"Come on over Saturday night. Rosalind's going to some law firm event, and I'm bringing home work to do over the weekend."

"Maybe I will."

"Do it," Anne said. "I could use another set of hands." She rose. "Who wants dessert? We brought ice cream."

"I've got ice cream," said Della.

"No one but you eats vanilla." Rosalind stacked the used plates.

"Isn't it thoughtful of them to make it just for me?"

"I mean no one else eats it plain. Vanilla ice cream is a side dish, to go with pie or cake. It should never be alone on a plate."

"You live your life by a bizarre set of rules, Rozzie."

"Oh please. You're the one who can't lay the pen down till the crossword puzzle is finished. You're the one who hides inside on the Fourth of July."

"Those aren't rules. Those are preferences."

"Those are weirdnesses."

Anne stood. "Rosalind, if you're finished tormenting your sister, let's bring in the dessert."

Della stayed with her mother, who sat perfectly erect, her eyes closed and her right hand resting on the table. Della studied her hand, the green veins pushing up through the pale gathered skin, the tiny puckers and scars that told of a lifetime in kitchens.

Placing her own hand next to Ruth's, Della noted their similar shape and blunt, capable fingers. She could visualize the delicate architecture of her mother's bones, her body's secret societies of blood vessels, its tangled neighborhoods of nerves. So much went on beneath the skin. So many processes, so many exchanges, so many connections made and missed. It was a wonder anyone survived into old age.

Rosalind carried in two round cartons. "Della, you need to turn up your freezer. Look what it did to my ice cream." She raised the scoop dramatically over the bowl and released a soft mound of peppermint with a *thomp.*

Della's stomach pitched. She lurched away from the table.

"Where are you going?" Rosalind asked. "This is for you."

"Coffee."

Leaning over the kitchen sink, Della turned on the cold water and let it cascade over her wrists. But her body was already ringing in alarm, and she knew nothing could stop it.

Oh fuck, she thought. *Incoming.*

Shivering, Della forced herself to reach for the coffeepot. Although she hadn't had an anxiety episode in well over a decade, the calming mantra she used to practice surfaced immediately. *I'm safe at home. I'm far from war.* Everything was familiar, she told herself, everything was fine. Here she was, scooping out the dark grounds. Here she was, pouring in the water. Behind the trickle of the brewing coffee, she could hear her family chatting just a few feet away, spoons chiming against bowls.

Della was doing all she could to hide her agitation, yet it made her feel terribly lonely that no one had noticed. A warm arm across her shoulders would comfort her—or maybe make her skin crawl. Damn her family. Damn that letter.

"Coffee's in the living room," she called out, and sprinted past the table, carrying the pot and a bouquet of mugs and spoons.

"No coffee for me," said Ruth. "I don't want to be up all night."

"It's decaf," Rosalind said.

"Decaf comes out the same as regular. I don't want to wake Della running to the bathroom all night."

"Got it."

Della sank into the big soft chair in front of the empty fireplace. Taking deep breaths, she inhaled the acrid smell of past blazes. Her blood slammed inside her head.

"Della, what's the matter?" Rosalind slipped off her black, pinstriped suit jacket and folded it over the back of the faded brown couch. "You're rushing around like someone's charging you by the minute."

Della saw Ruth lower herself into the wooden rocking chair. "I just...got the jitters, that's all."

"Why?" said Anne.

Della watched the overhead light reflected in her coffee cup shiver into fragments with each beat of her heart. "I was thinking about some things that happened a long time ago, in Vietnam."

"God." Anne took in a breath. "I keep forgetting you were ever there."

"Lucky you."

"Oh honey," said Ruth, "no one wants to hear those old stories." Her rocking chair halted with the slap of sneakers on the wooden floor. "If we have to talk about war, let's talk about the fresh one they're brewing in Iraq. I don't believe for one minute that Saddam had anything to do with 9/11."

"Neither do I," said Rosalind. "This war is about nothing but oil—if there even is a war."

"Of course there's going to be a war!" said Ruth. "I wouldn't be a bit surprised to wake up tomorrow and hear that Bush Jr. invaded Iraq already, without telling us. He's a sneaky one."

"I'd rather hear Della's stories," said Anne. Rosalind shot her a look Della couldn't read.

The liveliness drained from Ruth's face. "You girls can go traipsing down memory lane if you like." She pushed herself up with a grunt. "I'm going to bed."

After she left they were silent, like chastised children. Anne poured herself some coffee. Rosalind tugged off her leather boots and folded her legs underneath her on the couch. The silky lining of her trousers made a hissing sound when she moved. "Okay, Della, spill it," she said. "Don't think I didn't see you doing your little astral projection thing at the sink."

"What?"

"You left your body behind while the rest of you went God knows where. It's your special talent. What happened?"

"It's no big deal. I got a letter from someone I knew during the war. And it kind of ... I don't know. It stirs things up." Della folded her arms across her chest.

"So you're finally going to tell me about it." Rosalind's voice climbed.

"It just came in today's mail."

"No, I mean about Vietnam. All this time, Della—you've never talked about it."

"You never asked."

"Oh, come on. We must have. When you first got home?"

"When I first got home, you were a surly seventeen-year-old. Your only concern was staying out all night with your friends. Mom's whole goal in life was to keep you from getting pregnant."

Rosalind grinned. "Well, she sure did a good job."

"Why don't you tell us about it now?" said Anne.

"It's a little late for that, don't you think?" The edge in her voice surprised even Della. She tried to make her tone more neutral. "It was just a letter, Anne. I'd rather let it go."

"The Brown family is very good at letting things go." Anne walked over to the bookcase, packed with paperback mysteries, and reached for a thick white candle from the top shelf. "Too bad for you, I'm not a Brown." She set the candle on the coffee table and struck a match. They all watched as the flame trembled and took hold. Anne turned to Della and raised her eyebrows.

"I—I wouldn't know where to begin," said Della.

"Start anywhere," Anne said. "Just start talking, and you can fill in the rest later."

Start anywhere. Anne was right—it didn't make any difference. Because no matter where Della began to tell this story, there was no way she could make Anne and Rosalind understand. No one could understand who hadn't been there. And those who had been there were the most baffled of all.

CHAPTER 4

THE FIRST SHOCK was the airplane. Della couldn't believe the Army sent troops to battle in a regular commercial airliner staffed with friendly, hardworking flight attendants. It was May 1969, and the war had been dragging on for years—plenty of time for the Army to equip its own planes.

There were only two female passengers, Charlene Johnson and Della. They introduced themselves as they took seats in the front of the plane. Charlene was tall and slender, one of the few black nurses Della had met in the Army. She had a striking face with a broad forehead, large, luminous eyes, and prominent cheekbones tapering down to a sharp chin. The two women chatted for a few minutes, and then Charlene dozed off. Della figured they'd have plenty of time to talk later. The flight would take more than twenty hours.

Behind them stretched endless rows of soldiers in crew cuts and fatigues, partying their way across the world. Peering down the plane's length, Della saw that most of the guys had settled into groups made up of their own race. The bobbing faces merged into masses of brown, tan, and pink, like countries on an old-fashioned map of a narrow continent.

This, then, was her nation's fighting force. Della wasn't sure what she had expected combat troops to look like, but not this. During eight weeks of basic training in San Antonio, she had often observed the decorated officers, middle-aged men who strode the grounds of Fort Sam Houston with an air of command. This couldn't really be who they commanded.

She had seen the new recruits practice their ragged drills, had heard their ritual chants rise and fall in the dusty air. But somehow she had expected a transformation to take place before they shipped out, some last-moment infusion of steel that would turn them into warriors. It hadn't happened. These were only kids, boisterous boys with exaggerated gestures and loud voices.

Sprinkled among the young men were a few older ones with longer hair and lined faces, their fatigues faded. Maybe they were not so much older as more... weighty. There was a weariness about them, a gravity. Della guessed they were experienced soldiers, returning to Vietnam after a leave or to begin a second tour. And while they were as rowdy as the rest, these men held themselves aloof from the new soldiers. They chattered with one another, mingling freely across racial lines.

Della felt a surge of protectiveness for all these young men with their big guileless laughs and their long restless legs. How many would she see on the return flight a year from now?

She kept herself busy on the plane studying a map of South Vietnam and writing a letter home. Occasionally she peeked at Charlene. How the woman could sleep through all this commotion, wearing her uncomfortable uniform, Della couldn't imagine. The Army, with its typical attention to detail and disregard for logic, required nurses to travel in their light green "cord" uniforms—fitted short-sleeved top, trim skirt, and black leather pumps. Apparently it was important for the women to look ladylike on their way to hell.

Della could feel her feet beginning to swell in the stupid pumps to the point where she didn't dare take off her shoes for fear she'd have to hobble into Vietnam barefoot. It was a little cold on the airplane, but the flight attendants had already handed out all the blankets. Later, as she sweated through Vietnamese nights as hot and moist as the inside of a dog's mouth, she would try to soothe herself to sleep by recalling every cold sensation of that plane ride: the tensed muscles, the prickly skin, the fresh chill each movement brought.

It was nice to have some female company on the journey, even if Charlene was unconscious. Della had never been in such a male universe. Few women had. Still, she thought she probably knew less about men than most women her age. She'd grown up without brothers, and her father was gone before she developed an interest in boys. So there was no one to enlighten her about the alien species except her mother, whose advice boiled down to, "They can be a lot of fun, but a lot of trouble."

Of course Della was familiar with male anatomy from nursing school and, before that, from high school. She used to giggle with her girlfriends about the poor boys with their apparently uncontrollable erections and their mortifying attempts to hide them—the stack of books they'd hold in front of themselves, the sweatshirts they'd tie around their waists like aprons.

The first time Della had felt an erection pressed against her, she'd been surprised by how firm it was, how insistent and alive, like a trapped animal. She was slow dancing with Ronnie Schuyler, to a scratchy recording of Dusty Springfield singing "You Don't Have to Say You Love Me." All around them in the large dim family room, other couples swayed like underwater plants, their feet motionless on the thin carpet. Della could smell patchouli oil and perfume, the tang of onion dip, the musty odor of the basement world where teenage life was allowed to blossom.

She was thrilled to be dancing with Ronnie, one of the most popular boys in school. He had shoulder-length blond hair and sleepy blue eyes. She'd heard he carried a silver flask in the pocket of his ragged jeans, and now she believed it because she could feel something solid pressing against her hipbone. As the pleading music heightened, Ronnie slid his hands from her waist to her hips, pulling Della even closer. His breath grew hot on her neck. She had only a few moments to recognize what was happening before Ronnie clutched her to him, his hands squeezing her spasmodically as a long tremor coursed through his body.

He slumped against her, his chin resting on her shoulder, his breath choppy as if he had been running. They stood like that for several seconds, Della's arms around his neck, while his breathing slowed. Somehow, none of the nearby couples seemed to notice the magical event that had just occurred. Or maybe it was happening all around them in the dusk.

Ronnie straightened up and smiled at her, half bashful, half grateful. He took Della's hand and tugged her toward the dog-smelling couch. When they sat down he grabbed a record cover from the table and set it on his lap.

Della felt fizzy all over, like a giant soft drink. There was a tingling between her legs and down the back of her neck. Her brain was bubbling over with questions, like, how big was the wet spot Ronnie was hiding with the album cover, whether he could feel the wetness shooting out, whether it was thin like pee, or thicker like saliva, or slimy like the white of an egg. Whether his penis was still bulging, or had already gone back to its regular size, whatever that was. Did it deflate slowly, like a beach ball? There was no way she could ask him any of that.

Della was flattered to the point of dizziness that dancing with her had somehow turned Ronnie on so much that he had lost control. At the same time she suspected that his excitement had nothing to do with her. It was just an interaction of hormones and chemicals, nature playing out its patterns in the flesh of two young animals. Either way, she couldn't wait for it to happen again.

They dated throughout her junior and senior years, and while Della made sure they never went all the way—the phrase they earnestly used with one another—she did manage to learn the answers to her questions. Then he went to college and Della went to nursing school, where men were patients or doctors, and women were too busy to think of them otherwise. Now Ronnie was finishing his degree, and Della was the one hurtling through the night on her way to Vietnam, connected to home only by the flimsy airmail stationery beneath her fingers.

As Della finished her letter, Charlene finally stirred. She had been asleep for hours, and had missed the chicken dinner. They didn't know the airline would serve them the same meal twice more before the flight ended.

"Oh man, I'm going to need a neck brace," Charlene said, twisting her head slowly. "These seats are murder."

"Yeah, I guess they weren't built for such a long flight."

"I'll be right back." She stepped into the aisle, only to return a few seconds later. "Would you mind coming to the bathroom with me?"

Della looked up from her envelope. "What for?"

"The stewardess told me to come get you so you could guard the door."

"Guard you from what?"

"Gee, I dunno—two hundred sex-starved GIs, maybe?"

"How can they be sex-starved already? We just left California."

"You must not have any brothers. Could we please go before I do some serious damage to this uniform?"

Every man watched them as they edged their way down the long aisle. Della felt like she was pushing her way through peanut butter. They had almost reached the rear of the plane when a soldier leaned out and smacked Della on the bottom.

She whipped around, but couldn't tell who did it. All the men within reach were hooting and laughing. She stood paralyzed.

Charlene had no such uncertainty. She marched up to one of the chortling young men and pushed her face close to his. "Soldier, this woman is a U.S. Army nurse. She's not your playmate of the month."

"All I want is some of her tender lovin' care," he managed to choke out before doubling up in laughter. Della could see his pink scalp shining through his fresh crew cut.

"You just struck an officer. What you'll get is a tender lovin' court martial."

"What're they gonna do, send me to Vietnam?"

Derisive shouts broke out all around.

Charlene lowered her voice. "Boy, don't you realize that next week this woman could have your life in her hands?"

The young man sobered, but a voice nearby called out, "She can have me in her hands anytime, sugar, and so can you."

"Let's just go," Della whispered to Charlene, and they moved on with what dignity they could.

As they settled into their seats a few minutes later, Della asked, "Where'd you learn to talk to men like that?"

"Three younger brothers." Charlene rummaged around in her purse. "And you better learn how to do it, too." She opened her wallet and showed Della a photo of her family—three tall boys and Charlene, all with sharp cheekbones and toothy smiles, crowded around their bespectacled parents. It must have been some special occasion because everyone was dressed up, and Charlene's mother was wearing a corsage.

"What a good-looking family," said Della. "Looks like you all get along."

"Sure, my brothers can behave long enough for a snapshot. How about you—any pictures?"

Della pulled out a battered photo of her own family. "This is my mom, and here's my little sister, Rosalind. She's sixteen. Here's my Aunt Liz. We all live together." They were all laughing, leaning tipsily against each other as they perched on the steps of a narrow cement porch. Ruth looked goofy with a red bandana tied around her brown hair.

"No dad?" asked Charlene.

"Not since I was a kid." She slipped the photo back into her wallet. "Anyway, thanks for stepping in with that guy."

"For all the good it did. They don't mean any harm, you know. They just have to show off for each other."

"I know." Della looked down at her lap. "It just made me feel so … stupid."

"The way I figure it is, someone plucked this kid from his life, shaved his head, and shipped him off to Vietnam to get shot at. Talk about powerless. Now he made you feel small, so he feels a little better."

"What's your specialty? Philosophy?"

Charlene smiled. "O.R. nurse. I put in a couple of years in the operating room before joining the Army."

"I've only been working for six months," said Della. "Hope we get some training over there."

"Where are you from, Della?"

"A town in central New York that no one's ever heard of, called Sterling." She shifted in the scratchy seat and tugged her skirt down.

"Is it one of those places where everybody knows everyone else's business?"

"Well, it's not Bedford Falls, if that's what you mean. We've got a university, and the regional hospital. There's not much to do for entertainment, though. Drive fifteen minutes in any direction, and you're in farmland. What about you? I'm guessing you're a big city girl."

"Now I am. We live in Atlanta. But until I was twelve, we lived in a town a couple of hours outside Atlanta. That was some serious small-town soap opera."

"How'd you end up in Vietnam?"

Charlene sighed. "My brothers. As long as I'm here, they don't have to be."

"Really? The Army only sends one family member at a time to the war?"

"That's what my recruiter told me."

"My recruiter told me women only got sent to Vietnam if they volunteered."

"Well, I'm one of the dumb ones who did volunteer," said Charlene. "I'm the oldest kid in the family. My parents and brothers sacrificed so I could go to college. Now it's my turn."

"A college graduate and O.R. experience. That must account for the silver." A silver bar gleamed on the right collar of Charlene's uniform, indicating that she was a first lieutenant. Della was a second lieutenant, the lowest rank of officer, and she wore a gold bar that resembled a stick of butter—a "butterbar."

Charlene nodded. "What about you?"

"Diploma school, through the Army student nurse program. Got my RN, but no degree. No one in my family ever went to college. I hope my little sister will." Della peered out the window and tried to imagine what her town would look like from an airplane: the red brick university, the white church spires, the small, squat houses, all tiny and flat and merging into green and tan fields. If you flew over Sterling, the town would be gone in an instant. "Who knows, maybe I can finally save up some money this year to help her out."

"Probably not a lot to buy over there." Charlene reached up and fiddled with the metal nozzle in the overhead panel, which continued to blow a stream of stale, chilly air. "So what do you think about it—the war?"

"I haven't really thought about it all that much."

"Haven't thought about it?" Charlene swiveled to face her. "Girl, you can't turn on the tube without seeing the war. People are marching in the streets. What have you been thinking about?"

"Getting by." She felt a flush creep up her face. "It's not that I haven't noticed. Lots of guys from my high school went. I just haven't spent much time thinking about the right or wrong of it."

Charlene fell silent, biting her lower lip. "I'm sorry. I get kind of hot about this. In our neighborhood, so many guys have come back destroyed or not come back at all. There's so much death and misery, and for what? Who knows anymore? Who ever knew?"

"Well, somebody must know." Della glanced behind them at the soldiers. "I mean, those men in Congress, those generals—they're not stupid. They must know something we don't know."

"Yeah. They know their asses aren't going over there any time soon."

"But if you're so anti-war, what are you doing here?"

Charlene gestured around them. "Look at these guys. Most of them don't want to be here any more than I do. As a nurse, maybe I can help them. I'll be healing, not killing. And as long as I'm doing that, no one's going to be taking shots at my little brothers. They may get drafted—William already got his notice—but they won't get sent here."

"That sounds pretty noble. I'm just here to pay for my education."

"Nothing wrong with that."

Della tilted her seat as far back as it would go. From under half-closed lids, she watched the flight attendants work. They seemed to be in perpetual motion, serving drinks, handing out pillows, slipping out of reach of the young men's playful, prying hands. They spoke to the guys with kindness and authority, like a brisk mom. She wondered if that was how she would handle the men under her care. She wondered if the plane ever got shot at, if these women were ever afraid.

Della spoke softly, as if anyone could hear her above the rumble of engine noise and male conversation. "Charlene, are you scared?"

"Out of my mind. Are you?"

"I wasn't until you said that." She gave a weak smile. "I mean, I'm scared I won't be a good nurse. And I'm scared of being homesick. But I'm not scared for my life. I know the Army wouldn't send women where it's dangerous."

Chapter 5

Or at least that's the story Della tried to tell Anne and Rosalind. The memories throbbed against her skull, but she wasn't sure what she had actually managed to convey. Her words were a hopeful little rowboat, ferrying to shore a few salvaged scraps of meaning, while the main vessel slowly sank behind her.

"Why didn't you tell me about it when you got back?" Rosalind asked quietly. She had retreated to a corner of the couch, her arms wrapped around her knees.

The air tasted burnt from the stale coffee and the wavering candle flame. "You were a kid," said Della. "The last thing on your mind was hearing about whatever it was your ancient big sister had gone through."

"You know what? You *were* old. You came home from Vietnam and all of a sudden we weren't in the same generation anymore."

"I know." Heat spread across Della's skin; she felt like she was shrinking inside. Rosalind was accusing her of something, and she knew she was guilty—but of what?

"I've always been curious," Anne said, "about how you got to Vietnam in the first place. I've never heard you talk about it before and I didn't want to pry. But why *did* you sign up for Vietnam?"

"I didn't. My scholarship program required us to serve a year overseas, but I expected to go to Japan or the Philippines, where they were evacuating casualties from the war." Della pictured the thick manila envelope that held her orders for Vietnam. Pressing her fingers together, she could feel it still, the heft of it.

"Didn't you realize they were sending nurses to Vietnam?" asked Rosalind.

"Sure. But they told us nurses had to volunteer for the war, and there was already a long waiting list. It never occurred to me I could get sent there." Della laughed, a sharp sound that hurt her throat. "And from the way the Army prepared us, you'd think it had never occurred to them either. In basic training they taught us some skills, like how to read a compass, but mostly it was all about military ranks and rules. I remember we practiced doing a tracheotomy on a goat."

"A live goat?" Rosalind shuddered.

"The soldiers were live too, you know." Della watched out the window as the last bus of the evening trundled down the street, stamping its jumpy yellow light on the tidy house fronts. Even after all these years, she did not want to see that look of disgust on her sister's face.

"Oh, and they taught us how to march," said Della. "Every morning all the women had to march around this big quadrangle at Fort Sam Houston. All the men would watch us and laugh their heads off."

"What about, you know, guns?" said Anne.

"The whole time I was in the Army I never handled a weapon. In basic they showed us how to fire an M-16 rifle, but they didn't let us try it ourselves. In Vietnam, they kept a .45 in a cabinet in the E.R. The only instructions I ever got was to save the last round for myself."

Della fingered her temples, the soft indentations where a muzzle might fit snugly. "I realize there's no way you can really prepare anyone for—for that. But they didn't even try. They never had us talk with any of the nurses who had been there. Before we left, the Army sent us this packet of information with a map and all kinds of logistical details. What uniforms to bring, how much luggage, what time curfew began.

There was even a perky little list of do's and don'ts. 'DO be courteous and friendly! DON'T be overly familiar with the Vietnamese!' Like we were going on a class trip."

Anne, cross-legged on the edge of couch, leaned toward Della. "*Did* it ever feel like a class trip?"

Della turned her gaze to the silent, ashy fireplace. "The guys were very boisterous all the way over," she said. "But the second the captain announced we had entered Vietnamese airspace, everyone got quiet. It was eerie. We all stared out the windows. And the country— God, it was so beautiful. So green and innocent-looking. You couldn't believe anything ugly could happen there. Of course, by then we had defoliated half the land to death, but I hadn't seen that yet."

Della sat back on the sofa. So this is what it was like, she thought. Talking about Vietnam after all these years. It felt awkward and exhilarating and dangerous, like sharing intimate details of a love affair with people who had never met the lover, but disapproved of him anyway. She could only imagine how weird it must feel to her family.

"So I guess it was like a class trip," she said, "if your class liked to visit places where you could die."

"And where it was hellishly hot, from what I hear," Rosalind said.

She couldn't imagine who Rosalind had been talking to about the climate in Vietnam. "When you stepped off the plane, the heat just flattened you. And there was this smell… I almost wanted to turn around and get back on the plane, except for Charlene. I knew it would make her look bad if I chickened out. It would make all the women look bad."

"How many women were there?" asked Anne.

"No one bothered to count. Probably around ten thousand. Mostly nurses, but also translators, administrative people, you name it. And civilian women who ran recreation programs for the troops, and Red Cross volunteers who boosted morale."

"Like on *China Beach*," said Rosalind.

"Is that where you got your information? A TV show?"

"Certainly not from you."

Della's mother called from the bedroom and Della started, sloshing her cold coffee. She had forgotten Ruth was in the house.

"Dear, would you mind bringing me a glass of water?" Ruth said. "I should take my pills."

After a quick stop in the dim kitchen, Della set the water glass on her mother's bedside table. She let her glance rest on Ruth's white, shoulder-length hair spread across the periwinkle blue pillowcase. She thought Ruth looked lovely.

"Thanks, hon." Ruth reached out and cupped her hand against Della's cheek. "Della, that craziness about Vietnam? Don't get that started again."

"Okay, Mom."

From the kitchen came the sound of water running, then thumping bass notes as someone clicked on the radio to an oldies station. They heard Rosalind and Anne belting out, "What becomes of the brokenhearted?"

"Those two have too much fun, don't they?"

"I don't know." Della sat on the bed. "Is there such a thing?"

"Good point. If there is, I haven't had it yet."

"Me neither." She smiled.

"Do you ever think of your father?"

"Sometimes." A suitcase full of wind, hanging just under her heart. "What made you mention him?"

"Oh, I don't know. Something about the girls, the way they act together. It just reminded me, that's all."

"Of what?" Absently, Della touched each of her mother's pill bottles to make sure the lids were secured.

Ruth closed her eyes, revealing thin, veined lids. "Ancient history. Time to put it to rest."

"Time for you to rest, that's for sure."

"I went to the Vietnam Wall once, Della. Did you know that?"

"No. When?"

"Ten, twelve years ago. Aunt Liz and I went to Washington to see the cherry blossoms." Eyes still closed, Ruth turned her face toward

Della. "You should have seen it—that long, black wall, and all the visitors so quiet and somber. People left all kinds of messages for their loved ones. There were photos and teddy bears and wreaths all over the place. Made Liz weep, and you know she wasn't much of a crier."

"Why didn't you tell me you were there?"

"You seemed... content by then." Ruth fell silent for a moment. When she spoke again, her voice was soft with sleep. "That war's over now, Della. We've been at peace for years. You should be too."

The words fell a long way inside Della, ricocheting against her rib cage as they tumbled. She smoothed the blanket with new tenderness for her mother, this wise and sensible woman who still believed wars could end.

CHAPTER 6

THAT NIGHT Della dreamed she was about to sip a cup of coffee she had long craved. The earthy aroma embraced her. The warm, solid ceramic mug felt perfect between her cupped hands. She closed her eyes, inhaled, raised the mug.

Her lips had already parted to receive the hot liquid when her eyes fluttered open and she realized the cup was full of blood. A scream tore out of her throat but made no sound. She dropped the cup. The blood hovered in the air like a dancer's skirt. Then it fell to earth, splashing red everywhere. The white mug hit the ground, but as it shattered it made the wrong noise: a distinct, singular *thomp*. She had never heard it before, yet she knew the noise immediately.

She awoke sitting upright in bed, her heart hammering. She pressed her hand against the clammy skin of her chest. Years ago Della might have peered at her hand in the dimness, trying to see if that stickiness was blood. Now she knew it was only perspiration—not the drenching sweats of menopause, but a night terror. How peculiar, she thought for the thousandth time, that horror could become routine. Yet it happened more swiftly than anyone would imagine. She remembered some of the women she had tended in childbirth, women whose husbands beat them, the infants seared throughout gestation in the adrenaline of their mothers' terror.

Della glanced at the clock on her nightstand. Not quite four. The dream hadn't visited her in years, but now she knew it was still waiting for her, the bloody cup, just on the other side of sleep.

Shivering in her long cotton nightshirt, she pulled the blue comforter from the bed and drew it across her shoulders. The hardwood floor was chilly beneath her bare feet as she crossed the hall and opened the door to Abby's room. Her mother was asleep, snoring lightly; the room had taken on her sweet, powdery fragrance and a slight tang of unwashed hair. Della moved through the dark to her own room, then hesitated and tiptoed toward the living room.

Working the night shift in Vietnam, a nurse would never glide silently through the ward. The wounded soldiers had been in peril so long their battle reflexes were sharp and startling. Any furtive sound catapulted them awake, sending them snatching for weapons, or alarming the whole ward with cries of "Hit the dirt!" A night nurse learned to step firmly, to perform her tasks crisply, to wake men, if she had to, by shaking their big toe, standing far away from flailing arms and legs.

Della dragged her hand through her hair. She had to stop thinking about these things. She'd kept the memories at bay for so many years, and now they were ganging up on her.

I'm not going crazy, she told herself as she stretched out on the living room couch. It was just the surprise of that letter, the sound of that fucking ice cream.

Listen to me now, she thought. In country, every other word was "fuck." Since then she'd weaned herself from that vocabulary, especially after Abby was born. Now it was creeping back into her brain like an infection she'd managed to contain but not cure. And she was *beaucoup* tired of fighting it.

She turned onto her side and pulled the comforter up to her chin. Her mind skittered to the nightmare cup of coffee, and she yanked her attention away. Della tried to remember when drinking coffee had changed from a treat into a habit. Maybe in nursing school, when they all worked those rotating shifts. More likely high school, when each night she came home from her McDonald's job to begin her homework, still stinking of fries. She was an addict, no doubt about it—coffee, tea, sodas. And like all addicts she could clearly recall her first time.

It was a morning in April, the year Della was eleven. When she stumped sleepy-eyed into the kitchen, she found a strange sight. Her mother sat at the oval wooden table, the black telephone receiver pressed against her ear, one hand plunged into her messy brown hair. Her father's chair was empty. And Aunt Liz was at the house, already tipping the last of the coffee out of the pot.

Aunt Liz—her dad's younger sister—was the most glamorous person Della had ever met. She knew how to play the saxophone. She could pirouette on the tips of her toes. She had wavy, magnificent auburn hair that she would sometimes sweep up into a French twist. And she had lived in San Francisco, which to a child raised in central New York seemed as exotic as Mars.

One thing that really set Aunt Liz apart, that made Rosalind and Della look up at her with a mixture of excitement and sympathy, was the fact that she was a widow. "A *young* widow," Liz would always point out.

Her husband, Uncle George, had died in a fishing accident. "More like a drinking accident," Della had once heard her father mutter. But her mother had glared at him and glanced down at Della, so he gave his bark of a laugh and said no more.

Uncle George adored fishing. That was practically the only thing Della could remember about him. One summer when she was six, George had taken her out in his pointy silver boat with its red outboard motor.

It was early afternoon, a hot still day. Della had a cane pole with a red and white bobber on the end, and a worm wriggling just under the surface of the lake. Uncle George had a long blue pole that looked too spindly to hold a fish. He kept casting out and reeling in. She didn't understand how he hoped to catch anything that way.

He was drinking cans of beer from a small cooler under his seat. After a while Della got thirsty and reached for the thermos of water. It was the old-fashioned kind of thermos: a heavy cylinder, made of green metal with a glass liner inside. The thermos slipped from her sweaty hands onto the ridged aluminum floor of the boat. Della could hear the glass shatter. Suddenly she was desperately thirsty.

Uncle George assured her it was okay to drink the water, as long as she sucked it in through gritted teeth. Even at six, Della had known that didn't sound right. So she sat in that hot metal boat the rest of the afternoon, parched and silent, watching Uncle George slurp down beers and cast for fish that never bit. Her mother had turned white with fury when Della told her.

George had been fly-fishing when the river took him. It must have been that same year, or maybe the next. He had risked everything to teeter on slippery rocks and snatch the water's creatures out of their lives. Della wondered what he felt in that last instant of air, as the river yanked him from his rubber boots and thrashed him against the gravel. Whether he thought of beautiful Liz, of the children they might have had, or remembered the fish, their frantic struggle, their rich watery world sparkling beneath them as they dangled in the choking air.

But eleven-year-old Della had not been focused on any of that on the spring morning when she glanced from her mother to her aunt in the charged silence of the kitchen. "What's wrong?" she asked Aunt Liz.

Liz shook her head. A tendril of auburn hair caught on the side of her mouth, and she didn't bother to brush it away. "Did you sleep well?" she asked, reaching to make a second pot of coffee. Della watched her count out the scoops.

"How about some cereal?" She set a bowl on the table before Della could reply. Liz filled it too full of cornflakes, spilled in not enough milk. Della didn't dare object, mesmerized by her mother's tense, pale face.

"Yes, please call me right away if you hear anything," Ruth said in a singsong voice. She settled the heavy receiver into its cradle. "Well, that's that." She turned to Liz. "I've called every one of his friends.

Every one I know, that is." The two women exchanged a look. "And no one's heard a thing."

"Mom, what's wrong?"

She glanced at Della absently, the way her gaze sometimes slipped down the front page of the newspaper Della's dad held in front of his face at breakfast. Then she raised her chin. "Well, Della, your father's missing."

Della's empty spoon froze above the cereal bowl.

"He didn't come home last night," her mother went on. "I'm sure he's fine, but I don't know where he is."

Della's voice trembled. "He didn't go fishing, did he?"

"Of course not, sweetie." Still standing, Aunt Liz looked down at her with tender eyes, as if that distant tragedy had happened to Della instead of to her. "Tommy hates to fish. You know that."

"Where's Rozzie?" Ruth asked.

"Still sleeping," said Della. "I better go wake her. She'll miss the bus."

"No," said her mother. "Let her sleep."

And Della heard her add, as clearly as if she had spoken it aloud, *Let her stay a child a little longer.*

Aunt Liz must have heard it too, because without a word she poured a half cup of coffee, stirred in milk and sugar, and set it in front of Della. It was her first taste of coffee, sweet on the tip of her tongue and harsh on the back. She drank it all, enjoying the little jolts of electricity it sent through her chest and legs.

For weeks, detectives were as common in Della's life as teachers. At first it was the police detectives, with their narrow ties and thin smiles. Then it was a private detective with a small black vinyl notebook he snapped shut like disapproving lips. Soon the money ran out, and the detective pocketed his futile notebook. Nothing remained for Della's family but questions and the dwindling phone calls Ruth and Liz made to distant cities where someone thought they might have seen a man who resembled Della's father.

They never had a funeral. They never had an ending, never found out whether he had deserted them, or died, or was wandering the earth as an amnesiac. For all Della knew, her father had been abducted by aliens. She didn't believe in alien abductions. But then she didn't believe this world was large enough for a man to vanish in, either. She had seen enough of them try.

She strained to remember his last words to her. It was "Good night, *something*"— "Good night, sweetie pie," or "Good night, sugar pie." And what was a sugar pie, anyway?

Not that it mattered. Not that any of it mattered—what he said, where he went, how he felt. It was a comfort, really, that it was all so long ago and so meaningless. Don't mean nothin'.

"Well, what *does* mean something?" Della's mother had once snapped at her—oh, eons ago. "You've been saying that ignorant thing ever since you got home. Does anything matter to you? Anything except your booze and your precious car?"

That particular argument had had something to do with... bacon. Could that be right? It must have been breakfast time. No, it was afternoon, but she had just woken up and made her way into the kitchen, still dressed in the sweatpants and olive drab T-shirt she had slept in.

"Mom, thank you for making me bacon," Della had said, her voice rough with barely restrained irritation. "But I don't want it. I can't eat it."

"You always loved bacon. It was your favorite." Ruth pushed the thick white plate a little closer.

Della clung to her cup of black coffee, bare feet curled around the metal legs of the kitchen chair. She wondered how many beers she'd downed the night before. Even her hair hurt. "That was a long time ago."

"It was last year."

"Last year was a long time ago."

"Well, what am I supposed to do with all this bacon?" Ruth hefted the black iron skillet and poured the grease into an old coffee can.

"Why don't you eat it?"

"I can't eat bacon at this hour. It's the middle of the afternoon. Bacon is for breakfast."

"Don't you work at a restaurant that offers breakfast twenty-four hours a day?"

"That's for customers." She examined the plate. "What's the matter, not crisp enough for you?"

"Mom." Della peered down at the kitchen table, its white paint cracked like a dried riverbed. "I don't eat meat anymore. You know that. It doesn't matter how it's cooked."

"You've been home almost three weeks now. I thought you might change your mind once you got used to things again."

"Well, I won't."

"Did you meet some Army doctor that wouldn't eat meat?"

"Yeah, Mom. That's right. God knows I'd never have an idea of my own unless some man planted it in my brain." Without looking up, Della could feel the heat of her mother's blue eyes.

"You're all grown up, Della, but I am still your mother and you will treat me with respect. Don't you dare come into my kitchen and sass me." She snatched the plate and hurled the bacon into the trash. "There. Are you happy now? Good food and good money wasted. Do you think bacon grows on trees?"

"If it grew on trees, I could eat it!"

Della dropped her head into her hands. Her dog tags jangled against the table.

"Honey." Ruth sat down across from her. "Honey, look at me."

She lifted her head slowly. Pain zoomed around inside her skull. If only she could have a beer, maybe she could get through this conversation. "Mom, don't you have to go to work?"

"Not for a while yet."

Ruth was such a familiar sight in her uniform, a light blue polyester dress with a white scalloped collar. Her straight, shoulder-length brown hair was bobby-pinned behind her ears, ready for the hairnet. Ruth looked exactly the way Della had remembered during all those months when she used to envision this very kitchen and dream about how good it would be to return to the World. Now Della was back and nothing was right. She wanted to appease her mother, wanted to please her. But it was hopeless. The "Della" that Ruth kept appealing to no longer existed.

"Honey, you know I never believed in this war," her mother said. "I wrote letters against it. I called my Congressman. But I believe in you and what you did over there."

Tears burned behind Della's eyes.

"Healing the injured," Ruth continued. "It was a noble thing to do."

"We weren't there to heal anyone, Mom. We were there to preserve the fighting force. We nursed them back to hell."

Ruth reached out to her daughter, hesitated, and folded her hands on the table. "I know this will sound silly, Della, but I saw that new movie *M.A.S.H.*, and it made me understand a little bit about what it was like for you."

"For God's sake, Mom, that was a Hollywood movie. Those casualties got up and ate lunch."

"I know, dear, but what I meant was—"

"Our patients aren't just 'injured.' They're train wrecks. They've lost both their legs, and their thighs look like hamburger." Della heard herself talking faster and faster, but she didn't seem able to stop. "Their intestines are piled on top of their chest. Their brain's been shot up and they'll never so much as blink on their own again. And they're kids, Mom, eighteen- and nineteen-year-old kids!"

Della realized she was leaning across the table only when she saw how far her mother had drawn back. On Ruth's face was a look of horror and distaste—and fear. Della had seen that expression over and over during the past three weeks, every time she tried to tell her friends or family anything truthful about her life in Vietnam.

Oh, they loved learning about the parties and practical jokes. They clamored to hear about flirtations and romances. But anything real they recoiled from. Anything gory or wrenching they did not want to know. And Della had nothing to tell them that wasn't wrenching. She had brought back no pleasant souvenirs from the bloody borderland of life and death.

If you don't want to hear about wars, then don't fucking have them! she wanted to shout. But there was no one to shout at, certainly not her mother, who had marched against the war and thrown a fit in the administrator's office when Della got her orders for Vietnam.

No one was responsible for this war, no one was guilty. Only the dead truly knew their place.

"It all sounds awful," said Ruth after a long silence. The words floated away, airy as soap bubbles.

Della didn't blame her. What else was there to say? She focused on a crinkly, nickel-sized burn on her mother's left hand. "Mama, I saw so many of them die."

"All for nothing," Ruth murmured.

Della slammed her open palm on the table, knocking over the salt shaker. Ruth leapt off her chair.

"I *know* it was for nothing!" Della shouted. "*They* knew it was for nothing! Do you think those boys died just to prove how right you are?"

Della covered her mouth with her stinging hand. Never in her life had she spoken to her mother like that. "I'm sorry," she managed to say.

Della braced for her mother's anger, but Ruth merely reached over and righted the salt shaker. "I understand you're upset," she said. "But you're back home, and the war is all over now."

"Over? It's not over. People are still dying."

"I mean it's over for you. And soon it's going to be over for real. Look what happened at Kent State, just last month."

"Some college protesters get killed, and you think that's going to put a stop to the war?"

"I think people are furious all over this country. Nixon's a politician. He can't stand up to that for very long. He's got to end it."

An end to the war seemed impossible and almost irrelevant. All those snuffed-out soldiers, all those ravaged boys facing the rest of their lives limbless or paralyzed, all those Vietnamese children growing up burnt and mutilated. No one was going to put an end to that.

Ruth picked up her purse from the kitchen counter. "What will you do today, honey?"

"I don't know. Go swimming, I guess. Maybe see a movie."

"Haven't you seen every movie that's playing around here?"

"Only once, most of them."

"Why don't you pick up your sister after school and take her to that new shopping mall? You could use some clothes."

"Maybe," said Della. "But my leave is over soon. I'll be back in uniform."

"Don't you wear civilian clothes when you're off duty? If I were your age, I'd go out and buy myself some cute skirts. Now's the time to do it, while you still can. If you keep nursing, some day your legs will look like mine—covered in varicose veins." Ruth opened her wallet, counted out some coins for bus fare and slipped them into her pocket. "Well, I'm off, dear. It's a lovely day. Try to spend some time outdoors."

"It's freezing out."

Ruth sighed. "Honey, remember that Aunt Liz is having her card game over for supper tonight. Try to have your breakfast dishes out of the sink before she comes home from work."

"Roger that."

CHAPTER 7

ON THAT AFTERNOON so many years ago, Della had been mulling over the fight with her mother as she waited for Rosalind outside the high school. It hurt Della's heart to see how excited her little sister got when she spotted Della's red Camaro. Rosalind sprinted away from her friends and plopped into the low bucket seat. "Where are we going?" She tossed her books and soft Greek purse into the back.

"To the mall." Della handed her a can of Coke, scrutinizing the frizzy auburn waves that bordered Rosalind's narrow face and fell to her sharp shoulder blades. There was something soft and unformed about Rosalind in her flowing Indian print blouse, her fraying bell-bottomed jeans, her tender throat moving as she gulped the soda. Yet she was only months younger than the guys who were filling the hospital wards in Vietnam.

They rode mostly in silence, the wind roaring past the open windows while the radio thundered "Ain't No Mountain High Enough." Della drove fast, two fingers on the wheel, her head thrown back against the seat, eyes hidden by aviator sunglasses. Inside this chaos of speed and sound and motion was the only place she could find peace. Sharing it with her sister felt terribly intimate.

They careened into the sprawling parking lot. The mall was boiling with people. Cars trolled for parking spots, women towed children by the hand, gangs of hippie-ish teenagers sauntered across the asphalt. It used to be that the only place to buy clothes was the fading Main Street. Now Della was headed toward an enclosed shopping palace like it was an amusement park. While she had been gone, shopping had metamorphosed from a necessity to an entertainment. Della wished she had taken Rosalind somewhere, anywhere, else.

Rosalind held open the heavy glass door, chattering as if it took no effort to enter the strange canned world of the shopping mall. But Della found herself panting for air. The mall stood two stories high, shaped like a giant *X*. They had come in through the main entrance, right in the center of the *X*, where they could see everything—the clothing boutiques, the candy store, the fast food counters, the pipe shop, the kiosk that sold little ceramic animals. People swarmed everywhere, dressed in loud throbbing colors. Everyone was carefree. Whole. Everyone was busy buying pleasure.

Della could smell perfume, popcorn, the sour breath of strangers. Sounds clashed and swirled. A phone kept ringing, and spindly music pumped from overhead. The clamor of shoppers surged around her. Day-glo pinks and greens clanged out at her from store windows.

It was too much. She sank onto a bench. When Della glanced at Rosalind, her sister's face was swimming. Della knew if she didn't get out of there, she'd be sick.

"I've got to *didi*," she gasped, and ran for the exit.

When Rosalind caught up to her, Della was sitting on the curb, head between her knees.

Rosalind crouched beside her.

"Del, what's wrong?"

Della couldn't speak, so she waved in a way she hoped would be reassuring. After a little while, the swells of nausea subsided. She opened her eyes and watched a glossy black ant scale the mountain of her sneaker. Gingerly, she sat up.

"Are you okay?" asked Rosalind.

"I think so. At least I didn't puke."

"What's 'dee-dee'?"

"*Didi mau.* It's Vietnamese for, basically, get the hell out of here."

Della stood, and Rosalind jumped up to help her. Della gave her a weak smile. "Who do you think I am—Mom?"

"I don't know. You're acting like someone's grandma. What's wrong with you?"

"I—didn't feel well."

"Okay, don't tell me."

"It's not that. I just don't know how to explain it." Della tugged the keys out of her pocket. "Listen, I think there's a place nearby where we can get something to drink and some really bad food. Want to go?"

"Sounds great."

As they threaded through the hectic parking lot toward their car, Rosalind kept a hand on Della's arm, ready to catch her if she tottered.

"Hey, Roz, I just realized something," said Della.

"What's that?"

"You're taller than I am now."

"A little."

"No fair. You got Dad's hair and his height."

"Yeah, but you got his temperament."

"What do you mean?" Della unlocked the door and faced her sister across the warm red curve of the Camaro's roof.

"You're doing a disappearing act. But you're even better at it than he was. You're doing it right before our eyes."

Della ducked into the car. After a moment she unlocked the passenger door. Rosalind settled into her seat, fussed with her purse, set it on the floor. Still they sat in the bright baking silence. Finally Della turned the key and the car shuddered beneath them.

The bar was only about ten minutes from the mall, wedged into an industrial park where car repair shops shouldered against lumberyards and small factories. Della had discovered the place years ago with her high school boyfriend. She wasn't surprised that it was still in business; there was always a market for a bar that was casual about checking ID's. No one there would care that Rosalind was underage.

The building was ugly, a rectangle of unpainted concrete block. Inside it was cool and dim, reeking of cigarettes and cooking oil. A long wooden bar ran along one dingy wall, and six small round tables squeezed against the other. Someone had once tried to brighten the place with Yankee pennants and sports posters, but that must have been long ago. Now the posters were yellowed, and most of the pennants dangled from a single tack. A large American flag sagged across the mirror behind the bar.

They took a table near the door and examined the sticky plastic menus. Della hoped Rosalind was too engrossed with the long list of fried foods to notice how urgently she signaled for a beer. Across the room a sports announcer droned from the black-and-white TV that hung above the bar, now filling up with men just released from work.

"So," Della said, "tell me about your plans for next year." She licked foam off her upper lip. "I'm really proud of you, going away to college."

"I'm not going all that far. Just to Ithaca."

"It's not the distance that matters," said Della. "You're the first in the family to make it. Mom and Aunt Liz must have been beside themselves."

"Yeah, they were pretty happy. And the scholarship helps too. It's not a full ride, but pretty close." Rosalind sipped her Coke. "It'll be weird."

"Why?"

"Well, I'll be with all kinds of kids from all over. And the classes will be serious, not like high school. I'll have to do some heavy studying."

"But you're so smart, that can't be what's really worrying you."

Rosalind dragged a french fry through the pool of ketchup on her chipped plate. "I've never lived away from home before. Other kids go to camp, or they spend summers at Grandma's house or something. I never did any of that. What if I'm homesick? Or maybe I'll hate my roommate. You know, they just stick you with a stranger."

"She can't be any stranger than your old roommate, can she?"

Rosalind smiled. "She won't be as bossy, that's for sure. But once you were gone I kind of got used to having my own room."

"Well, thanks for sleeping on the couch while I'm home on leave. It's great to have a room to myself after sharing a hooch for so long. I forgot what it's like not to hear other people snoring and talking in their sleep."

"Did you hear anything else?" Rosalind wiggled her eyebrows suggestively.

"Everything. The walls were plywood. Not exactly soundproof."

"What was it like? Your hooch?"

"A low building with sandbags piled all around it. Windows up near the roof. There was a living room and a bunch of tiny bedrooms that could hardly hold more than a cot."

"No bathrooms?"

"Nope. We used latrines—outhouses with big metal barrels to hold the waste. Some poor soldiers had to burn the shit every day."

"Yuck."

"No bathrooms and no baths," said Della. "Just a showerhead hanging over a slimy concrete slab. The water came from a tank overhead. In the morning it was freezing, but it warmed up during the day."

"You must have missed those long, hot baths where you'd hog the bathroom for hours."

"Yeah, I did." Della emptied her glass. "Tell me about you, Rosalind. Doing anything evil with your life these days?"

"Like what?"

"Oh, you know. Drinking, drugs, fucking around?"

"Not too much. But that's what I plan to major in once I get to college."

"Good choice. Make Mom proud." Della relaxed into the knobby wooden chair. For the first time that day, nothing hurt.

"It's hard to know what would make Mom proud," said Rosalind.

"True. But I'm pretty sure a degree in sex and drugs isn't it."

"She might not care, as long as I end up with an M.R.S."

"Really?" She waved for another drink. "You think she has her hopes set on marrying you off?"

"Well, not right away. But she does keep dropping these little hints. You know, 'Someday, when you're married and have children of your own...'"

"Man. You'd think having an older sister would shield you from all that."

"You weren't here, so I got all the attention." Rosalind jabbed her straw into her glass, making the ice cubes dance. "But don't worry, I won't run off and get hitched. I have other plans."

"What are they?"

"Getting through college, for one thing."

"Good for you." Della lowered her voice. "Rozzie, if you have any questions about guys or sex or anything..."

Rosalind's lips twitched. "No thanks."

"You're sure?"

"Positive."

"Okay."

Rosalind had a pack of friends; maybe she learned everything she needed to know from them. Or maybe she had more experience than Della thought.

"So, how's Mom been doing in the dating game?" asked Della.

"She's slacking off a little. I think she only went out with a couple of guys while you were gone."

"And Aunt Liz?"

Rosalind shrugged. "Nothing new there. She still plays cards and bingo with that same old crowd. Every few months they go to Atlantic City for the weekend. There's no telling how they divvy up the hotel rooms."

A chorus of shouts arose from the bar as the men watched a pivotal baseball moment played and replayed on TV. Rosalind twisted in her chair to see what was happening.

"You know, you're not off the hook either with this marriage thing." She turned back to Della, grinning. "Mom and Aunt Liz used to weave these big fantasies about you, how you'd meet some handsome wounded soldier in Vietnam and heal him, and then you two would come home and live happily ever after. Next door, of course."

"I used to have those kinds of daydreams too, till I got over there. Turns out it's not like that at all."

"Why not?"

"First of all, no one sticks around long enough to fall in love. The injured guys are brought in by helicopter. They're in their fatigues, all covered with mud and blood and this sweaty, earthy, jungly smell. We treat them and stabilize them and they're gone like *that*." She snapped her fingers. "Back to the field, if their wounds aren't too severe. Or to Japan if they need more treatment. Or on to the graves registration unit."

"Oh." Rosalind looked down at her plate.

"So you can see, there's no relaxed recuperation period when a nurse and a patient might get to know each other. No time for intimate talks."

"No, I guess not." Rosalind reached for her purse. "Hey, do you want to get out of here? It's getting smoky."

"A lot of the time we don't even know their names. We don't want to know their names. They die too quickly."

Rosalind scraped her chair back from the cluttered table, but Della gripped her wrist. "Let me tell you something about men, Rozzie." Della could tell that her mouth was moving faster than her brain, but it was crucial to impart this wisdom to her sister. "Men are frail. Most women don't realize that, because guys seem so big and strong. But really, they're fragile as insects. They die or they fly away. You can't keep them."

"Got it, Della."

"No, Rosalind, this is important. You have to know this. Men don't last."

Rosalind scooted closer to the table and lowered her voice. "Della, stop it. You're talking like a crazy person. What happened to you over there? Did you lose someone?"

Suddenly Della was exhausted. There was no point talking, trying to make anyone understand. With sickening effort, she moved her lips. "Lots of people."

"But I mean, someone special?"

"Everyone. Every one was special. That was the whole problem." Rosalind pulled her arm out of Della's grasp. "I've got homework to do. Can we please go?"

Della reached into her pocket, momentarily surprised not to find Military Payment Certificates, the paper scrip that replaced cash on Army bases in Vietnam. American money felt unfamiliar—the sharp-smelling coins, the greasy bills softened by the skin of strangers. She tossed a handful onto the table.

They didn't speak all the way home. Della gripped the steering wheel with both fists. Finally, as their house grew larger through the bug-spattered windshield, Rosalind leaned over and clicked off the radio.

"You know, I missed you like crazy while you were gone. I always thought we'd have so much to talk about when you got back."

"Don't we?" Della slipped the Camaro against the curb.

"I don't know," said Rosalind. "Are you back?"

CHAPTER 8

EVEN NOW, a lifetime later, Della still couldn't answer that question. She had spent the night clenched on her couch, fending off sleep. Here it was, three years into a new century and Della was still fighting an ancient war. She could think of only one person who was certain to understand, who would require no explanations. But in the endless night Charlene felt lost to her still, as out of reach as a name etched high on a granite wall.

Dawn found Della pacing in front of the green steel door of the recreation center, preparing to douse the shards of her dreams in the blue, bleached water of the public pool. She had recognized the raw ingredients of her nightmare—the cup of warm blood, the horrifying sound as it shattered—and knew that if she did not act, she could meet that vision every night for weeks. It had happened before. But it wasn't easy to fight against your own dreams. Della could think of only one way, and there was no place on the dry earth where she felt safe enough to try it.

Her breath rose in silky plumes as she clustered with half a dozen other early risers, pale as moths in the murky light, gym bags bumping against their hips. Finally a young man in a janitor's jumpsuit unlocked the door and stood aside to let them in, meeting no one's eyes.

Della's body had once been a slender blade, slicing through the water as she swam her tireless laps. She was still fit, but the water let her know she was thicker and broader. She found herself working to part heavy curtains of blue with each stroke. Della stayed underwater, breast-stroking down the length of the pool, until the craving for oxygen sent her shooting to the surface. She sucked in air, adjusted her goggles, and pushed off from the end of the pool, moving down her empty lane in a steady crawl.

Della had always thought the bright water was akin to faith: it looked like something you could hold onto, but each time you reached for it, it ran through your fingers. Yet somehow, effort after effort, loss after loss, you made it to the end of the pool. Della could feel the comforting pressure of the water against her skin. With her ear below the surface, she could hear the dull percussion of her heart. It called up the nightmare sound that had driven her to the pool in the first place.

☙

The Twelfth Evacuation Hospital in Cu Chi was like no hospital Della could ever have imagined: a cluster of corrugated metal Quonset huts, surrounded by barbed wire and connected by walkways made of wooden pallets. Around the hospital sprawled a massive Army base, a dismal landscape of metal and canvas and lumbering vehicles. The trees had been scraped away and the flat earth coughed up powdery red dust.

Tenement towns built of discarded American packing cases spread like a rash around the base. Beyond that, Vietnam's Highway One followed the country's curve: south, toward Saigon, or north, through the Central Highlands.

The hospital compound held an emergency ward, an operating room with six suites, several convalescent wards, a pharmacy, and X-ray area. At the heart of it was a landing area where helicopters delivered the wounded.

Major Ada Throop, chief nurse of the Twelfth Evacuation Hospital, stood outside the hospital, facing Della and Charlene. They had arrived in Vietnam just two days ago. Now they squinted in the morning glare, already wilting in their stiff boots and fatigues. The powdered egg breakfast lay heavy in Della's stomach.

"The first few days you'll spend a little time in each department," the major told them. Above her, heat waves shimmered off the arched metal roof. "You'll begin in the emergency room. Then you'll move to the O.R., the recovery room, and the I.C.U. I want you to follow the journey a typical patient makes here, from triage to discharge."

Della could not stop staring at the chief nurse. Of course all the nurses dressed alike—olive drab fatigues brightened only by the insignia and embroidered patches that signified their place within the military. But something about the way Major Throop carried herself held Della's attention. Graying hair peeked out from her olive drab baseball cap, ending a tidy inch above her collar. A stethoscope looped around her neck like a friend's arm. A set of keys dangled off one hip pocket; her leg pocket bristled with ballpoint pens. In her sleeve pocket, the major carried a pair of bandage scissors with a length of yellow rubber tubing tied to the finger hole—a tourniquet, Della figured out after a few moments. Major Throop seemed both at ease and poised for disaster.

"You should observe the first case, then pitch in where you can." The major rocked slightly on her heels, hands clasped behind her back. "It's important for you to learn our standard procedures. I know it seems overwhelming at first, but you'll soon catch on."

She had started the orientation by telling them that the Twelfth Evac could handle more than three hundred patients, who would come mostly from the Army's Twenty-Fifth Infantry Division. Della was surprised to hear that they would also be expected to treat Vietnamese patients—local women and children, the allied Army of the Republic of Vietnam, even the occasional Viet Cong prisoner of war.

"When you're off duty," Major Throop continued, "I want you to get as much rest as you can, especially these first few days. Tomorrow you'll begin your shifts promptly at 0630." She spoke quietly, but the authority in her voice was unmistakable. "Now we'll move quickly and quietly through the I.C.U. The emergency room is on the other side."

With that she turned and pushed open the double swinging doors. Della and Charlene followed her down a long aisle bordered by two rows of cots. Almost all the beds were in use, occupied by haggard young men wearing light blue pajamas, or swathed in white gauze with red blood seeping through. One of the patients, lying on his back, glared up unblinking. The bundled stumps of his amputated arms poked out from his shoulders like raw wings.

IV lines ran into the men, and hoses trailed out of them. Glass bottles hung from metal poles and wires. Glass jars of various sizes stood taped to the concrete floor beside the beds, tape marks measuring the bodily fluids they collected.

Della wanted to stop and gawk, but Major Throop moved swiftly through the ward and into another Quonset hut. With a sweep of her hand, she pointed out where the hospital received the wounded, a large area ringed with supply shelves. Against one wall, a cabinet held drugs. Pairs of sawhorses stood in rows across the floor, a bucket waiting beneath each set.

"You'll need to learn quickly what supplies and equipment we use and where we keep them," said the major. "We may not have the same materials you were used to stateside."

A green canvas litter holding a wounded soldier rested across one set of sawhorses. Della couldn't see his face from where she was standing. He was still wearing his muddy fatigue pants and combat boots, but his bloody shirt lay heaped on the floor. The man's chest was stippled with black, pitted wounds. A nurse and a doctor, both in faded green fatigues, bent over him, picking pieces of metal from his flesh with long-nosed instruments and dropping them with a clang into a metal bowl.

"Shrapnel," said Major Throop. "Michelle," she called out, "I'll leave these two to your tender mercies."

"Yes, ma'am," replied the nurse. She gave them a friendly nod and turned back to her patient. Her blonde hair was swept up into a knot held in place by a ballpoint pen plunged through the center. A hemostat glinted from her sleeve pocket.

"Watch and learn, Lieutenants." The major strode away.

Watching and learning was about all Della felt capable of doing. She had barely slept, partly because of anxiety and partly because the night was unbelievably hot and loud. The hours were pierced by terrifying explosions and gunfire, and furtive noises she could only hope were not rodents.

Now it was early morning, but already she could feel the heat and humidity crushing her. And she couldn't be the only one in this place who noticed the smell. As they had made their way through the ward behind Major Throop, Della had identified so many warring odors—blood, bandages, feces, ointments, infection, vomit—that they merged into one horrible stench.

As if in answer to her thoughts, a breeze swept through the room, accompanied by a low throbbing sound. Della was relieved until the wind began to blow more violently, sending pieces of paper skittering across the floor. Uniformed women and men appeared from nowhere, filling the room with an urgent buzz. The clamor from outside grew louder as the swinging doors at the far end burst open and soldiers rushed in, bearing litters that held bloody bodies. Della realized that the noise was the sound of helicopters ferrying in casualties from the field.

She shrank against the wall. In minutes all the sawhorses were in use, and the soldiers began to lay injured men on the floor. Soon it was clear they had run out of stretchers too, because they carried the next wave of wounded in sagging ponchos.

Some of the injured soldiers groaned and writhed; one was shrieking in pain. A few called out to one another.

"Lookin' good, bro."

"That's a million-dollar wound or I don't know shit."

Many of the wounded were silent, and Della couldn't tell if they were stoic or dead.

The room erupted. Nurses raced through the ward, took vital signs, cut off uniforms black with blood, started IVs, applied pressure bandages, gave tetanus vaccines, asked questions of the soldiers who could speak. A couple of nurses with clipboards circulated, seeming to assess each soldier with a single glance. Doctors and nurses consulted tersely, while corpsmen set up equipment and supplies.

Everything happened at once. Everyone worked with incredible speed. They all knew exactly what to do, and they worked together as smoothly as if they shared one brain. Della knew she would never be able to measure up.

"This is triage," Michelle shouted in their general direction. Although Charlene and Della had made themselves as small as possible, they had not managed to become invisible. "That's when we sort out who needs what treatment and in what priority. You have any questions, ask me. I'm Micky."

A doctor looked up from his patient. "Micky, you've got spare nurses? Good. I need some help over here."

They hurried over, stepping around the bodies and blood on the floor. The patient was red-haired and probably freckled, although his face was so filthy Della couldn't tell. Two clean tracks meandered down his cheeks. He was unconscious, his eyes closed, his arms wrapped in tourniquets and tucked along the edge of the litter. One arm seemed longer than the other. With a gasp, she realized that his left hand was hanging free, attached to his wrist by a single tendon.

"That's right, the hand has to come off." The doctor nodded toward a wheeled metal table that held an array of tools. "Grab a scissors and cut it off. There's a bucket to drop it in."

Della reached for the scissors. Or at least she tried to reach for them, yet her arm stayed rooted to her side.

"Come on, ladies, this isn't surgery. It just needs one snip."

But Della had turned to wood.

Slowly, so slowly, Charlene stepped forward and lifted the scissors. She held the pail under the boy's dangling hand and brought the sharp blades together. Long moments later, the hand hit the bottom of the bucket. It made a strange noise, sort of a *thomp*.

A black dot floated across Della's field of vision, followed by another. Soon a swarm of dots hovered before her eyes. Then she understood. This wasn't really happening; it was only a news photo. The black dots would form a picture, and she could study the picture but she would not be in it.

Just before she folded to the floor she heard Micky say, "Jesus Christ, these poor fuckin' FNGs." The words reached Della in a muffled way, as if her ears were stuffed with cotton. It seemed a mean thing to say, yet Micky's voice didn't sound angry; it sounded sad. Della wondered what FNG meant, and if "fucking" was strictly necessary. She felt herself sink until blackness covered her like a quilt.

When Della opened her eyes she was face to face with a boy who had a bloody hole where his mouth used to be. Before she could scream she felt someone's fingers dig into her wrist. She looked up to see Charlene squatting beside her.

"Are you okay?"

She had fainted. She was a nurse and she had fainted in front of everybody. Della tried to bolt to her feet, but Charlene's grip held her down. "Slowly," Charlene said in a low voice. "Take it easy."

Della rose unsteadily. Her pants stuck to her leg, soaked with blood from the floor.

"Everything okay?" Micky called from across the room.

"Yes. I'm really sorry." With a shudder, she plucked the sodden fabric away from her skin.

"Go sit behind the desk and keep your head between your knees for a couple of minutes," said Micky.

"I'm fine."

"You're in the way," Micky pointed out, not unkindly.

That evening, Della sprawled face down on her cot. Her hair was damp from the shower. The sheets were damp too, as if someone had taken them out of the dryer too soon. But that couldn't be the problem because they had been wet last night as well. Maybe the humidity was so high in this horrible place that she would have to spend every night in slimy sheets. For some reason that seemed too much to bear on top of everything else. Very quietly, she began to weep, pressing her face into the musty pillowcase.

But she must not have been quiet enough, because soon Charlene was knocking on the door, followed by Micky. The two women filled the tiny room. Della sat up on the bed, clutching the pillow to her stomach.

"Want a beer?" Micky said. She had a lively face with pale blue eyes, bright, even teeth, hair pulled back into a ponytail. Della thought she must have been a cheerleader in high school.

"No thanks." Della swiped a hand across her cheeks. "I don't drink."

"Not yet," Micky said, punching two holes in a can of Budweiser with a bottle opener she fished out of her leg pocket. She sat on the floor, leaning back against the flimsy wall. "That's pretty much all there is to drink around here. Good water is hard to come by, but liquor is everywhere and dirt cheap. Sodas too."

Charlene sat cross-legged on the end of the bed. "So, how're you holding up?" she asked Della.

"Did you hear me blubbering?"

"I think we can hear each other breathe in this place."

"Oh God, I'm so embarrassed." Tears pricked her eyes again. "This isn't like me. Normally I'm someone who can do things. Normally I don't cry, and I never faint."

Micky shrugged. "This isn't normal."

Della turned to Charlene. "What about you? You're new here too. How come I'm the only one freaking out?"

"I am freaking out, I'm just doing it differently. Besides, I've been working in an O.R. for a couple of years, so I've seen more gore than you have."

"No one's seen this."

"You have to be tough," Micky said, "if you're going to make it here. Practically indestructible. But no one starts out that way." She swigged some beer. "My first week, I couldn't eat. It was a big mistake, because you need all the fuel you can get. And sometimes you gotta think of it as fuel, 'cause it sure doesn't resemble food. Did you guys have dinner tonight?"

"I did," said Charlene. "It wasn't too bad."

"I wasn't hungry." The sight of hamburger had made Della gag after all the raw meat she had seen that day.

"I've got some Ritz crackers and Cheez Whiz in my room," said Micky. "Want some?"

"No thanks," said Della. "I'm not a big fan of cheese in a spray can. Now, whipped cream in a can, that would be different."

Charlene nodded. "I'm with you on that one."

Micky rolled the beer can between her hands and studied it as if she could read the future in its dull gold curves. "Someday soon, you two will look back on this night and wonder. Because junk food—any kind of junk food—will seem like a treat to you by then. But me and my Cheez Whiz, we'll be long gone."

"Where will you be?" Della asked.

Micky shrugged. "Back in the World, if it's still there. Back to Michelle. I'm short, ladies, getting shorter by the minute."

"What's that supposed to mean?" Charlene said.

"It means we probably won't get to be friends," said the cheerleader. "It means my tour is up in exactly twenty-six days." She drained her beer and set the empty can twirling on the concrete floor. "So if there's anything you want to know about this place, I'll tell you. I'll tell you the God's awful truth. I'll gladly share my food with you, and my booze, and the little tricks I've learned about how to get by. But my heart, my confidences, my innermost feelings? Too fucking late for all that."

She stood and swayed. "Night, ladies. Welcome to Hell's Lobby. Don't worry about the rockets, by the way—the VC can't aim worth a damn." She giggled. "'Course, that can be good or bad, depending on what they're aiming at."

"Wait a minute," Della said as Micky reached for the door. "That name you called me today. FNT?"

"FNG." There it was again, that note of compassion in Micky's weary voice. "Fucking new guy. That's what we call everyone who can still cry."

"What do you call us when we stop crying?"

Micky tossed her can into the wastebasket with a clatter. "Then we call you 'Nurse.'"

Charlene and Della stared at each other through the vacant air Micky left behind. Finally Charlene unfolded her long legs and rested her elbows on her knees, her head sagging. "Well, guess I'll go write a letter home. We don't need stamps, did you know that? Free mail. It's the one perk of serving in a war zone." She looked at her boots. "How the hell did I end up in a war zone?"

"I don't want to be here," Della blurted. "I never wanted to be in the Army, I just wanted an education."

Charlene rose, pushing her hands against her thighs like an old woman. "Girl, looks like that's exactly what we're going to get."

CHAPTER 9

RIDING HOME from work on the swaying bus, Della took stock. Charlene's letter had been in her house only twenty-four hours, and already it had sent her twisting through ugly memories and trying to drown her nightmares in the local swimming pool. The one thing she longed to do—call Charlene—would have to wait until Della's mother moved back to her own apartment. Della would feel too exposed to make the call while Ruth was in the house; it would be almost like having sex while her mother was in the next room. She ran her fingers through her hair, releasing the sharp scent of chlorine. All in all, it had been a trying day.

A twenty-nine-year-old woman had spent fifteen minutes that morning sobbing in Della's arms. The blood test patients took before each chemotherapy treatment revealed that her white cell count was too low today for her to tolerate chemo without risking infection. This would throw off her treatment schedule—not a big deal, usually, but it meant that she would not reach her goal of completing her cancer treatments before she turned thirty. Clearly the woman had made some magical bargain with herself: if she finished chemo in her twenties, she would survive. Now all bets were off.

Later Della saw Mr. Sutton, an elderly patient who had dropped so much weight since his last treatment that she had to recalculate his body surface area and reduce his chemo dosage. As Mr. Sutton dozed in the blue vinyl lounge chair, toxic drugs dripping into his vein, she stood in the hallway, carrying on an intense, murmured conversation with his son Daniel.

His children, Daniel confessed, were scared to be in the same room with their grandfather. And he couldn't blame them; he was a little scared himself. His father was now like a walking agony. The bare skull, the huge, suffering eyes, the scabs around his lips …

Della told him about nutrition drinks to ease his father's weight loss and ointments to help with the mouth sores, problems that were caused not by the cancer but by the treatment. Mostly she assured him that his feelings of revulsion were natural—just as natural as the son's tenderness when he had helped his dad into the chair and unfolded a blanket across his lap.

None of this was out of the ordinary for the oncology ward, but even the norm was hard to take when she was so tired. Now Della felt like leaning her head on the window and nodding off. The greasy smudges from passengers who had already done so kept her upright.

Across the aisle a man murmured into a cell phone. He was in his late thirties, dressed in a charcoal gray suit and stiff white shirt. His tie was firmly knotted, his shoes polished. Only his black hair seemed to rebel, spiking up into a cowlick.

You didn't see many business types on the bus. You didn't see many white men at all. It was just past rush hour, and the passengers were a mother with a fussy toddler, a couple of elderly people with single sacks of groceries, and several weary workers like herself, with empty lunch bags and sore feet, making their way home after a long shift.

The businessman slipped the phone into his pocket and pulled a *Wall Street Journal* from his briefcase. As he stretched out his arms, Della saw a slim leather thong knotted around his right wrist. So he still had a little wildness in him, something he kept close to his skin, hidden beneath starched white cuffs.

She had snipped off many of those bracelets in Vietnam. Leather bands, twisted shoelaces, braided strips of jungle grasses—the guys were endlessly inventive. Back in the World, POW bracelets were the fashion. In country, the soldiers wore all kinds of adornments, heavy with the power of hope, to protect themselves from ending up as a casualty or a name on some stranger's wrist.

She remembered one man who wore a beautiful band made of tiny beads in the red, green, and black colors of African unity. When she cut through the bracelet, all the beads had rained down onto the concrete floor. In one snip she had destroyed hours of someone's painstaking work. But it had to be done. There was no time to unbutton his uniform or unknot his bracelet. Everything came off the same way—with scissors.

Strange, Della could envision perfectly his broad wrist beating with a faint, thready pulse, the colorful bracelet against his bronze skin, his curled fingers with their caked, broken nails. But she couldn't recall his face or his injury. She did remember hearing beads crunch under combat boots, hours after you would have thought they had all been crushed.

"Combat boots can be your best friend or your worst enemy here," Major Ada Throop had told them. Charlene and Della sat facing her in their oversized fatigues, still stunned by the strangeness of their new world. Through the open window of the small, spare office, Della could hear men shouting, and trucks roaring past, and the urgent whine of heavy equipment doing who knew what. A small black fan rotated noisily on its wall mount but failed to move the sweltering air.

Major Throop strode to the front of her gray metal desk. She leaned against it, crossing her feet at the ankles. Della noted her tidy salt-and-pepper hair, her weary brown eyes, slightly large for her face and so dark Della couldn't see the pupils. In the movies, Della thought, this woman would be the heroine's wise best friend, or maybe the mother of a troubled teen.

Here in Vietnam, Ada Throop was a small woman with a large job. Briefing the newly arrived nurses was only a sliver of it, yet from the way she focused on the two recruits, Della might have concluded that easing her anxiety was Major Throop's primary mission in life.

"You must change your boots regularly. Wash your feet and change your socks daily, no matter how exhausted you are. You've heard the expression, 'An army travels on its stomach'?"

Della glanced at Charlene. She had never heard the phrase and couldn't imagine what it meant.

"Well, this army travels on its feet," Major Throop continued. "In World War I the men got trench foot. In Korea it was frostbite. Here, it's jungle rot. It may sound silly, but foot care is crucial. For the soldier, certainly. But also for the nurse." Major Throop leaned forward confidentially. "Most of these fellows will be a soldier for only a year or two. But a nurse? A nurse will be on her feet the rest of her life."

Della looked at her feet. While Charlene and the major were wearing sturdy jungle boots, somehow she had been issued pink high-top sneakers instead. They would be no protection against the rivulets of blood that were beginning to snake across the floor. And what were those light flecks floating in the blood? Bending closer, she smelled the blood's iron tang and recognized the freight it carried: bits of bone and brain matter, and tiny white beads. Wrenching herself back in her chair, Della tried to lift her feet off the floor, but it was too late. Her sneakers were already mired in the pooling blood.

Della awakened on the bus with a gasp. It took her a panicked moment to realize that she'd dozed off, traveling unnoticed from memory into nightmare, not so long a journey as one might expect.

She was wide awake now, but something was still not right. Everything Della saw through the grimy window was familiar but out of place somehow. The bus passed a gas station, then a brightly lit McDonald's. They lumbered past the entrance to a shadowy park and she figured it out.

She had missed her stop, that was all, had slept through her own neighborhood and several others. Now the bus was entering an area called Olive Hill, where she'd spent her childhood.

There were no olive trees in Olive Hill, of course, nor was there a hill. When Della was a child this was a community of small, neat bungalows, purchased by young World War II veterans with the help of the GI Bill and maintained by their hardworking wives. In the years since she had last visited, the neighborhood had been transformed. Where once she had played kickball with her friends, grand new houses hulked above sculpted lawns, remnants of snow glittering in the streetlights. Some of the familiar old bungalows had sprouted second stories and three-car garages. It looked bizarre, as if an epidemic of elephantiasis had swept through the streets.

Della knew she should get home, where her mother was waiting. But she couldn't resist taking a few more minutes to see what had happened to their old house. She yanked on the bell cord and the bus jerked to a stop.

In the cold she hurried down the narrow sidewalk, her progress marked by sudden spurts of light from motion detectors. Most of the familiar landmarks had disappeared. The Greek bakery had been replaced by a Starbucks. The children's shoe store was gone, and so was the family pharmacy that delivered prescriptions by bicycle. A few blocks later she recognized the house, although it was bloated with new additions on either side of the original structure. But the owners had preserved the wide front porch with its distinctive railings that Della's father and Uncle George had built one summer.

As a child, she had spent hours on that porch, lying on her stomach, feet in the air, peering so closely at the newspaper that Ruth took her to get her eyes checked. Della didn't need glasses; she simply loved to stare at newspaper photos until they revealed their true nature: nothing but little dots of ink.

The summer after Della's father went missing, Ruth spent most of her time on the porch, reading magazines, poring over bills, glancing up frequently as if any moment he might stride down the street. Della too hated to be indoors, surrounded by dwindling furniture and growing silence. She was amazed to come home from school one afternoon and find strange men carrying away the TV set while her mom leaned in the doorway and watched, an old blue cardigan of her husband's wrapped around her. After that the living room sofa evaporated, and then the matching dressers from her parents' bedroom.

It was so swift, their fall from the middle class. One day Della was dreaming of the flute lessons she'd get to take when she was twelve. The next day she watched her swim team clamber onto a bus and leave for the statewide competition without her. Ruth could not come up with the fare.

By July, they had sold almost all the familiar items of Della's childhood, and moved into two cramped bedrooms in Aunt Liz's house, far away in a new school district. The world she knew disintegrated. For the life of her, Della could not understand how a bank could take back their old house or where they would put it.

Years later, as she was struggling to sort out the financial details of her own divorce, Della tried to pin down what had happened with her parents' finances. "When Dad left, how did you manage in terms of money?" she asked her mother one evening. They were in Della's living room, the one room in the house that did not look denuded by Ben's departure.

"It wasn't easy," Ruth replied, setting down a plastic basket piled with clean, fragrant laundry. She had started washing her clothes at Della's house to avoid the dim, musty laundry room in her apartment building, she said, although Della suspected it might also be to help her daughter ease into the loneliness of her newly single life.

"We lived paycheck to paycheck—his paycheck," Ruth said. "I was earning peanuts, waitressing part-time so I could be home for you kids. Once your dad disappeared, so did his wages."

"What about savings?"

"We never had more than two hundred dollars in the bank." Ruth began to fold her laundry—snap, crease, smooth; snap, crease, smooth. "It didn't go far, even back then."

She pulled out a crumpled white sheet and tossed one end to Della, keeping hold of the other end. They faced each other, shook out the sheet and folded it in unison, like a flag over a casket. "Thank goodness for your Aunt Liz," Ruth continued. "I don't know what we would have done without her."

"How is it Aunt Liz was able to keep their house when George died?" Della moved closer to her mother with each fold.

"Because her husband had the foresight to buy life insurance."

"And she had the foresight not to have children."

Ruth laughed. "Children aren't cheap, that's for sure."

"Yeah, Mom, I know this story," Della had said, smiling too. "We ate you out of house and home, took the best years of your life, etc."

"Exactly."

Even one child wasn't cheap, it turned out. From the instant she was born, Abby had required an astonishing number of *things*— pacifiers and playpens giving way in moments to rollerblades and books and bicycles, computers and CDs and an unending stream of clothing, all of it turning obsolete almost before it was paid for. Ben and Della would be chipping away at Abby's college loans long after she had forgotten the names of her professors.

As she stood on the narrow sidewalk and faced her childhood home in the dark, Della imagined a parade of all the things she had given up for Abby's sake. She never traveled after Abby was born, never saw Europe or the Grand Canyon. New cars, a remodeled kitchen, graduate school, weekend getaways, clothes-buying sprees, fancy restaurant meals—all of those luxuries remained out of reach once she had a child.

Della's love for her daughter was a wild thing that sometimes bullied them both. Even now, with Abby newly grown and flown away, it clawed at her heart. Della couldn't understand how people without children managed, how they fed the fierce human hunger for connection. Rosalind and Anne: how did they get through their days? Where could they place their desperate energies?

In all the years she had spent raising Abby, Della's life had never been her own. Thank God. Now it had been handed back to her, and she wasn't sure what to do with it.

Della stared for a few more moments at the familiar porch. She could not say what it was she had hoped to find at their old house, but it wasn't there. Pulling up her coat collar, she turned away from the house, into the biting wind.

CHAPTER 10

"How about a game of Scrabble?" Ruth asked that evening after dinner, turning to her daughter next to her on the couch. This would be their last evening together. By tomorrow, Saturday, her apartment would be freshly painted and aired out enough for her to move back in.

Della glanced up from her mystery novel. Her mother, in flannel bathrobe and quilted slippers that barely touched the floor, seemed relaxed for once. But then Ruth slapped her magazine closed. "Bet I can still beat the pants off you," she declared.

"Bet you can too." Della took off her tortoiseshell reading glasses and tucked one earpiece into the neck of her navy sweatshirt. "The question is whether I can find the game. Last time I saw it was in Abby's closet."

"Think she took it with her?"

"Who knows? She stripped her room to the bone, but the closet is still a mess."

"Time never rests, does it? Seems like only last week Abby was begging me to bake her cupcakes, and just yesterday Liz was carping at me not to open my umbrella in the house or it would bring bad luck."

A flash of grief pulled down the corners of her mouth. "Maybe she was right at that."

"I'll go look for the game." In Abby's closet Della found stacks of T-shirts, athletic shoes in varying degrees of decay, abandoned school books, and finally, the dusty maroon box with its taped cardboard corners.

"Should I light a fire?" she asked, setting the Scrabble board on the coffee table.

"No need to go to all that trouble just for us."

"Who are we saving it for?" Della crumpled the newspaper, laid it in the iron grate, and built the tidy cross-hatch of kindling and logs. As she swiped the wooden match against the stone hearth and touched the small flame to paper, she felt a bubbling excitement. The pleasure was tinged with shame; she kept it private, the thrill she got from unleashing destruction.

Ruth selected her letter tiles and lined them up on the small wooden tray. Della pulled over the rocking chair so she could face her mother. It was strange, Della thought: she was intimately familiar with her mother's expressions, her habits, her mannerisms. Yet there must be so much she didn't know of Ruth's inner life.

Ruth didn't look up from her letters. "If you're trying to eyeball me into submission, it isn't going to work."

"Oh, I think it might."

"Nope." She laid down each wooden tile with a click. "There. T-H-R-E-A-D. Hah! Twenty-eight points. Not too bad for starters."

"Don't thread on me." Della jotted down the score.

"Give us this day our daily thread."

"Shoot if you must this old gray thread."

Ruth craned her neck, trying to spy on Della's letters. "Are you ever going to play?"

"C-L-E-V-E-R. It took me a while, but better late than cl—"

"Please don't say it." Ruth slipped her hand into the gray vinyl bag and drew out a new batch of tiles. "You're worse than your father with those puns. Well, you are," she said in response to Della's surprised look. Ruth sighed. "I know I'm being punished for something with these letters."

"Since you won't let me say anything, why don't you tell me a story?"

Ruth's face lit up. "Why, Della, you haven't asked me for a story since you were five years old. What do you want to hear?"

"Something about you. Maybe a story about you and your mother."

"Well, let's see. You know, my mother's been gone forty years now, and I still think about her every day. Sometimes I remind myself about things to tell her—you know, in the hereafter."

"Really? Do you think there is one?"

"I surely hope so," said Ruth. "Mostly I just remember times we had together."

"Like what?"

Ruth squinted at the ceiling. "I remember that every Sunday when I was a little girl, my father would take the boys to church and my mother and I would stay home. We'd darn socks or sew on patches or replace buttons. This was during the Depression, you know. We had to make do or do without. Lots of times we did both. Every piece of clothing got handed down from one of my brothers to the next. If there was anything left after all four boys had outgrown it, it got passed on to a neighbor. I got dresses from the girl who lived upstairs. She was three years older than me, so everything had to be taken in before I could wear it. And that's what my mother and I did on Sundays."

"So the men worshipped while the women worked."

"It wasn't like that." Ruth glanced at Della, a mild reprimand. "My mother was very high-minded. She just wasn't a churchy kind of woman. She didn't believe the Lord lived in a brick building on Fourteenth and Maple. And our minister's wife was my mother's best friend. So she happened to know the man did not take his work home with him."

"You didn't mind being left at home with the sewing basket?"

"Oh, no. It was a treat for me to be alone with my mother. We'd talk and listen to the radio while we worked. The apartment was empty, the whole building was quiet. It was better than church. When I was a mother myself I figured out those Sunday mornings must have been the only time she got any peace from children and their needs."

Rocking slowly, Della could easily imagine those cozy Sundays. "What about you? You were a child."

"Little girls weren't raised to have needs back then, but to fill them."

"Tell that to Abby."

"I wouldn't dare." Ruth swooped forward and laid out her tiles. "P-L-E-A-D. Only twenty points, but I couldn't think of anything better, with you distracting me."

"You know what I remember? Going door to door with you when I was a little kid, getting people to sign those 'Ban the Bomb' petitions. It was kind of fun."

"You liked that? Then why did you make me bribe you with candy?"

"I liked the candy too." Della felt herself easing into the rhythm of the game. She loved the feel of the smooth wooden tiles, the thoughtful silences, the satisfying click of each letter claiming its place on the board. To Della, Scrabble was a kind of meditation.

To her mother, Della knew, Scrabble was a blood sport. Almost as soon as Della could visualize a play, Ruth planted a word to block it. Her pleasure seemed to be not in creating the words, but in thwarting her opponent. It was a coldhearted and singularly successful way to play the game. And while Della was amused by her mother's competitive glee, deep down it irked her to lose time after time.

Della laid down T-E-N-S-E-D and added her meager sixteen points to the score pad. But instead of pouncing, Ruth leaned back against the couch.

"Your grandmother lived through a world of change," she said. "She saw those first rickety airplanes barnstorming above the fields, and she saw men walking on the moon. But do you know what she said made the biggest difference in her own life?"

Della thought for a moment. "Television?"

"Sanitary napkins."

"*What?*"

"She said sanitary napkins gave women a whole new freedom. Before that, everyone used rags that had to be laundered and bleached. And I guess it wasn't very comfortable to go around with a wad of rags pinned to your underwear."

"It's not. When I was in Vietnam we couldn't get tampons a lot of the time, so we had to stuff bandage material into our underwear. It was miserable. The PX hardly ever carried any products for women. And whenever they would miraculously get in a shipment of tampons, the guys bought them up."

"Whatever for?"

"To clean their M-16s with. They'd take their rifles apart, shove the tampon into the barrel and hook the string with a cleaning rod to pull it out."

"Oh, my." Ruth turned back to the game. Apparently sharing time was over, thought Della.

She tried again. "So the big event in Grandma's life was Kotex. What were the big events in your life, Mom? The real turning points?"

"Well, now, let's see." She examined her letters, then spread out A-X-E-D for thirty-six points. "I'd have to say World War II. Especially Hiroshima. And after that, the Rosenberg trial. Those two things taught me that if you love your country, you can't just sit by and watch it go wrong." She nodded toward the score pad to remind Della of her duty. "You know what else was a real big event for me?"

"What?"

"Well, when you girls were born, of course. But before that, my wedding day." Ruth smiled. "Especially my wedding night. Oh, you can't imagine what it was like in those days, Della. Your father and me—we were a hot item. And there was nowhere for us to go. I lived with my family and so did he. We spent a lot of time at the movies, but there was only so far you could go there. That almost made it worse."

"What about the back seat of a car?"

"What car? The streetcar? No, our wedding night was the first time. For me, anyway. First time I was ever in a hotel room. First time

I was alone with a man. Tommy and I left our wedding party early because we couldn't wait. My mother was furious."

"You told her that's why you were leaving?"

"She knew. Guess it wasn't that hard to figure out, the way he had his hands all over me when we were dancing." Ruth fingered one of the smooth wooden tiles. "One thing about that man—he kept me wet every day, till the day he disappeared."

"Mom!"

"Oh, Della, don't be such a prude. Are you going to tell me the facts of life make you blush?"

"Just the facts of *your* life."

"That's why your generation hasn't accomplished much, Della. You think you invented everything—sex, politics, unhappiness. You're not so special. You're no different from every other generation. We all have the same needs: food, shelter. Love. Or what passes for it."

Della rose and shoved another log onto the fire, squatting in front of the screen as the dry wood spit out sparks. She didn't know why her mother said such mean-spirited things. As if Della was supposed to be insulted on behalf of her generation. It was so childish. And what was that comment supposed to mean, anyway? That Ruth had known love once, and nothing since had been genuine? That didn't say much for the men in her life who followed Tommy Brown. It didn't say much for her family, either, if the only person who had ever kindled authentic emotion was the man who abandoned her.

Maybe everyone created some story for their lives, some heroic tale they told themselves to make sense of their days. Ruth's might be "I have had a grand love."

Della thought hers could be "I never smacked my mother."

But something else disturbed Della, something she couldn't define. It was as if not only her mother's sentiment but the words themselves unnerved her. The words were trying to pull her under, to take her on some kind of journey, but Della refused to go.

"Don't get me wrong," Ruth called out to her daughter's back. "I'm not up to any gymnastics any more. Haven't been for years. But I wouldn't mind sleeping in a strong man's arms, I can tell you that.

Now come back here and let's finish the game. We know I'm going to whup you, but it's always fun to see how bad it can be."

"Fun for you, maybe." She dusted off her hands and rose, knees creaking, to watch tendrils of flame curl around the new log.

"So what were your turning points, Della? I bet I can guess one of them."

"Go ahead." Reluctantly, Della returned to the rocker.

"Abby's birth. That sure turned you around."

"That's right." She studied the board, trying to push away her irritation. For all she knew, a perfectly obvious Welsh noun was staring back at her, but the letters certainly didn't suggest any word she had ever seen. "And going to Vietnam," said Della. "That changed my life in a big way."

"You always say that, like change is a bad thing. Did you want to stay the way you were at twenty-one?"

"Of course not. But you enter adult life surrounded by death and mutilation … It molds you. It ages you. I don't think I ever really knew what it felt like to be young."

Ruth snorted. "If you want to know what it feels like to age a hundred years in a day, have your husband disappear, and you with two kids to feed."

Della tossed down an S at the end of T-H-R-E-A-D. "You know, you ask me what was the big deal in my life, and then you tell me not to make such a big deal of it."

"Maybe I'm just tired of hearing about Vietnam."

"How could you be tired? I haven't mentioned it five times since the day I got back."

"Maybe not, but they've all been in this last week." Ruth rattled the few remaining tiles in the bag. "It was over thirty years ago, Della. Thirty years!"

"So what? Hiroshima happened sixty years ago, and it didn't even happen to you."

"Yes it did. Hiroshima happened to all of us."

Della gripped the wooden arms of her chair to keep herself from bolting out of the room. "Well, Vietnam didn't happen to all of us. It happened to me."

"It's ancient history, Della. I'll be the first to say that war is horrible, and we should all be worked up about it—especially this new war they're cooking up in Iraq. War is a sin and a shame. But it's not personal. It's not aimed at you."

"War is completely personal." Her jaw ached as if she were chewing on gravel. "It's as personal as love or sex or—or childbirth, even. If you don't believe that, it's only because you weren't there. But I was there, Mother. And I don't understand why you can't even bear to hear about it."

"Because every time the subject comes up, you bite my head off." Ruth held up a hand to silence her. "Did it ever occur to you, Della, that maybe I feel guilty?"

"Why in the world would you feel guilty?"

"Because I couldn't keep a man."

"That has nothing to do with—"

"If your father had stayed, we could've sent you to college. And he was a veteran, he knew what war was like. Maybe he would have stopped you. You ended up in Vietnam because I couldn't hold on to my husband. I wasn't enough for him. There was something he needed that I couldn't give him." She touched each tile on her tray. "After all this time, I'd sure like to know what it was."

"Oh for God's sake, Mom, we don't even know that he left on purpose, much less why. He could have been forced to leave. He could have died."

"He left. Of course he left." Her voice shook.

"So what stopped you from remarrying?"

"There was never anyone serious. Who's going to get serious about a gal with two kids who doesn't even know where her husband is? I couldn't do what you did, Della, go to school after I was all grown up. I knew there was only so far I could go without an education, but I didn't have a sharp mind like you girls. All I had was this." She held up her kitchen-scarred hands.

"That was plenty, Mom."

"No. If I could have provided for you better, you wouldn't have needed the Army to pay for school. They wouldn't have sent you to that godforsaken country. You'd be a happier woman than you are today, and we'd be a happier family." Ruth shook out the bag of letters over the Scrabble game. The wooden tiles spattered onto the cardboard.

Della flinched at the sound. "Mom, what are you doing? We're not finished."

"Close enough," she said.

CHAPTER 11

LATE SATURDAY afternoon, Della sat alone on the bed in her blessedly empty house, clutching the phone in one hand and Charlene's letter in the other. It felt like so much time had passed since she received it that Della was surprised the single page hadn't turned yellow and brittle. She skimmed the printed lines as if they could reveal something new.

On the second try, she managed to press all the numbers in the proper order. The phone rang. She wanted to swallow, but her mouth was too dry. This must be what it used to be like for Rosalind, she thought, calling up women to ask them out on a date. At the third ring, Della pressed her fingers against her lips and resolved not to hang up until the sixth ring or until her heart had flung itself out of her chest, whichever happened first.

Finally she heard a man's cheerful voice. "You've reached the Randalls," he said. "We can't take your call right now, but—" Della shoved the phone away. She did not want Charlene's first contact with her after thirty years to be the sound of Della's shaky, stammering voice on an answering machine. It was astonishing how even the effort of making this thwarted call had wearied her—so much yearning and anxiety crammed into a handful of numbers.

Cracking the bedroom window open, Della smelled the complex aroma of a fading winter: stale snow, fresh air, damp earth. In a few weeks she would no longer be a captive of rooms, but could turn over the dense soil of her yard and watch new life spring up around her. Now as the daylight drained, she made a cup of tea in her quiet kitchen and read the newspaper. Her breath caught with each mention of weapons of mass destruction and the imminence of war. She wondered if she should cancel her evening with Anne and just go to bed, but then she remembered the promise of how soothing it would be to work with her hands when the only lives at stake would belong to flowers.

❧

"What's all this?" Della asked as she walked into Anne and Rosalind's living room.

"Oh, Della, I'm sorry." Anne picked up her glass of red wine and moved it to the far side of the table. "I meant to finish this before you got here."

Della laughed. "Don't worry, I wouldn't lose all my chips for a lousy glass of wine. It would have to be a single malt whiskey at the very least. Anyway, I meant this." She gestured toward Anne. Slabs of white styrofoam were stacked on the black slate coffee table; large cardboard spools of pastel ribbon lay in heaps on the L-shaped black leather sofa, like piles of discarded cotton candy.

"Our agenda for tonight." Anne reached for a roll of slim pink ribbon. "We're making bows to use in flower arrangements." With a pair of shears, she cut identical lengths of pink ribbon and dropped them onto the coffee table.

Della picked up one of the strips and fingered the smooth satin. "Is this for some kind of breast cancer event?"

"You are such an oncology nurse. It's for Mother's Day." Anne passed her a stack of green wires, each about a foot long, and thick as a straightened paper clip. "Here, make yourself useful. Cut each of these in half." She pushed over a pair of wire clippers with red rubber handles.

"But Mother's Day is two months from now."

"I know. And I have lots of bows to make before things get busy."

Della watched in awe as Anne plucked a piece of wire, bent it in half and, with incredible swiftness, twisted the ribbon around the wire in six even loops that fanned out into a perfect little bow. "Anne, you've got talent."

"Why, thank you, Della." She inserted the bow on its wire stem into a slab of styrofoam.

For a few minutes they worked in peaceful silence. Della listened to the rustle of the ribbon, the brief hiss as Anne stuck the thin metal into foam, the pleasing *snip* of the wire cutters. She could hear no traffic sounds, no music from the people next door. This house, so much larger and sleeker than her own, could have been a lone ship, its broad decks lit up and the world around it a fading mystery.

"Today a customer came into the shop," Anne said, "and showed me a swatch of rust-colored fabric. He was having a party, and he wanted to buy two dozen roses of that exact shade, to match his curtains." Small pink bows seemed to blossom in her hands. "I had to explain that roses grow in a lot of colors, but rust isn't one of them."

"Would he settle for a complementary color, like mold or mildew?"

"Ha. He thought I was just being lazy, refusing to special order them. I offered to spray some roses with a rust-colored floral paint, but that wasn't good enough. He walked out in a huff."

"My customers are usually happy with any flowers they get." Della reached for another batch of wires. "I don't think I've ever heard a cancer patient complain about flowers. The nurses are a little more particular."

"Speaking of nurses, what happened with your friend from Vietnam?" Anne covered the white rectangle with bows so quickly, it looked as if the styrofoam was growing a sickly pink skin.

This is how it happens, thought Della. Even her favorite pastime with Anne—gossiping about their respective workplaces with all the detail and fervor of soap opera addicts–had been pushed aside.

Suddenly every conversation was about Vietnam. After all this time, she finally wanted her family to ask her about it, but when they did she didn't like it, or she didn't like the questions they asked or the way they squirmed when she answered. Or maybe it was herself she didn't like–the way she was suddenly gushing about Vietnam, the things she said, or failed to say, or refused to say. Della felt as jumbled as the spools of ribbon on the couch.

"I called Charlene today," she said, "but she wasn't home."

"Oh, too bad."

"It was almost a relief. Her letter kind of … knocked me off my feet."

"Yeah, your mom told Rosalind you didn't sleep the whole time she was at your house. She thought maybe she was snoring too loud."

"Well, she does snore." Della watched her silver clippers bite into the thin green metal. "The thing is, ever since I got the letter, I've been remembering things I'd rather forget. I'm having nightmares, the same ones I used to have the first few years after I first got back."

"You know this sounds a lot like post-traumatic stress disorder."

"Yeah, I know."

"So this isn't news," said Anne.

"I've always thought I might have it, ever since I first heard about PTSD. I don't mean I always *have* it," she added quickly. "I've gone for years without a twinge. But then something happens and—" Della snipped a wire in half. "I even went to a medical library to study the literature and see if I could diagnose myself. As far as I could tell, not a single study on Vietnam vets included women."

"Della, when was this?"

"I'd been home around ten years by then, so it must have been '80 or '81."

"But that was ages ago," said Anne. "That shouldn't stop you from getting some help now. So much has changed since then."

Della smiled at her fierceness. "I already got some help, Anne. Lots of it. First I tried a rap group for veterans." Della looked at the clippers, the red rubber handles now warm and giving to her touch, and turned them over and over in her hands. "There was this technique—

walking through Vietnam, they called it—that I thought might help. Basically you talk about your memories over and over again, and hope that makes them settle down."

"Did it work?"

"I don't know. After one session, the group leader took me aside and told me he couldn't let me take time and attention away from the real veterans."

"Jackass." Anne jabbed a wire stem into the corner of the board and a chunk of styrofoam crumbled off.

"So then I joined a therapy group for women. But I still didn't fit in. The group was for women who had been victims of violent crimes."

"War is a violent crime," said Anne.

"I know that, but they didn't."

Della remembered the distinctive smell of the crowded room. Even though the therapist lit a strawberry-scented candle at the beginning of each session, the scents hovered: stale coffee, cigarette smoke trapped in clothing, and too many people breathing the same still air.

"When are you going to talk, Della?" a woman named Justine had demanded. "You've been here like three weeks now, and you haven't said a word. This isn't a damn TV show. "

Della had glanced at the therapist, an earth mother type in long skirts and large hoop earrings, but the older woman said nothing. It was clear the therapist had been expecting this challenge.

Another woman spoke up. "Leave her alone. Y'all pushed me to tell my story last week, and I haven't slept through the night since then."

"I haven't slept through the night since 1970," Della said in a quiet voice. She wasn't trying to trump the woman who had defended her, just trying to claim her place in the group.

"Then how about you let us in on it." Justine peered at Della from behind a hedge of black bangs that hung below her eyebrows. Her eyelids were dusted with purple, her blue eyes heavily circled by thick black eyeliner. It was as if she had found a way to wear her wounds.

"There's nothing to tell," said Della.

"So what are you doing here?"

"I mean there's no *one* thing. I don't have a day, a moment when it happened, like you do."

"Well, tell us *something*," said Justine. "The rule is no one has to share all the time, but everyone has to share sometime."

Della talked then. It seemed like she would never stop talking. She told the group about treating all the mutilated young men, about filling the body bags, about the endless, pointless hopelessness of it all.

"Everyone knew that war was crazy," said Justine. "Why did you even go there?"

Della's face burned. "Why did you wear that short skirt the day you were raped?"

"Fuck you!"

"Don't you see? It's the same question."

"Like hell it is. I was raped. You were fucked over. *Big* difference."

All this she told Anne very quickly. "But at least I learned some techniques to cope with the anxiety," Della added. "That's why it's ticking me off so much that my little tricks don't seem to be working anymore."

"I have a friend who's a therapist," said Anne, "and she told me treatments for PTSD have progressed a lot."

"This week I've been trying a do-it-yourself approach," said Della. "Water therapy."

"You're swimming again?"

Della nodded. "Just started. But so far it hasn't helped with the nightmares."

"Maybe now that you're beginning to talk about it, you'll feel better. Talking helps, really. Or at least I think so, and I've been in therapy a looong time."

Anne put aside her styrofoam board, half covered in bows. She collected the wire, ribbons, and tools, and set them all in a box behind the black sofa. Della felt naked with nothing in her hands. Anne came over and sat beside her. "What keeps you awake, Della? What is it you're thinking about in the middle of the night?"

In the mellow glow of lamplight, Della saw Anne leaning toward her. It occurred to her that, aside from her husband and child, Anne was the only person in Della's life who knew she had been in Vietnam but hadn't met her back then. That made her perhaps the one person that Della had not yet disappointed.

Della drew in a breath. "Sometimes I worry because I can't figure out which is worse: the boys I let die, or the ones I saved. What in God's name was I saving them for?"

"To go home," said Anne. "To have experiences, to raise kids. To love somebody."

"Some of them, maybe. But lots of them I patched up and sent back into battle. That was our mission; that was what we were there for. To save soldiers' lives so they could go back to kill and be killed."

Anne rose, pulled a yellow fleece blanket from the other end of the sofa, and wrapped it around Della's shoulders. Only then did Della notice she was shivering. The blanket was soft and warm, but weightless. Della wished she had something heavier to hold against her skin.

"That wasn't your decision," Anne said. "You didn't get to choose what would happen to them."

"It was the Army. You didn't get to choose much." She looked toward the small lights set like stars in the vaulted ceiling. "I worked in an intensive care unit. We treated some spinal injuries, but mostly amputees and burns. Hideous, unimaginable burns."

Della's hands twisted in her lap. "We spent our days debriding charred skin. I can't even tell you about the odors. I felt like my mother in those restaurant kitchens, working with the cooked meats. Only my meat could still shriek."

Anne shuddered.

"Should I stop?"

"No, go on."

"There was one patient who came in with a burned arm. It wasn't serious; all he needed was a few days of treatment. But this guy begged me not to release him. I can still remember every word he said." Under the blanket, Della pulled her knees to her chest and clasped her arms around them. "'You don't understand,' he told me. 'If you say I'm healed, I'll be back in the bush by tomorrow night. And I won't make it this time. Look, I've been in country five and a half months, and already I'm the oldest man in my unit.'"

"How old was he?" asked Anne.

"He meant he'd been in country the longest. He was only twenty. Every guy in his unit who had come to Vietnam with him was dead or wounded. He had the most beautiful brown skin, and these black, black eyes that you couldn't look away from. 'I can't hold out another six and a half months,' he told me. 'No one can. I'm no tougher than all those other guys were.' He grasped my hand so hard, I could feel the life in him.

"'Lieutenant. Nurse. *Della*,' he said. 'I'm not saying I don't want to go. I'm not saying send someone else instead of me.' He sat up in bed; he pushed himself up with his bad arm. My reflex was to help him, but he was holding my hand so tightly I couldn't. Still, I had to lean in close to hear him. 'What I'm saying is, no one can stay alive out there for six and a half months. Listen to me, Lieutenant: *It's—not— possible.*'"

"And did you keep him in the hospital?" Anne asked after a few moments.

Della could hear the flatness in her own voice. "His injury wasn't severe enough. We had to release him."

But she had always wondered whether that was really true. Surely Della could have figured out something. *Making a way out of no way*, Charlene used to say. If it happened now, she would manage to hold him, crafty as she was after decades of navigating hospital bureaucracies. But in 1969 Della had had less than a year of nursing experience, and the entire military hierarchy pressing on her to send him back to battle. So she kept him the only way she could: as an image in a ghastly album of blunders and regrets, held close to her heart.

"Did he survive?" Anne asked.

Della felt so tired she could barely move her lips. "Oh yes. He was awarded a Silver Star."

"Then you did the right thing."

"He was wounded again, and they brought him back to the hospital," said Della. "A few days later, a general came onto the ward to present the medal. The soldier turned his head away. Maybe he wanted to shake the general's hand or maybe he wanted to give him the finger, I don't know. All he did was turn his head. That was all he would ever be able to do. He was paralyzed from the neck down."

CHAPTER 12

THE SILVER STAR award ceremony took place on a Sunday in October, during the tail end of Cu Chi's rainy season. For months water had thundered from the skies and turned the world to mud. Della thought she would go mad from the din of monsoon rain pounding on metal roofs.

There was no escape from the soggy heat. Mildew bloomed everywhere—on her clothes, her sheets, her toothbrush. As she dashed from the mess hall to the hospital, only the wooden pallets that served as sidewalks saved her from sinking up to her ankles in red mud. It was impossible to keep the glutinous mess out of the hospital, no matter how often they mopped the floors and rinsed them with water mixed with aromatic peppermint oil to mask the odors of seared flesh and suppurating wounds.

The general planned to arrive at the ward in midafternoon, and he expected the universe to stop and attend to his visit. He had forwarded a lengthy checklist of items he wanted to be in place when he stepped out of the chopper, fans and cold drinks being among the most reasonable. Then he sent an assistant to inspect the hospital on the morning of his arrival.

As Della worked her way from bed to bed, checking vital signs and changing dressings and IVs, she snuck glances at the negotiations taking place near the doorway of the Quonset hut. The general's aide clutched his clipboard and gaped down at Major Throop while she told him how it was going to be.

"I'm sorry, Captain, but my nurses are medical professionals, here to serve patients, not generals. We are happy to change any bloodstained linens as the general requested. But we will not be moving any patients, no matter how unsightly their wounds."

"Ma'am, the general's got a tight schedule and a short fuse," he said urgently.

"I understand you to mean that the general will take it out on you if everything doesn't go as he wishes, and for that I am very sorry. But this is a hospital, not a movie set. My nurses will not take time away from their patients to pretty up the ward."

"Look, ma'am, the general's been wounded himself, more than once. He's a tough man, but he's tenderhearted. He doesn't like to see other people's blood and pain."

"Then perhaps he should think about a new line of work where the product is more to his liking. Now, if there's nothing else, Captain, I have patients to attend to."

He snapped to attention and gave her a salute. "You oughta be a general yourself, ma'am."

"Not very likely in this man's Army." Major Throop's mouth turned up slightly as she returned his salute.

At 1400 hours, the general swept into the hospital trailed by his entourage, including the anxious, clipboard-toting captain. The general strode down the wide central aisle of the ward, tossing salutes like candy, barely glancing at the wounded men. He paused by the side of the paralyzed young soldier, who lay strapped into an apparatus called a Stryker frame that enabled the staff to change his position.

The general looked ridiculous in his crisp, starched uniform with its rows of colorful ribbons, his polished boots gleaming like patent leather. Maybe he had been a soldier once, but now he was nothing more than a REMF, a rear echelon motherfucker who caused more trouble than he was worth and had no idea what was really going on.

The high-ranking career officers, Della knew, rarely spent a whole year in Vietnam, but rotated in and out within a few months. That way as many officers as possible could claim the all-important combat duty on their résumés. "Punching their ticket," they called it—the ticket to promotion.

"Son, a grateful nation thanks you for your heroism," the general began in his booming voice. The young man, whose strong body was now just a circulatory system for fluids and wastes, turned his head away. His trembling lips bunched up as he fought back tears. Della saw his eyes lock onto Charlene's, who was tending to a post-op patient a few beds away.

The general continued, "It is my distinct privilege to present you with this honor." He pinned the medal to the soldier's light blue pajama top. "May you take pride and comfort in all you've accomplished and all you've sacrificed for love of your country."

Across the cots, Charlene spoke to the soldier as if they were alone in the room. "Isn't it crazy what passes for love around this place?"

"Crazy," he whispered, and he smiled. A tear trickled out of his eye and slid across the bridge of his nose. Della thought it must itch, the slow progress of saltwater across his skin. It took her a few seconds to remember that he could not reach up to wipe his face.

That night in the officers' club, Della bought a round of drinks for everyone in honor of Charlene's demotion. At the insistence of the red-faced general, Charlene had gotten busted from first to second lieutenant. It was a laughable punishment for a woman who was not planning to make a career in the Army. Even the reduction in pay meant nothing in a land where a can of beer cost fifteen cents.

Della handed the bartender a thick pile of colorful Military Payment Certificates. "Everyone, raise your glasses," she called out, standing on a chair, "to Second Lieutenant Johnson, Cu Chi's newest butterbar."

She hopped down amidst the cheers and brought a bottle of Gordon's gin over to the small round table where Charlene waited. They gulped down their drinks. Della barely grimaced at the bolts of lightning that scorched her throat and belly.

"Let's have another toast." Charlene refilled the glasses. "To my little brothers, who landed me here in Hell's Lobby. Thanks a lot, guys."

"They're gonna owe you big when you get back to the World."

"Especially William. He's in Fort Riley right now, going through basic. Hope they're training him for some cushy stateside assignment to make up for what they're doing to me."

"Seems only fair."

Charlene swirled the clear, sharp-smelling liquid in the small glass. "I can't decide if he should wash my car for the rest of his life or mow my lawn."

"Why not both?"

"Roger that." She tipped her glass to Della. "Let him take care of me for a change."

They had to drink fast. For one thing, 0630 rolled around quickly, and they needed to be sober in time to begin their shifts. For another, in this world of sexually deprived young men, two women could expect to have only moments together before being begged to dance, to talk, to take a walk, to let a lonely soldier sniff their hair.

"You're the first roundeye I've seen in months," they would hear over and over, and "Couldn't I just hold your hand for a minute?" and "You smell like home." Very possibly it was all true and all heartfelt, but oh, what pressure when all Della wanted to do was put up her feet and relax with a woman friend after a tiring day.

Sometimes the pressure was less subtle. Rumors about the female nurses flourished. They were all sleeping with doctors, which is why they thought they were too good for everyone else. Or they were all prostitutes, serving men by day and, for a fee, servicing them by night. Donut Dollies, on the other hand, gave it up for free. Sometimes the rumors were reversed, and it was the Red Cross volunteers who were coining it while the nurses offered themselves as a public service. And of course, any woman who was not readily available to her country's fighting men was obviously a lesbian who needed a man to show her the light.

The rumors were hilarious and at the same time menacing. After all, in Vietnam the women were constantly surrounded by men and vastly outnumbered. And while the medical staff or the patients might think of the nurses as sisters or saviors, it was clear that plenty of other men thought of them as meat. A decent woman wouldn't be here, they seemed to believe, so any woman in country was here for the taking.

And so Della learned to be wary. She learned that the distance between a joke and a threat was not all that great when the joke ran along the lines of, "OK, sugar, I'll let you go this time, but next time you won't get away so easy." She learned that if she wanted to get loaded in the O club with Charlene, she'd better do it quickly.

That night she got so drunk she decided to drop in on Major Throop. Della found the major in her quarters, hunched over a narrow table as she wrote a letter.

In the oval of ivory light cast by a desk lamp, the energetic woman looked drained, the lines of her face pulled down as if by a special gravity all her own. Della glanced at the major's small hand gripping the pen, and it occurred to her for the first time that maybe Ada Throop had a life and loves beyond the barbed-wire boundaries of Cu Chi base. Yet she'd volunteered to stay on for a second tour.

"What can I do for you, Lieutenant? Come in and close the door. You're letting in the entire insect world."

"Thank you, ma'am." Della leaned against the door and eyed the cramped room with its concrete floor and bare plywood walls. "I wanted to ask you about a patient, the guy who got the Silver Star today." She was pleased to get the words out without slurring.

"He's stable. Tomorrow he'll be air evacked to Japan."

"And after that?"

"Then home, to a VA hospital near his family."

"And then what?"

Major Throop laid down her pen. "You can imagine that as well as I can, Lieutenant. A lifetime of dependency, infections, frustration, isolation. Probably a short lifetime, but perhaps not short enough for his liking. Is that what you came here to ask?"

"No ma'am. What I want to know is *why?*"

The major blinked up at her. Then she sighed and her face softened. "Della, that's how most people spend their entire adult lives—seeking an answer to your question."

"But what if you can't find an answer?"

"Then you learn to live with the unknown." She scraped back her chair and stood, filling the room. "It's a big question, Lieutenant. Try to give it some time."

彩

"SHE SOUNDS very wise, your major." Anne sat cross-legged on the couch, facing Della, so close Della could smell the faint almond fragrance of her hair.

"She was certainly ancient," said Della. "She must have been at least forty."

"Wow, it's amazing she could still totter around."

"I do wonder where she got her stamina. Nurses worked twelve-hour shifts, six days a week, and we were on call four times a week. When there were mass casualties, we worked around the clock. I was worn out, and I was only twenty-two." The extravagant energy of youth—Vietnam had burned through it in a single year. "By the time I got home I was exhausted. I feel like I've been tired ever since."

"What happened when you got home?" asked Anne. "Some kind of re-entry program?"

Della shook her head. "The Army put you on a plane in Vietnam and twenty hours later you found yourself alone with your duffel bag and your heat rash, plunked down into the everyday world. I landed in May of 1970."

"Oh my God," said Anne. "Kent State. Jackson State."

"Exactly. By the time I made my way from the Oakland army base to the San Francisco airport, kids my own age had called me every name in the book, from whore to—" Della stopped.

"Let me guess. Dyke?"

Della nodded. "At the airport, I ran into the first bathroom I could find and tore off my uniform. I threw on some civvies, went to the airport bar and got drunk."

She remembered seeing two middle-aged men in business suits at the other end of the bar, guzzling tall glasses of beer. "We oughta get the hell out of Vietnam," the shorter man had declared. "Just pull out."

"Yeah," said the other, "like you do when your wife is just about to come."

They had both laughed like cartoon characters—har har har!—and Della had banged her glass on the counter for a refill.

"Rosalind says you were pretty messed up when you got back."

Della ducked her head, wondering which of the shameful stories Rosalind had chosen to tell her. She hoped it wasn't about the time Rosalind had tracked her down and found her in her car at dawn, passed out behind the wheel in the deserted parking lot of a dingy bar.

"If you want to kill yourself, go ahead!" Rosalind had screamed, slapping the keys out of her hand. "But don't do it here in town. And don't do it in a car 'cause you'll probably screw up and kill someone else instead."

"Why do you hate me?" Della had mumbled.

"I don't hate you. I don't even know you." Sobbing with rage, Rosalind had shaken her by the shoulders until Della thought her spine would crack. "You are not my sister. You are not my sister!"

Della squeezed her eyes shut against the memory. "I was drinking a lot, changing jobs, moving around. I never got fired, though, for the drinking. I just quit."

"Why?"

"I would get bored," said Della. "Or somebody would piss me off. I worked in the E.R. at first, but in those days they wouldn't let nurses do anything. Here I had been debriding wounds and clamping bleeders, and they wouldn't even let me start an IV. And then they expected me to take orders from little rich boys fresh out of medical school."

Anne smiled. "Sounds like you didn't treat the young doctors with much respect."

"I gave them exactly the respect they earned," said Della. "Finally I had to get out of E.R. I trained for labor and delivery and moved to another city where they didn't know I was so evil."

"Rosalind has this theory that it's all about fathers."

"Oh, please. Rosalind and her theories," said Della, prepared to laugh. But then it struck her that she *had* believed in them, the men in suits who stood before the flag and spoke with such assurance, the steel-jawed officers with their tidy racks of ribbons, the heroes and victors of World War II. She was certain they would remember their own battle terror, the brothers they had lost. She had trusted them to treat their sons with tenderness, to risk them wisely in combat, to recognize in each young soldier a precious, irreplaceable life.

The fathers had abandoned them all.

"My first few weeks in country," Della said, "I kept thinking there must be some terrible misunderstanding. You see these horrible wounds, these ruined boys, and you can't believe this is what they really intended."

"*They*, meaning…"

"The politicians, the generals, the men who made these decisions. Did they really say to each other, 'We have a policy problem with another country. Let's solve it by maiming and slaughtering their children'?"

"I know. I've been thinking about that a lot, with all the talk about Iraq." Anne kneaded the yellow blanket between her fingers. "In the movies, when you see the leaders decide to go to war, they're all sitting around a conference table looking grim. But really, someone must love it. Otherwise we'd have found a better way. There must be something irresistible about war—the sick glamour of it all."

"It's more than glamour." Della had glimpsed the grinning skull beneath the bland smile. It still made her dizzy to think of it. "It's money. I mean, take napalm—a flaming jelly that sticks to the skin. You can't wipe it off; it just keeps burning wherever you spread it. Who would create such a monstrous weapon? Someone made that decision. Someone said, 'You know, I think I could put more money in my pocket if I manufactured a product that made human beings scream in agony.'

"I want that person to know what I know," Della said. "I want him to live the way I live, with that odor trapped inside his head—the stench of charred flesh mixed with the jet-fuel stink of napalm." She wanted Anne to smell it too, to taste the lingering foulness in the back of her throat—just for one moment. Because in that moment, Della would not be so alone.

"Della, I never knew you were so furious."

"I wasn't. I used to believe we had learned something from Vietnam. Now we're rushing into Iraq to do it all over again, and it makes me so fucking angry I can barely stay inside my skin." She flung off the blanket. "Stop telling me to talk about this shit, Anne. It doesn't help. It's like I puke it out but there's always more there."

"Maybe you're not talking about the memories that really make you sick."

"Who says I'm sick?" Della asked sharply.

"Hey, you brought up the puking metaphor."

"Oh. Right."

"Della, you have to talk to someone about this, someone who can help you."

"Do you mean a shrink?"

"I mean Charlene. Because when you talk to me, you sound like a closeted lesbian."

"Well, that's a first. What does a closeted lesbian sound like?"

"You have all these thoughts and feelings and memories that seem to set you apart from everyone else, and you think you're the only one in the world. But you're not. You simply haven't figured out how to identify the others. I can tell you from my own life, sometimes I just want to hang out with other lesbians because it's so much easier. You share assumptions and experiences, and you don't have to explain anything."

"Gee, the lesbian thing works much better than the vomit thing."

Anne didn't smile or pull away. "I'm not joking, Della. You're in pain, and it's not funny to me."

"All right, all right. I'll call Charlene again. Soon."

"And then call my therapist friend." Anne pulled a slip of paper from her pocket. "She's expecting you. I didn't tell her anything, just that you might call."

"Man, I feel so *easy*. You had this all planned before you even invited me over."

"No, I didn't," said Anne. "I didn't know what to expect, but I came prepared. You can tell your mother those years in law school weren't wasted after all."

CHAPTER 13

THE NEXT MORNING, Della found herself in her fragrant kitchen, talking with her ex-husband. Ben had layered the table with newspaper and removed the cover from the old VCR. Now he bent over its shiny, delicate internal organs, the small screwdriver in his large hand making a rhythmic squeak like a baby bird.

Tapping her fingers on her knees, Della watched Ben work. His profile was so familiar: the square chin, the bushy brown mustache, the blue eyes squinting in concentration. Even his ever-receding hairline was familiar, as it now looked exactly like his father's.

"There. She ought to run fine now." Ben ran a clean cloth across the face of the machine. "Hey, Del, didn't I fix this old girl last year?"

"No, you told me you would fix it last year."

"Oh. Sorry."

"Don't be." She rose and stirred the soup that simmered on the stove, watching chunks of onion, carrot, and celery tumble over one another in the amber broth. "The fact that it was broken is the only reason Abby didn't take it with her when she moved."

"That and the fact that I got her a DVD player." He gave his lopsided smile. "What are you making? Smells good."

"Vegetable soup."

"The kind with the lentils? I never liked that."

"You'll notice you don't live here anymore."

He took a spoon from the drawer and dipped it into the soup. "Ugh. I still don't like it. Those lentils look like floating mouse turds."

"Thanks a lot. Now I'll think of that whenever I make this soup." With her hip, she shoved him away from the stove.

"Why are you making such a big pot, anyway?"

"My book club is coming over this week."

"A book club?" He sat and tipped his chair back until the front legs hovered in the air. "Kim belongs to one too. She kicks me out of the house when it's her turn to host. Makes me wonder what goes on at those things."

"It's not that mysterious. We have dinner together and talk about what's happened in our lives, and then we discuss the book."

"Who decides what you read?"

"Well, it used to be Oprah." Charlene's letter crackled in the back pocket of her jeans as Della squatted to reach the pot lid on a low shelf. "Then we decided to strike out on our own."

"I can't believe it. Not only does she own all the money in the world, but you women let her tell you what to read."

"Oprah recommends good books. If that was what made her rich, there'd be a lot more male librarians."

Ben let his chair fall with a thump. "I hope you didn't teach our daughter your twisted way of thinking."

"I tried, but it didn't take. Have you talked to Abby lately?"

"Last week. She told me she's trying out for a play that calls for total nudity. How can I go see my daughter in a play if she's going to be buck-naked?"

"You can hide your eyes."

"But everyone else will be looking!"

"You can beat them up afterwards." Della leaned against the sink and looked down at him. A circle of scalp shone, pink and vulnerable, at the crown of his head. "Ben, Abby goes to a lot of auditions and so far she hasn't gotten very many jobs. There's no point in getting upset about this one until she lands the part."

"Yeah, you're right."

"I left a message for her a few days ago," Della said, "and I still haven't heard from her."

"You really should get a computer if you want to keep in touch with Abby. She's not good with phone calls, but she does answer emails."

"I once had a computer exactly like the one Abby's using now. Unless you got her a new one?"

"Working on it." Ben gathered the newspapers into a pile. "You look tired, Del. Having trouble sleeping?"

"Some."

"My guess is you're just not getting enough."

"You better mean sleep."

"I mean whatever you think I mean. Seriously, though. Are you having any fun?"

"Sure. I'm having fun right now." She sat at the table again and watched threads of steam escape from under the trembling lid of the soup pot.

"No, visiting with your ex on a Sunday morning is pleasant," he said. "I'm talking about the lift-your-spirits kind of fun. What makes your heart pound these days?"

"Running for the bus?"

"That's my point. You're so damn virtuous. Why don't you do something useless for a change? Go sky diving. Learn to belly dance."

"I thought this was supposed to be fun for me."

"So what would you enjoy?"

"I'm not sure." She thought for a moment. "Maybe you're right. It might be fun to learn something new just for the sake of learning. Maybe … Latin?"

"Well, that's definitely useless."

"Actually, it would help with crossword puzzles. And a lot of medical terms are Latin."

"See, that's no good. It has to be just for fun, nothing you can use at work."

She listened to the quiet murmur of the soup. "When I was a kid, I really wanted to learn to play a musical instrument."

"Now you're talking. Music might be just the thing to help you sleep, too."

"Anne thinks the insomnia is getting out of hand. She thinks I should see a counselor, someone who works with PTSD."

Ben stood and shoved the stack of newspapers into the recycling bin. "Della, you can't have PTSD. You didn't see any combat."

"Maybe what I saw was worse than combat."

"There's no such thing. I was in Nam too, remember?"

"You spent your tour stacking boxes in a PX at Long Binh."

Della pulled the letter out and smoothed it against her knee under the table. Maybe if she showed it to him, he would understand. "Something is happening to me, Ben. I'm coming unglued. I'm being overrun by memories—things I haven't thought about in years. Things I never told anybody, not even you. It makes me feel kind of sick, like there's all this fear and guilt churning around, eating away from the inside. Do you know what I mean?"

He shook his head.

"I hoped you might understand because... Well, do you ever think about, you know, why you? Why were you assigned to the PX instead of the field? What happened to the guy who got sent into the bush instead of you?"

"It was the luck of the draw, Della." He dropped into the chair. "I got lucky, some other guy didn't. I don't have anything to apologize for, and neither do you."

"Maybe I do." She twisted to face him. Here was a man who knew her like no other, who had heard her moan in passion, and scream profanities in childbirth, and hum tunelessly as she sewed curtains. And now, for the first time in years when she needed him to truly hear her, she looked into his eyes and saw—nothing. He had no idea what she was talking about. The man had left her once again.

"Listen, Del." He covered her hand with his own. "We were kids when they sent us over there, and kids make mistakes. Now we're looking back at fifty. It's only natural we have regrets and bad memories and things we'd give anything to do over."

"I guess." Her hand was still warm where he had touched her. She remembered, like a thump of fist against breastbone, the tense, effortful sex they had in the latter years of their marriage, as if each was frantically searching for something in the other. Afterwards she would fall back, spent and silent, never having found what she needed or even a way to name it.

There was no point in showing the letter to Ben. With the best will in the world, he would read the few printed words and miss the white space where all the meaning hid.

"I better go," he said. "Kim's probably getting ready to sizzle up some burgers." Ben reached for the VCR. "Where do you want this?"

"Leave it there. Rosalind's coming over later to take it to Mom's apartment, along with a stack of Cary Grant videos."

"That ought to make Ruth happy." He slipped the screwdriver into his shirt pocket. "Listen, Della. You've got a killer job, you can't sleep—that would drive anyone nuts. Not to mention the fact that the world's a scary place right now. Try to cut yourself some slack."

"Okay."

"And stop taking medical advice from your florist," he said.

"My florist?"

"Your whatever-she-is. Anne."

"My sister-in-law."

"Kinda more like an outlaw, don't you think?"

"Oh, I don't know. In my family, you're more like the outlaw. After all, Anne's still married to my sister."

He clutched his heart. "Guess I'll stagger on home now."

"You do that. And thanks for the house call."

The house throbbed with quiet after Ben left. She remembered the first time she noticed silence had a voice, on the day seven years ago when he had moved out.

"I can't believe you're doing this," she had told Ben that morning, her words stretched thin with the effort not to scream at him. They stood on either side of the bed, his suitcase open between them like a patient on an operating table.

"Della, I'm just making it official. We both know you left me long ago." He closed his suitcase, and the sound of the zipper sent a surge of panic through her.

She clutched the handle with both hands. "What are you talking about? Look at me, I'm right here."

"No, you're not." He sounded exhausted. "You never have been."

Late that afternoon, Abby had marched into Della's denuded bedroom and announced her intention to get an after-school job. Della studied her somber, dark-eyed daughter and did not explain about child labor laws or her lack of marketable skills. Instead she patted the bed and rested her hands on Abby's thin shoulders.

"Abby, I have a job for you. It's a big responsibility, and it's the most important job in the house."

"What is it?"

"Your job is to be a fourteen-year-old. That means you're supposed to study hard, and sweat on the basketball court, and hang out with your friends, and play really ugly music as loud as you can. That's the best way you can help our family now."

"So you just want me to be a kid?" Abby had squirmed away from her touch.

"Exactly."

"Then you should have waited. You should have waited until I was grown up before you split. What was the big hurry, anyway?"

There had been no hurry. Little by little, like so many household items, their love had gotten lost. Until the end, Della kept thinking it would turn up again.

She and Ben had failed each other in ways large and small, ways that she could catalog but even now didn't fully understand. But at least they had managed to be good parents. She was pretty sure of that.

"Abby's got two parents who love her and a good education, which is more than either of us ever got," he had consoled her when she fretted about how Abby would manage alone in New York. Now she and Ben had embarked on their last and longest project together—learning to master all the open-handed ways you can love a grown child.

CHAPTER 14

ON SUNDAY afternoon Rosalind rushed into Della's house, her face bright with cold, her unbuttoned leather coat flying behind her like a cape. "Where's the VCR?"

"Well, hello to you too," said Della.

"Sorry. It's just that we need to get going. Mom's been waiting all day for her Cary-fest."

"And whose fault is that?" asked Anne, on the doorstep behind her.

"Um, yours," Rosalind said. "If you recall."

Anne actually blushed as she looked down to wipe her boots on the mat.

"Oh please," said Della, stepping aside to let them in. "Is there something about my house that makes people come here and talk about sex?"

"Who's been talking about sex?" Rosalind said.

"Suddenly you're not in a hurry. Anyway, it was Mom."

"Ew," said Rosalind. "Never mind."

"I know." Della gestured to the open door. "Staying or going?"

"If it's OK with you, I'm staying," said Anne. "I don't want to spend the rest of the afternoon with Ruth."

"But I'm just going to set up the VCR for Mom," Rosalind protested. "Then we'll leave."

"No, we won't." Anne pulled off her boots. "You'll put in a tape just to get it going, and then you'll both get engrossed in the movie, and I'll be stuck there until Cary Grant makes that goofy expression at the end of *Charade*. I can drop you off or I can stay here."

"I'd love the company," Della said. After dealing with Ben's incomprehension, it would be good to spend time with people who were at least more sympathetic, even if they were just as discomfited by this strange new need to talk about her experiences. "I could make coffee."

"We won't stay that long," Rosalind said. "I'll get us some water."

"*You* won't stay that long. *I* just got invited." Anne took Della's wrist and tugged her into the living room.

"Let me run this past you," Anne said. She and Della faced each other across the dead fireplace. They were in their accustomed places, Anne on the sagging brown couch, Della in the wooden rocker. They could hear Rosalind in the kitchen, murmuring into her cell phone. "We were debating this on the way over. Didn't you ever wonder about Ruth and Liz?"

It took Della a moment to figure out what Anne meant. "Good God, no."

"I mean, they weren't technically related. Liz was your dad's sister."

"They were sisters-in-law," Della said pointedly. "Like us."

"They lived together all those years," said Anne. "They were only in their thirties when they moved in together, and neither one ever lived with a man again."

"No, no, and no. I don't know about Liz, but Mom got around pretty good."

"Is Anne regaling you with her Liz and Mom theory?" Rosalind set down three glasses of water and stretched out on the couch, resting her stockinged feet in Anne's lap. Della thought Rosalind looked her most relaxed and lovable in jeans and a hooded sweatshirt, her curly auburn hair freed from the large silver clip that subdued it during the day. Most striking, she had traded her contact lenses for the solid, brown-rimmed glasses she wore only in front of family.

"You're not a believer?" asked Della.

"Certainly not," said Rosalind. "I don't even want to think about it. Nobody wants to hear about their parents' sex lives."

"Or anybody else's," Della added.

"Although fictional characters and celebrities are OK," Rosalind said.

"I love to hear real people's stories," Anne said.

"Yeah, but your own parents'?" She nudged Anne with her feet, which, in their hot pink socks, resembled a pair of exotic birds.

"Fortunately, my parents never had sex. But other people's stories can be sweet and romantic. Especially stories about the first time."

"Was your first time sweet and romantic?" Della asked.

"Absolutely. It was on a summer night, outside under the stars. The air was sparkling with fireflies, and the soundtrack was crickets and Barry White."

"Barry White! What a funny choice for two women."

Anne smiled at her. "What makes you think my first love was a woman?"

Della glanced at her sister. "Well, I just assumed. I mean, I know Rosalind hasn't been with any men."

"Unlike Rosalind, I had to go through some trial and error."

"I had plenty of that," said Rosalind. "The first time I had sex it was in a dorm room, in the middle of a snowstorm that knocked out power to the whole campus. For one night, Maureen and I were in our own little world, lit by candles and hormones. The next morning, she freaked out at the thought of being gay. Broke my heart in pieces. By the end of the semester, she was engaged to a football player."

"Talk about being scared straight," Anne said.

"Anne loves that story," said Rosalind. "I've never understood why."

"What about you, Della?" Anne asked.

"You don't want to hear my story. It's not sweet."

"I knew it," declared Rosalind. "That blond guy, Ronnie. You could tell he thought he was quite the catch."

"No, it was much later, when I was overseas," said Della.

"You were a virgin? You were twenty-one when you went over there. Abby's age."

"But it was a different world," Della said. "I was in nursing school. I lived in a dorm with forty other girls, and we had a housemother who made sure men left the building by ten o'clock."

"Sounds like heaven."

"You are such a pervert, Rosalind."

"Don't I know it."

"Tell us," said Anne. "I don't care if it's not pretty."

Della hesitated, but only for a moment. "His name was Mac. He flew a dustoff chopper, one of the helicopters that fly into battle zones and pick up the injured. The nurses were close with the dustoff pilots. They handed off their wounded to us, and they saw the same kind of carnage we did day after day. Mac had been flirting with me for a long time, and I had been resisting. Then one day I decided to go ahead with it."

"That sounds a little cold," said Rosalind.

"You could say I reassessed my future."

"Della, is there a reason why you have to be so cryptic? Either tell us or don't." Rosalind took off her glasses and tossed them onto the coffee table. Della jumped a little at the sound.

"All right." The familiar agitation ran like ants along her nerves. "The first time I decided to have sex," she said, "it was because I had just watched a boy die. And in a way it was my fault."

Della gulped some water, but it couldn't seem to reach the parched place in her throat. She gripped the glass with both hands.

"It was early morning. Charlene and I were just completing the overnight shift. The fighting had been pretty heavy, and the ward was completely packed. There was this one patient who had sustained so much damage…."

"We had all these clinical abbreviations to describe wounds. GSW for gunshot wound. AEA for above-the-elbow amputation. But cases like his, well, some nurses just called them 'horriblectomies' because there was so much wrong with him. He had lost a leg and an arm. His genitals had been blown off. There was a crater where his right eye used to be, and his left eye was all bandaged. Flies had laid eggs in his open wounds, and the surgeons were letting the maggots debride his wounds."

Rosalind turned her face away as if she could see the wounds on Della. "What is that?"

"The maggots ate the pus and the decaying flesh. It's an ancient medical technique, and some of the surgeons found it helpful. But I could never get used to it. It made me gag every time."

Della glanced at Anne to see if she should continue. Anne gave a slight nod. "I passed near this patient's cot, and he called out, 'Nurse? Did I get a letter or did I dream that?' He asked me to read it to him.

"I opened the letter. He was so new in country that this was the first letter he had received. As soon as I started reading it out loud, I knew it was a mistake. Charlene kept signaling at me to be quiet, but I couldn't figure out what to tell him if I stopped reading.

"The letter was from his girlfriend. She was kicking herself because she had been too afraid to sleep with him before he left for Vietnam. I read each word to him, words she never intended anyone else to hear." Della could see the round careful writing, blue ink on flimsy lined paper.

"She wrote, 'Next time I see you it's going to be different. I'm going to hold you so tight and never let go. Oh, honey, I get hot just thinking about it. I don't care what Mama says. If we end up having a baby I don't mind, as long as he has your beautiful blue eyes.'"

Della rested her forehead in her hand. "When I looked up from the letter, I could tell he wanted to die. That was no figure of speech. There's a light people have when they're struggling to live, and I watched his flicker out. He would never make love with this girl who was longing for him. No child would have his beautiful blue eyes.

"What kind of life could he look forward to, with chronic pain and only half a body? You can talk about healing, you can talk about the miracle of prosthetics. And I did. But who can believe that when he can smell his own flesh rotting?"

She looked up. Rosalind was no longer prone on the couch, but sitting upright, hands clenched in her lap. Della remembered that they had been expecting a lighthearted story about her own first romance, not this detour into horror. But it was all so connected there was no way to talk about one without the other.

"Anyway. After our shift ended, Charlene and I went to the hooch and sat on the floor with a bottle of Jim Beam. And we decided to let go of all the good girl/bad girl ideas we had been raised with. You know, 'one true love.' 'Saving myself for my husband.' We could die any minute. Might as well live while we could."

Della pictured her young self, slumped against the dusty wall in her worn fatigues. *Some day my prince will come,* Charlene had sung, and Della had completed the sentence, *And he'll be in a body bag.*

We're putting an end to that shit right now, Charlene had declared. She took a swig of bourbon and pushed the bottle toward Della to seal their agreement. Della welcomed the bite of liquor in her throat, the way it shot fire through her legs.

"That afternoon," she told Anne and Rosalind, "I ran to Mac."

It was monsoon weather, inside and out. Rain and wind battered Della's hooch, where she and Mac stood inches apart. A sudden gust blew open the tin flap that covered the window, and water pelted the small room. They barely noticed, reaching for one another. She felt dazed and stupid with desire.

They grappled, sweaty and urgent on Della's narrow cot, sandwiched between flimsy plywood walls that carried every sound. He told her everything he wanted to do before he did it. She thought it was tenderness, some kind of deference to her inexperience. Later she wondered if it had been a form of seduction, his breath hot in her ear as he whispered what the next moment would bring.

There was no way to tell what was his frenzy, what was hers, what was the wildness of the Southeast Asian summer, spending itself in the late afternoon. Above the battering of the rain she caught a moaning sound, like nothing she had ever heard. It was rising from her own throat. Della could no more have stopped it than she could stop the storm. At the end Mac had to clamp his hand over her mouth.

The war vanished, the world was wiped clean, and all that remained were two young animals, healthy and whole and driven towards life. Sleep pulled her under.

A few hours later, the war snatched her back. Della and Mac were awakened by sirens, by the *whump* and crash of mortars, by one of her hoochmates muttering, "Where the fuck's my flak jacket?" Incoming, she thought. Of course. She hardly had time to register the sweetness of his arms wrapped around her before Mac released her and began to feel around on the floor for his clothes.

"You're not going to the bunker, are you?" She sat up in the cot.

He zipped his pants. "Nah. But I gotta go." Mac sat on the bed and looked frankly at her breasts in the dimness. She pushed away the sheet. "Wow," he said. "You are a beauty, Della Brown."

The words meant nothing, she knew, but his fervent voice thrilled her. Mac looked different to her now: his face appeared softer, like a pencil sketch smudged by someone's hand. Della wondered if she looked different too, or if that was just how everyone looked after they'd had sex and their body and mind were filled with light.

Another explosion ripped the night, farther away this time. Mac leaned in to kiss her, crushing her breasts against his bare chest. She could feel the muscles of his back move under her fingertips. Cool air rushed between them when he pulled away.

"I have to get some sleep," he said, reaching for his shirt. "Tomorrow morning I'm on call for twenty-four hours. Can't fly when my brain is mush."

"You can sleep here."

Mac grinned. "With you looking like that? I wouldn't be able to shut my eyes. Besides, I'm not supposed to be in the women's hooch past 2300 hours."

"What are they going to do, send you to Vietnam?"

"No, but your roommates might kick my ass."

"That's true." But she scooted over to make room for him in the bed.

"Baby, if I stay here one more minute, no one's going to get any sleep tonight." He took her hand, pressed it against his beating heart, and left.

Della had been in Vietnam four months by then, long enough to know she was in trouble. You didn't rest your happiness in a man, much less a man who belonged to the sky.

❧

THE SUN SLIPPED behind the houses across the street from Della, surrounding them with bright halos that flared in her living room window. Her hands squeezed her empty glass. She had never told that story before, never revealed the way sex and death and love and remorse were all knotted up inside her.

Anne was the first to speak. "Did he survive the war?"

"He did. I almost lost him once, and then I did lose him—he DEROSed. 'Date of expected return from overseas.' "

"He went home," said Rosalind.

She nodded. "By now, he could be somebody's grandpa."

Anne stretched her arms along the back of the couch. "And his grandchildren will never be able to imagine him as the dashing pilot who swept a young nurse off her feet."

"I have no idea where he is now. When he left, he didn't want to give me a way to contact him."

"Maybe he was married," said Anne.

"Probably. He said he wasn't, but I really didn't care. The time when those things mattered seemed very remote by then."

"Well, let's go Google him," Rosalind said.

"The thing is, I can't remember his name." Della felt a flush of shame, as if she had been caught in a lie. "Everyone called him Mac, but that was just a nickname. His last name was Mac-Something. McCall, MacDougall—I've tried to think of it a million times. There are a lot of things I don't remember from those days, and names are a big one."

Rosalind gave her a skeptical look. "You say you thought you could die any minute. I thought you weren't near the front."

"There was no front. The war was all around us. Cu Chi was a huge army base, with all kinds of targets. We got rocketed and mortared a lot. They may not have been aiming for the hospital, but sometimes they hit it. Every time there was a red alert, we had to get the patients into bunkers, and if they couldn't walk we covered them with mattresses."

"That seems a little pointless," said Anne, "like those school drills where they taught us to squat under our desks during a nuclear attack."

Della shrugged. "At least a mattress could protect the guys from falling debris. The nurses were supposed to run to a bunker too. But most of us stayed on the ward to take care of the patients. Before long, I stopped going to the bunker even when I was off duty. I learned to sleep under my cot, in my flak jacket and helmet, curled up in all this gritty yellow dust that was everywhere."

"I can't imagine even trying to sleep in the middle of an emergency," Rosalind said.

"After a while it didn't feel like an emergency, it just felt like—how things were. The whole time I was in Vietnam, artillery blasted throughout the night. Sometimes a few of us nurses would climb on top of a latrine and watch the light show." She closed her eyes. They were still there: the rockets with their terrifying cartoon whistle, tracer bullets slicing neon trails of red and green through the black sky.

"I don't understand how a U.S. Army base could be so dangerous," Rosalind said. "You were surrounded by armed soldiers."

"Sure, but we still got hit. Cu Chi was vulnerable; the Viet Cong had dug tunnels throughout the whole area. They had kitchens and hospitals and sleeping quarters right below us. They could get anywhere underground. It was an amazing achievement."

"I always thought that was some kind of urban legend."

"No, they had more than a hundred miles of tunnels. We only found a fraction of them."

"I guess I never realized you were in such danger," Rosalind said in a small voice.

"Where did you think I was, Girl Scout camp?"

"I probably pictured you in a sparkling clean hospital, miles from any action, helping wounded soldiers sip lemonade through a bent straw. Give me a break, Della. I was just a kid."

"I was just a kid, too. We all were. They had nurses Abby's age doing triage—assessing these hideously wounded boys and deciding who could be saved and who would die." Della snapped on the lamp, and Rosalind covered her eyes with her hand. "Would you want Abby making life and death judgments about you?" Della said. "Abby, who thought it was a good idea to get a pink flamingo tattooed on the back of her neck?"

"She would grow up fast," said Rosalind. "Just like you did."

"I suppose that's one good thing that came out of it," said Della. "And I saved up enough money to help my kid sister through college. That meant a lot to me."

Rosalind picked up a small, square gold cushion from the couch and clutched it to her stomach. "Please don't say you did it for me."

"What?"

"It was a big help that I didn't have to hold down a job while I was in school. That's the only reason I was able to get the grades to go to law school, and I've always been grateful. But don't say you went to Vietnam for me."

"I didn't say that."

Rosalind's knuckles turned white as she kneaded the cushion. "That whole era was just one big misplaced modifier. Johnson spraying napalm. Nixon bombing Cambodia. They all swore they did it for us. I didn't ask for any of that, and I sure as hell didn't ask my sister to go over there and earn money for my college career. I won't take responsibility for your nightmares, Della, or the way you stare into space sometimes like you're waiting for the mother ship to come back and get you."

"All I said was, it made me feel good to be able to help you." Feeling a sudden surge of nausea, Della planted her feet on the floor to still the rocking chair. She turned to Anne. "Help me out here."

"I wouldn't dare wade into your family history. But do you want to hear what Vietnam cost me?"

"Please."

"Four years in night school," said Anne. "When I was in college, some of my professors bumped up the boys' grades so they could keep their student deferments. That meant the teachers had to cut back the girls' scores to keep the grade spread balanced. I never got an A no matter how hard I studied." Anne smiled slightly, as if the memory amused her.

"By the middle of my sophomore year," she continued, "the draft changed to the lottery system, and that ended student deferments. Eventually the grading system got back to normal. But by then it was too late. It was hard enough for women to get into law school in those days, and with a grade point average weighted down by the war ... well, that's why I spent four years taking dictation by day and law classes at night."

"Did the girls agree to sacrifice their grades to keep boys out of the draft?" Della asked.

"No one consulted us. It was just understood."

"Yeah, there was a lot of that going around. In Vietnam there was an 'understanding' that nurses would rather die than be taken prisoner by the Viet Cong. I heard there were actually American soldiers whose assignment was to shoot the nurses if the base was about to be overrun. No one consulted us either."

"How would the soldier know if the base was about to be overrun?" asked Anne.

"That teenaged boy with a deadly weapon, hyped up on terror and adrenaline? I guess he was supposed to use his own judgment."

"Okay, that's it for me." Rosalind slapped her knees. "Time to go."

Della felt heat flare on her cheeks, as if the blow had reached her. "What's the problem, Rosalind?"

"No problem. I just don't understand why we're talking about war again."

"Have you read the newspapers lately?"

"I mean your war. It was so long ago, Della. Why can't you just leave it in the past?" Rosalind threw her cushion on the couch and stalked into the kitchen.

Della watched her disappear. "I don't get it, Anne. Why is she so mad?"

"I'm not sure. Did you ever ask Rosalind what life was like for her back then?"

"Probably not."

"Well, maybe you should."

It was not quite six o'clock when they left, still too early to call Charlene, who might be having dinner with her family. Della made herself a cup of tea and settled on the couch with a book, but soon nodded off. Much later she awoke from a dream about the pilot, his breath on her throat, his muscled thighs, the soft skin on the inside of his arms. She reached down to finish what the dream had started, only to find herself as dry and indifferent as a folded slip of paper.

With a sigh, Della sat up. The living room was murky with its single lamp, but the air was alive with sound. The refrigerator cycled on with its reassuring hum. A car whished by on some urgent errand, not bothering to slow for the stop sign on the corner. The kitchen clock chimed the half hour, solemn and distant as a church bell. She closed her eyes and replayed the afternoon's conversation.

It was true that there was a long chunk of time when she'd lost sight of her sister's life. Shortly after Della returned from Vietnam, Rosalind left for college. She must have felt like an immigrant trying to find her place in a new country, Della thought.

Abby had grown up with the expectation that she would get a higher education, in part because Aunt Rosalind had broken the path. It was Rosalind who helped Abby shape her application essays and collect her recommendations. But no one had shown Rosalind the way. Somehow she'd managed, alone on that hilly campus in Ithaca. Della could imagine Rosalind, with her watchful brown eyes, studying the older, richer students to learn how to fit in. But she would never truly fit in; her love of women would always make her an outsider. And that too she must have learned in school.

Della felt a bolt of grief for those years she'd missed, the times when Rosalind might have needed an older sister and had no one to turn to. Della had been on a mission to anesthetize herself—with drink, with distance, with men. She saw Rosalind at Christmas, and kept in touch with her mainly through the news that Ruth or Liz would share in their infrequent phone calls. Only now did it occur to her what bland pieces of information could have made it through all those filters.

Maybe that was why Rosalind seemed so bitter. Della thought she could read it on her sister's face: *You can't remember the name of the man you loved, but you remember every awful thing you saw there.*

But she didn't know if she had really loved Mac. Maybe she'd been in love only with his healthy limbs, his unbroken skin, the sharp intake of his breath when she touched him. She'd probably been a little in love with her patients too, all the young warriors, each pursuing a private vision of manhood that would perish with him.

The soldiers she had lost, the ones whose final home was the Twelfth Evacuation Hospital—Della couldn't remember their names, but she knew them. These men never surfed the Internet or sent an email. The names Watergate, Chernobyl, World Trade Center meant nothing to them. Most had never known a longtime love or held a child of their own. They hadn't learned that you could spread death by making love. They had never grown old and they never would.

Why can't you just leave it in the past, Rosalind had asked, and she was right. Vietnam was long past. But it was not yet over. Della pulled Charlene's letter from her pocket and reached for the phone.

CHAPTER 15

SITTING ON THE edge of her bed with every light in the room turned up high, Della punched in Charlene's number. The phone rang once, twice.

"Hello?" A voice, low and mellow, sliced through the years.

"Charlene?"

"Yes?"

"It's Della. Della Brown."

Silence. Della's blood thudded in her ears. Finally she heard Charlene inhale.

"Girl, where in the world have you been?"

"Right here." The words rushed out in a strange, choking breath. "Right here in Podunk, New York, like you always said."

"You got my letter."

"Yes. I couldn't believe it. After all these years."

"I didn't know if you were ever going to call," said Charlene.

"I didn't know either." Della waited a moment. It seemed to be still her turn to talk. "How'd you find me?"

"Online. You signed an anti-war petition. I knew it was you because I recognized the name of your town."

"Oh my God." She gave a breathy laugh. "My mother made me do that. She hasn't entered the computer age herself, but she read in the newspaper about these online petitions, and nagged me until I signed one."

"Well, that was lucky for me. Glad to hear your Mom's still at it, too."

"What about your folks?" Della wished she could bite back the words, because as soon as she uttered them, she and Charlene veered into a strained kind of chitchat, like guests at a class reunion who couldn't quite place one another. They talked briefly about parents and husbands, about Della's daughter and Charlene's two sons, all the children grown and gone.

"Abby just left a few weeks ago," Della told her. "It still feels strange. I haven't lived alone in more than twenty years."

"When my boys left, I had such mixed feelings," said Charlene. "Arthur and I miss the kids, but we love the quiet. And the tidiness. Boys are chaos theory in motion."

"Girls can be pretty good at creating chaos too." Della wanted to climb through the phone, to shake the other woman by the shoulders and yell, "Charlene, it's me!" Instead, finding herself exhausted by the superficial conversation, she flopped back onto the bed.

"Charlene," Della said finally, "can we meet somewhere?"

"Yes." The relief in Charlene's voice was unmistakable. "We can. But you know, it's not going to be some breezy little get-together. You, me, Vietnam—it's a lot."

"I know." Della wished she could float up to the ceiling. The clean white plane and sharp corners looked so inviting and peaceful. But it felt as if a double dose of gravity had pinned her against the mattress. "The thing is, I'm having kind of a life crisis. Your letter kicked it off."

"I'm so sorry, I didn't mean—"

"No, I know," Della said quickly. "It's just that...all this stuff about Vietnam, and then Iraq... and it's crazy, but I feel like you might be the only person in the world who truly understands me."

"Della," said Charlene, "I don't even know you."

"Right." A strange pang spiraled through her. "But you knew me then, and that's what I need."

"Let's keep it simple," said Charlene. "Why don't we meet for coffee and see how it goes."

"I'll come to Boston. Do you live near a Starbucks?"

"Do I live in America?"

"Tell me where it is. I'll meet you there."

"There's a quieter place. It's a little restaurant I like, called Amanda's, in the Newbury Street area. You get off the subway at Copley Square."

"I can find it."

"This way," Charlene added, "if it's not going well you can just excuse yourself, head for the ladies' room and duck out the door. I know you've had practice at that."

"What? I'm sorry, I don't—"

"Those god-awful officers' parties? Where they figured nurses were the main dish?" Charlene said. "You have to admit, we worked out some pretty good escape strategies."

"Oh, right. After you left, I heard some other nurses weren't so lucky."

"I guess a lot happened after I left," she said.

Della opened her mouth to reply but only air came out. "Okay, see you on Saturday," she said after a moment, and they hung up.

With a dull ache in her chest, Della slid open her top dresser drawer and felt around behind worn-out bras and folded socks. It was still there. She pulled out the tiny glass vial and held it up to the light. Climbing back onto the bed, she unscrewed the small black cap and peered inside. The aromatic oil had dried into a cracked paste.

Many of the nurses in Vietnam wore perfume when they worked. The patients loved it; they said the fragrance reminded them of home. For the nurses, the perfume helped cover the odor of blood, feces, and decomposing flesh that they inhaled daily. Della's favorite, she remembered, was something called Hypnotique. But while the other women doused themselves in flowery fragrances, Charlene used to wear a touch of sandalwood oil on each wrist and behind her ears. It was her signature, as distinctive as her warm voice or melodic laugh.

Della sniffed the glass vial. Here was a substance never meant to last, yet thirty years later it was still potent.

◊

"Wᴇʟʟ, ᴄ'ᴍᴏɴ, Della! Are you going to show us what's in there, or do we have to take matters into our own hands?" Charlene pretended to lunge for the dented cardboard carton labeled in Ruth Brown's bold purple print.

"Get your paws off my package, or there's going to be one more amputee in Vietnam." Della pulled an envelope from the box.

"Do you girls have to be so rude?" Mary Grace smoothed her fingernails with an emery board. The sound sent chills skittering up Della's back.

They were relaxing in the community room of their hooch, a drab dorm-like space enlivened by colorful posters, beat-up chairs with tie-dye fabrics thrown over them, and a slatted wooden coffee table painted egg-yolk yellow. The haphazard decorating reflected contributions from most of the fifteen women who shared the quarters, as well as many who had lived there before.

"Charlene, you know Della's going to divvy up," said Mary Grace. "Keep your pants on."

"Repeat that to yourself later," said Charlene, "when Larry comes to pick you up."

"You are so bad."

"I've heard you're good."

"You heard that right," Mary Grace exclaimed, and they both cackled. "Della, Charlene has a point, for once. Read the letter on your own time. Let's see what we got."

"You're going to be disappointed. I didn't ask for food, I asked for supplies."

"What kind of supplies?"

"Arts and crafts. Water colors, or colored pencils, or needlepoint. I don't care what it is, I just want something to take my mind off the war."

Charlene peeked into the box. "Well, if that's all you wanted, you could have found it on base for two bucks a bag, with the rolling papers thrown in for free."

Della pulled a mangled package out of the carton. "Here's a bag of what used to be Oreos."

Mary Grace scooped up a handful of cookie fragments. "Perfectly good," she announced thickly.

"What else did you get?" asked Charlene.

"Well, let's see." Della set each item on the table. "Chef Boyardee pizza mix. Noodle soup. Pancake mix. Syrup."

Charlene reached for the package of pancake mix. "Look at this. Aunt Jemima in her do-rag, grinnin' in delight 'cause she gets to cook flapjacks for de white folk."

"That is pretty offensive." Della took the box and set it on the table, face down. "I'll be sure to make the pancakes when you're not around."

"Don't you dare. What else is in there?"

"The nectar of the astronauts." She held up a jar of orange powder.

"Cu Chi punch!" Mary Grace and Charlene said at the same time. The sweet, powerful punch could be made with any alcohol that was around, as long as it was mixed with one particular taste enhancer—Tang.

"Hey, I wonder what this is." Della plucked out a crumpled ball of newspaper, crisscrossed with masking tape, and squinted at the note scribbled across a strip of tape. "It's for you, Charlene. From my sister."

"Well, bless her heart. What is it?"

"I don't know." She tossed her the ball.

"This is all very nice, but where are your craft supplies, Della?" Mary Grace brushed cookie crumbs from her fatigue shirt.

"That's what I was wondering, before I got distracted by the sight of an O.R. nurse wrestling with a wad of newspaper."

"You just attend to your own business." Charlene struggled to peel off the masking tape. "That big box isn't empty already, is it?"

"Damn near." Della pulled out a round metal canister. "Oh, good. Rat-proof snack storage." She pried open the lid and shook the canister over the coffee table. Out slid two magazine-sized paperbacks filled with crossword puzzles. "I don't get it." Della picked up a book and riffled the pages. "I've never done a crossword puzzle in my life. Why would they send me this? All I asked for was some art supplies."

Charlene gave up on delicacy and tore through the tape. "I know how you feel. Now and then you need something to help you get through the day, and a big bucket of gin isn't always the answer."

"Not always," Mary Grace said. "Sometimes a simple beer will do."

"Hey, look at this!" Charlene held up a small glass vial. "Your sister got me my scent." She unscrewed the cap and sniffed. "It's me, all right. Sandalwood, straight up. How'd she know?"

"You told me you were almost out. And I was pretty sure the PX wouldn't carry it."

"If we want it, they don't carry it." Mary Grace rose and stepped over the low coffee table on the way to her room. "I have to put on my civvies. Larry will be here soon. What are you two doing tonight?"

Della flipped through the books. "Crossword puzzles, it appears."

"Maybe we'll drop in at Joey Z's going away party," said Charlene. "He's got two days and a wake-up, and then he's freedom bound."

"Lucky guy." Mary Grace closed the door.

Della unfolded her letter and scanned the two pages, dense with Rosalind's round, upright handwriting. "Listen to this, Charlene. Rosalind says my mom decided art supplies would get ruined in this climate."

"Probably true," she said, dabbing sandalwood behind her ears. "Look what happened to our clothes."

They had learned to protect their clothes from mildew during the rainy season by keeping them in a wooden box with a light bulb that burned all day to combat the incessant moisture. "And get this," Della continued. "My aunt decided that crossword puzzles would be a good way to 'expand my vocabulary in more helpful directions.'"

"What does she mean by that?"

"I have no fucking idea."

"My mother would shit a brick if she heard the way I talk now." Charlene tossed the ball of crumpled newsprint from hand to hand. "And my father…I can't even imagine his reaction if he heard his darling daughter cussing like a damn grunt."

"Let's not talk about our families. Let's talk about how much fun we'll have tonight, making sure Joey Z re-enters the World with a hangover he'll never forget."

"Those crossword puzzles are sounding better and better."

"I know. Charlene, did you have coloring books when you were little?"

"Sure."

"Remember that feeling you had as a kid, of being so engrossed that the whole rest of the world faded away?"

"Sort of. But I can definitely remember watching my little brothers, the way they'd lie on their stomachs, their little feet swinging in the air, tongues sticking out. They'd get so absorbed they even forgot to fight over the crayons."

Della nodded. "I'd give anything to have that feeling for just a few minutes. I guess that's what I was hoping for when I asked for art supplies."

"Your mom didn't know. There's no way our families can understand what this place is like, no matter what we tell them. And I've seen your letters, Della. You don't tell them much."

"Yeah, but still."

"I know."

Della sighed and turned a page. "Okay. What's a ten-letter word for 'destroy'?"

They never made it to the party. The phone emitted its harsh ring, and they were ordered back to work.

Charlene shrugged. "That's why they call it 'on call.'"

"TPRS," Della muttered as she laced up her boots. In the nursing world these initials stood for "temperature, pulse, and respirations," but in Vietnam it was universally understood to mean "This place really sucks."

Della spent much of the night with two burn patients. One had second-degree burns over 30 percent of his body, and his pain was so intense it seemed no amount of morphine could stop his screaming. The other patient was in even worse shape, his nose and lips seared off, the skin down to his hips scorched leathery and black. He, at least, was not suffering; he was unconscious, not yet aware that the life he had known was over.

Della drew blood for testing, pulled off the men's boots and started IVs in both legs. She hung bottle after bottle of saline solution, plasma, and blood to replace the fluids that leaked copiously from their exposed flesh. Through the night the medical staff pumped antibiotics and painkillers into the men, but it was not enough; the more serious patient developed pseudomonas, a life-threatening bacterial infection that turned burnt tissue blue and produced an odor so foul it overpowered the stench of charred flesh and hair. Della had to breathe shallowly through her mouth so she wouldn't vomit.

It was after three o'clock in the morning before things finally quieted down in the I.C.U. Della sagged in the wheeled chair behind the nurses' desk, resting her arms on the metal desktop as she filled out patients' charts beneath the piercing light of a gooseneck lamp.

There was no sound, but something made her look up to find J-Rag, a friend of Mac's, standing in the doorway. Mac's unit was a small one, only twelve pilots, and by now she knew them all. How they got their strange nicknames she had no idea. For an instant she scrutinized J-Rag to see where he was wounded, until it struck her that injured men did not walk into the I.C.U. and wait silently for attention. She rose so suddenly that the desk chair went careening toward the wall. She turned to Hillary, the charge nurse, who nodded across the still row of cots, giving Della permission to leave the ward.

Outside the Quonset hut, J-Rag got right to the point. "Mac's late," he said, slapping a mosquito on his neck.

Della's brain seemed to have entered its own time zone, a few seconds behind everything else. Mac was late, she puzzled. Did that mean she was pregnant? Her body seemed to understand first; she found herself squatting Vietnamese-style in the powdery dust before she absorbed the information that he had not returned from his mission on schedule.

"What happened?" she whispered.

"We don't know yet." J-Rag squatted in front of Della, but he addressed himself to her boots. "He's only a couple of hours late. It's some kinda trouble, but maybe nothing deep. Could be some minor fuckup. It's happened."

She glanced at her boots and noticed they were spattered with blood. "When will you hear something?"

"Can't say. Could be any minute." For the first time he looked at her, and she saw troubled, rheumy eyes in his young, tanned face. "Thought Mac would want you to know." He stood, and Della clutched at his arm.

"Will you call me as soon as you hear anything?"

"No sweat."

Back in the I.C.U., she stood over the first burn patient and prepared to check his central venous pressure to assess his blood flow. The usual sites for testing—the carotid artery in the neck, inside the elbow—were a mass of scorched tissue, so she pressed her fingers against the pulse under his ankle. But with panic thrashing inside her gut, Della could not summon the stillness to stand there for thirty seconds and count out the beats of the man's blood.

She tried to hang a fresh IV bottle for him, but her shaking hands missed the hook. The glass bottle crashed to the concrete floor, waking several of the patients. Hillary calmed the patients while Della replaced the IV and cleaned up the mess. Then Hillary steered her to the desk and pushed her into the wheeled chair.

"What's going on here, Lieutenant?" Hillary Hammond was a captain in the Army Nurse Corps, destined to be a lifer, and as STRAC as they came: upright and impeccable, outraged by trivial infractions of dress or demeanor, and intolerant of the notion that rules could be relaxed in a war zone. She stood rigid, her green eyes narrowed. Even her chin-length red hair looked angry.

"My boyfriend is missing." Della felt a laugh bubble up in her throat. She had never before called Mac her boyfriend, and it sounded ridiculous. The urge to laugh quickly dissipated, leaving her hollow. If only Charlene were here with me, she thought, or anyone other than Chilly Hilly.

But Hillary sank to the floor in front of her and rested her hands on Della's knees. "Oh, Della, I'm so sorry," she said. "Not to know— that's the worst feeling in the world."

To Della's horror, Hillary's eyes filled with tears. The captain tipped up her chin, and the tears did not spill over. The move was so practiced Della realized she must have relied upon it many times.

Chew me out, Della begged silently, give me demerits. This was worse than anything. To know that Hillary, of all people, had suffered; that the Ice Queen carried pain so close to the surface it brought instant tears of compassion—well, how was Della supposed to hold it together after that? And hold it together she must, no matter what. That was the one thing she was sure of. Della felt a flash of anger at Mac for thrusting her into this sorority of suffering women she had known all her life and vowed to avoid.

"Della," said Hillary, "I'm going to send you home."

"But I don't want to go home."

"We'll be fine here. The morning shift begins in a couple of hours."

"I'm on the morning shift," said Della.

"Not today, you're not. Go get some rest. Find out what you can about your boyfriend. Do what you need to do."

Della never would have expected that Chilly Hilly had such warm hands, or that her light touch could be such a comfort.

"But Della, listen. I want you to understand this. You're hurting now because you gave your heart to someone." The captain nodded toward the sleeping ward. "Every man in here carries some woman's heart. Maybe it's his mother or his wife. Maybe it's, I don't know, a teacher who had high hopes for him. Do you understand what I'm saying?"

Della shook her head.

Hillary rose, but her voice remained gentle. "I'm saying take today for yourself. But after that, return to duty. These men need you here, a hundred percent focused and professional. Not a grieving girlfriend. A nurse."

Della stood outside the Quonset hut and listened to the night whine of insects, the hum of generators, the boom of artillery. There was nowhere she could go. She would not be allowed to do the one thing she craved, which was to bang on the door of Mac's commanding officer and plead for news. She couldn't bear to go to any of the places where she'd spent time with Mac: the mess tent, the officers' club, her hooch, and certainly not her bedroom. There was only one place Della could think of that she had never gone with Mac, one place that would not echo with his absence. She headed there without hesitation.

It was not a room, really, but a destination: a three-piece folding screen, each panel covered with pleated yellow fabric, like a curtain. In an old movie, the nightclub singer would change her clothes behind a screen like this, just beyond the view of her male admirers. Here in Vietnam, the screen hid a different kind of transformation. This was where patients came to die.

The boy behind the screen lay on the gurney, a green sheet pulled up to his smooth, hairless chest. He was still breathing, but Della could tell that he had slipped below consciousness. His body shocked her: no wounds, no burns, no mutilation. Just a swelling of the abdomen where the percussion of a bomb had turned his internal organs to jelly.

It was always surprisingly quiet behind the screen, considering that the pleated curtain and a few feet of space were all that separated this area from the rest of the I.C.U. Della knew she would be safe here, and that someone would find her if there was news about Mac. She sat down next to the gurney and let the silence sink into her.

The ethos behind the screen was the same as on the ward: no crying, and no false assurances. In a way, a nurse's task back here was even more difficult, because she must stifle every instinct to fight against death. Death was the guest they were waiting for, and all a nurse could do was try to make sure the visit was painless. To make the bargain explicit, the men behind the screen were called "expectants."

She found the expectant's name on the evacuation tag that was tied to his toe. "Hi, Carlos," she said. "You don't know me, but I'm Della and I'm going to sit with you for a while."

His expression did not change, of course; his black eyebrows and firm, full lips held a look of concentration that she had often noticed on unconscious patients. His eyes were closed, but one eyelid did not quite reach the lower lid, revealing a slit of white. Carlos's thick black hair was studded with debris from the explosion. His square jaw was rough with stubble.

"I know you can't speak, but maybe you can hear me. Or maybe you can feel this." She took his hand, still warm but inert.

"Carlos, you don't need to be scared or worried about anything. Your family will never forget you. They'll always love you and be proud of you. And they'll always remember you the way you are now: handsome and strong and brave."

She didn't know who she was reassuring, Carlos or Mac. With each word, she could feel something inside of her break. It was a new, wild pain, made of equal parts loss, fear, and fury. Yet each fragment that fell away from Della seemed to join something larger, some force that was greater than grief, or war, or the flimsy hope of humans.

She remembered, suddenly, one winter dawn years ago when she had walked alone through glittering woods. Small sounds piled on top of one another: the packed snow squeaking under her boots, dry branches clacking in the breeze, a pine cone falling to earth, her own breath, taking in the sharp air. In that moment Della realized that the earth was singing—a glorious, complex chord she was never meant to hear. And she couldn't exactly *hear* it, but she could feel it vibrating in her own body. She had known, with a teenager's certainty, that somehow she was a part of that melody and it was a part of her.

Here in this steamy land, where nothing cold could live, she could almost sense that chord thrumming in the strange, pulsing silence behind the screen. She looked at Carlos and thought maybe the music was what he was studying so intently.

"You can hold on as long as you want, Carlos." She gave his hand a squeeze. "But when you're ready, just let go. It'll be okay. Everyone does it. I know it's terribly unfair you have to go so soon, but it will be all right. You'll see."

It wasn't as though Della couldn't survive without Mac. She could, and she expected to, as soon as his tour was over. But a life without Mac was one thing; a world without him was too awful to imagine. Still, it was far more bearable to face her own abandonment than to envision Mac frightened or in pain or—oh God!—burning to death in the carcass of his beloved Huey.

All right, this is not useful, she told herself. This is fucked up. He's just late, not gone.

"Look, Carlos, it's getting light out." His chest had stopped moving, but Della kept talking to him. "It's always pretty gray back here, but you can still tell when the sun comes up." She could hear people begin to stir in the main section of the ward. It seemed very far away.

"I know your family and friends will be sad, Carlos. But you can rest now. What you did here was so difficult, and now it's time to rest."

One of the yellow curtains billowed slightly, and Charlene slipped behind the screen. In the dimness she smiled brilliantly and raised both her thumbs. A sob of relief erupted from Della, and she clasped Carlos's hand to her chest to silence herself. Charlene nodded and withdrew. Della knew Charlene would wait for her on the other side of the screen, where the living belonged.

She could feel the cold creeping up Carlos's arm. It happened so quickly, even here where the air was warmer than the human body.

"People can say what they want about this war, Carlos." She released his waxy hand and set it gently on the gurney. "But you should be proud. You did your best, and that's not a small thing."

For the first and last time behind the yellow screen, she dropped her head and let herself weep. For Carlos, for Mac, for Hillary. For the next man to enter this silence. For those who would never know why they had been called to this country, and those who would never wonder. For everyone who had donned a uniform and done what was asked of them, the most bitter duty of all.

CHAPTER 16

AFTER HER PHONE call with Charlene the days marched past smartly, pulling Della closer to their meeting. Still the nights lingered, delivering gruesome dreams and gritty, weary dawns. But on this Wednesday evening, as she pushed a wobbly grocery cart, Della felt hopeful. On Saturday she would see Charlene. The following Monday she had an appointment with Anne's therapist friend. Maybe she was finally ready to give peace a chance.

"I'll get that for you, Mom." She stooped to pull a box of cereal off the metal shelf. "They're on sale. Do you want two?"

"At my age there's no point in buying backups." Ruth reached for the red plastic handle of the cart.

"You've been saying that for years. I think we could take the risk."

"Well, that's about it." Ruth checked her shopping list. "You know, Della, it's very sweet of you to buy my groceries for me. But it's not necessary."

"I'm glad to do it, Mom. Do you have all the basics at home? Toothpaste, toilet paper?"

"Yes, dear. When did you become such a fussbudget?"

"I can't help it. I inherited it from my mother."

They were next in line to check out, and Della began to unload groceries onto the moving belt. Oranges, eggs, cottage cheese. A plastic bag bulging with broccoli, dimpled red potatoes the size of a child's fist.

All progress stopped as the elderly man in front of them examined his receipt. Money must have been tight for him, or maybe he didn't trust the electronic scanner. At any rate, he wouldn't budge till he was satisfied. Della didn't mind the delay, but the people behind her sighed and shuffled their feet like a herd of ponies.

"Your father's as bald as that man," her mother whispered.

"Yes, I imagine he could be by now."

"Not could be. Is."

She turned to Ruth. "How do you know that?"

"I saw him."

"What are you talking about? When?"

"At Liz's funeral. I saw him after the service, when we all turned to walk back up the aisle. He was standing in the last row, in a navy blue suit. Remember all that beautiful red hair he had? Gone. Nothing left but a few wisps of white, like little bits of cloud."

Della gaped at her. A man's voice called out, "Hey lady, you gonna move up or what?"

She glanced at her mother's purchases, now gliding past on the damp black belt: the bloody cuts of beef, the pallid chicken breast. The floor felt spongy under her feet. Della grabbed her mother's wrist and yanked her out of line, past the exclaiming cashier and the staring customers.

"What about my groceries?" Ruth protested.

"I don't give a damn about your groceries." Della pulled her through the bright, noisy supermarket, past the ranks of checkout lines, past the displays of dog food piled against the wall like sandbags, and into the chilly night. The still, damp air felt soothing on her face, and even that infuriated Della, as if some feathery hand was trying to pacify her.

"What are we doing?" Ruth's voice sounded a little tremulous, but her pose was bold. She stood hands on hip, one foot in the parking lot and one on the curb, a slim leg clad in navy pants angling through her long gray coat.

"We're talking, for once. Sit down." She pointed to the green plastic bench near the store's entrance. Ruth pulled her coat around herself and sat.

"If you saw Dad at the funeral, why the hell didn't you say something?" Della stood directly in front of her mother, forcing Ruth to look up at her. Ruth put a hand to her eyes to blot out the pinkish halogen lights in the parking lot behind them.

"I couldn't. My mouth opened, but nothing came out. From all the way across the room he looked right into my eyes and he smiled, just a little bit. Then he shook his head. One of Liz's friends came up and hugged me, and when I looked up he was gone."

"Why didn't you tell me? I could have chased after him."

"He asked me not to."

"When?"

"When he shook his head."

Della sank onto the green bench. "Are you sure it was him?"

"Of course I'm sure. After all the years I spent looking into that man's eyes? Eyes don't change, you know. I'm looking at them right now. You have his eyes."

Della's father was gone, evaporated. It had always been a fact of life, something you could rely on, like the expectation that Rosalind would argue with the television throughout the evening news. Only now it seemed her father was not gone. Or maybe he was, in which case it was her mother who was slipping away.

"Do you know what I kept thinking after I saw your father?" Ruth gripped the curved armrest between them. "I kept thinking, I can't wait to get home and tell Liz." Her eyes glistened. "Then I would remember that Liz wasn't there. And a few minutes later I would think about telling her again, and I would have to remember all over again that she was gone. It was so strange, the way that lesson just couldn't stick in my brain."

"But why did you want to tell Aunt Liz and not us?" Della hated how childish she sounded.

"I would have told her afterwards, after he left."

"Well, you could have told us then, too."

"But Liz wouldn't try to find him if I asked her not to. I wasn't so sure about you and Rosalind."

"Did you know he was alive, before the funeral?"

"I never knew. But I always thought I would feel it—" Ruth pressed both hands against her chest—"if he was dead."

"So you weren't surprised to see him there?"

"I was and I wasn't."

In the artificial light, Ruth's hair was the same color as the wire shopping carts that sat abandoned on the sidewalk around them. Even on this ersatz park bench, her posture was erect. Her hands were clasped in her lap, and her blue eyes looked defiant. But what could she be defying—Della? Her husband? The family mythology she herself created? Della wondered if she would ever be able to see Ruth as the woman she was, without the yearning and resentment that shimmered the air between mothers and daughters.

Ruth sighed and let herself slump against the hard green slats. "He called me. After the funeral."

"You've *talked* to him?"

"Turns out he lives in Lockhart. Been living there for years."

"Lockhart is less than two hours away!"

For the first time, Della's mother turned to face her. "I know."

"He didn't even have the decency to run to Montana, or at least Canada?"

"Matter of fact, he did. He went to Canada first. But he left later, when all the Americans coming to Canada were draft dodgers."

"Of course," Della said with an exaggerated, palms-up gesture. "He wouldn't want to be mistaken for a draft dodger. The man's only a family deserter. No shame in that!"

"Don't you think I know that?" Ruth snapped. "I'm the one he deserted."

"So what did he do for all those years?"

"He was a salesman. Appliances, hardware, plumbing supplies, I forget what else he said. You know how he is. He can sell anything to anyone."

Della didn't bother to point out that she did not know how he was. All she knew was the jagged hole he left in their lives, the festering questions. And one more thing. "But he loved us," she said slowly. "I know he did."

"Yes," said Ruth. "He loved his daughters. And he loved his wife." She pressed her lips together. "But he just didn't have the stamina."

From the way Ruth spoke, Della could tell her mother had heard that sentence a hundred times since her husband first uttered it, had tumbled the words over and over in her mind.

"He didn't have the stamina," Della repeated.

"That's what he said. Not everyone is cut out for married life, Della." Ruth gave her a level look. "As you know."

She nodded. It seemed no one in their family was cut out for married life, except for Rosalind. "Did he ask about us?"

"Of course. I told him all about you and Rosalind. He's very proud."

"Proud!" She snorted.

"He wanted to know about everything, about you girls and me and Liz. All of it."

Why, how wonderful, Della thought, slowly unzipping her purse and watching the silver teeth pull apart. One conversation and the man catches up on forty years! Who needs Christmas letters?

She pictured her father old, diminished, with tufts of white hair and her own hazel eyes. She thought of war criminals tracked down after a lifetime, of corporate titans whose days of selling poisons had long ago ended. She had seen them on TV: feeble old men, coughing into crinkled handkerchiefs. It hardly seemed possible to bring such men to justice, to make them recognize, just once, the ruin they had spent their lives creating.

"Did he ask you how you managed after he left?" Della said, her voice rising. "Did he ever say he was sorry?"

"Della, that's enough. What we said was between me and him."

"Then why are you telling me now, three years later?"

"I got tired of keeping it inside. And you're already so busy chasing ghosts, I figure you don't have time to go after him." She looked out across the parking lot. "Maybe I shouldn't have. He begged me not to tell anyone."

"So what? Why should you do what he wanted?"

"Because I owed him."

"You *owed* him? He abandoned you with two small children and a pile of debt! You owed your daughters the truth, not him. The man fucked you over, Mom, don't you get that? What could you possibly owe him?"

Ruth's face looked gray and exhausted. "Oh, Tommy wronged me terribly, I know that. But he still left me with something precious."

"What was that?"

"You, dear. You and your sister."

Her generosity astonished Della. But what did she really know of what passed between her parents? As a father, Tommy Brown had been like so many dads of that era: awkward, affectionate, largely absent. Now it seemed he was alive, living nearby, able to learn about his sister's death in time to pull on a suit and add a dose of shock to the day's sadness. At least he didn't disrupt the funeral. At least he had stayed true to his nature and disappeared.

"Do you think it's possible?" Rosalind slid the iron down the sleeve of the white blouse. The smell of hot cotton rose in the air. "God, I hope Mom isn't losing it."

"I thought of that myself, but no, she was perfectly lucid. That's why I rushed over here." Della looked around Rosalind's laundry room, a temple to tidiness. Shelves surrounded the washer and dryer, stocked with rows of detergent and dryer sheets. A counter ran the length of the room, at the perfect height for folding clothes.

"Man. I can't believe it." Rosalind set down the iron and looked at Della. "Dad is alive?"

"That's what Mom says."

"Mom caught sight of him and he's still alive?"

"That part is hard to believe."

"No wonder she never tried to establish his death legally." Rosalind hung up the finished blouse on a metal rack. "I offered to do all the paperwork, but Mom said she didn't see the point."

"I always thought she was just being sentimental, holding out hope," said Della. "But I guess she had her reasons. Do you think she gave him her patented rap about how hard it was to raise two girls on her own?"

"I hope so. Of course, Mom didn't exactly raise us alone," Rosalind said. "Aunt Liz was there the whole time. She was the one who made us breakfast and got us off to school when Mom worked the day shift. And she paid half the bills. Probably more than half, since she earned more than Mom did."

"I think when Mom says 'alone,' she means without a man."

Rosalind nodded. "Isn't it funny how some women can't tell the difference?" She picked up a crumpled russet blouse.

"What I can't get over is, he must be in touch with people here in town. Otherwise how would he know about Liz's funeral?"

"Unless he read the death notice online," said Rosalind.

"Our local paper is online?"

"The high school newsletter is online. Get with the times, Della." Rosalind picked up a plastic bottle and sprayed water on the blouse. The hot iron met the drops with a pleasing hiss.

Della watched the steam evaporate. "Does Dad seem like the type of person who would keep up with the news over the Internet?"

"We don't have any way to know what kind of person he is," said Rosalind. "We never did."

"That's true. Remember how he told us his job was to sell time? I never understood that. How could you sell time? Who would buy it, when there was so much of it lying around for free?"

"I sell *air* time," he had once explained, which only deepened her confusion. Wasn't air free too? Later Ruth had sat Della down at the kitchen table and turned on the brown, rectangular radio. "Hear that commercial for Pepsodent?"

"Yes."

"Well, your father sold the Pepsodent company fifteen seconds of time on the radio so they could play that commercial."

"But the radio is free."

"It's free to listen to. But it costs money for the radio station to hire the men who play the music and read the news. The station gets that money from advertisers—people like the Pepsodent company who want to play their commercials on the radio."

"Why?"

"So everyone will go out and buy their toothpaste," Ruth had said. "And your father makes it all possible, because he brings the advertisers to the radio station."

Rosalind nosed the iron around the white buttons. "I got tripped up on the concept of time too. After he left, I didn't understand why all our furniture got taken away just because Mom and Dad had bought it on time."

"Rosalind, how many shirts do you have?"

"A lot. I'm very wealthy, you know."

"Yeah, tell me about it. Look at this excess."

"What's wrong with my basement?"

"Not your basement, your house. You and Anne have two of everything. Two bedrooms. Two bathrooms. Two studies. A two-car garage. Your kitchen even has two ovens."

"We have two incomes. So sue me."

"I can't. You're two lawyers."

"Not really; Anne is a lapsed lawyer. Besides, she'd be the first to agree that enough is enough, and we passed that point long ago." Rosalind slipped the blouse onto a hanger. "I'm the one who likes to acquire things."

"Why?"

"I don't know. I like having extras—extra paper towels, extra laundry soap, extra batteries—things like that. And when it comes to clothes, there's no stopping me. I could make do with five suits, but I have twenty. It drives Anne crazy, but shopping is my idea of fun."

"My friend Charlene was a little like that," Della said cautiously. "One time we went on R and R together in Hong Kong, and all she wanted to do was shop. I wanted to spend the whole time soaking in a hot bath and sleeping in air conditioning, but Charlene kept dragging me out to shop for clothes."

"I thought with the uniforms, you wouldn't need a lot of clothes over there."

"It was the shopping itself she loved. Charlene grew up in Georgia, and she told me that most shopkeepers wouldn't let black people try anything on."

"You mean the whites didn't even want their money?"

"Oh, no. Charlene said you could buy whatever you wanted. You just couldn't try it on beforehand. Dresses, shoes, hats—even overcoats. And if the garment didn't fit after you'd taken it home, you sure couldn't return it. There was only one store that let black people try on clothes. It was forty miles away from their town, and it was owned by a Jewish family. Everyone called it the Jew store."

"Nice."

"Charlene and her mother went there twice a year. It was the only place they shopped, until they moved to Atlanta when she was older."

"No wonder she went wild in Hong Kong."

"I didn't buy much, though. I got you a camera—"

"Oh, yeah. I loved that."

"And I got Mom and Aunt Liz some silk bathrobes."

"Which they never wore." Rosalind ran the iron along the collar.

"So I noticed. Mom said it was too fancy to wear around the house."

"I guess she was saving it for all those formal occasions that call for a bathrobe."

"I wonder where those robes are now," Della said.

"Mom got rid of a lot of stuff when she sold Aunt Liz's house. She must have given me six boxes to take to the women's shelter."

"I should do that too, now that Abby's gone. I still haven't gotten used to Abby being off living a grown-up life."

"You sound like you were changing her diapers just yesterday. She spent the last four years in college, remember?"

"But she lived at home, so I still got to mother her a little. Now it's like going cold turkey."

"Which reminds me, I'm starving." Rosalind clicked off the iron. "Want a turkey sandwich? I'll make one without the turkey for you."

"You mean a mayonnaise sandwich like we used to take to school sometimes? No thanks."

"Not even if I throw in some cheese and lettuce?"

"It's getting late. I have to get going."

"Of course you do. How are you getting to Boston this weekend?" She led the way up the basement steps.

"The train."

"Let me know if you need a ride to the station."

"My train leaves early Saturday morning."

"Let me know if you need cab fare."

"That's what I figured." Della gave Rosalind a quick hug and pulled her jacket off the wooden coat stand.

"Della, wait. What about Dad?"

"What about him?" Della's hand dropped from the doorknob.

"Well, don't you think we should do something? Go see him?"

She pulled her keys out of her purse. "Why would we want to?"

"Aren't you even curious about what happened?"

"Rosalind, you have this touching faith that mysteries can be solved."

"It's a little late in life to be using your big sister tone on me." Rosalind's voice thinned to a blade of irritation. "This isn't some ineffable mystery, it's a question of fact."

"I didn't suggest it was *ineffable*. I don't think I've ever said anything was *ineffable*."

Rosalind sighed. "Let's not fight over my vocabulary, Della. All I'm saying is, this is probably our last chance to answer the big question mark that's hung over our entire lives."

"I don't doubt that, but I just can't make room for him right now."

Rosalind moved closer until they were almost face to face. "I don't understand you, Della. Your own father is alive and nearby, and you don't even care. He's deader to you than those dead soldiers you can't stop talking about."

"I don't think we owe Dad anything, not even our attention."

"What do you owe those soldiers?"

"That's what I need to find out." The jagged edge of her keys bit into her palm. "I want to be there for you, Rosalind, I really do. But I'm in trouble, can't you see that? I need to deal with my own life first."

Rosalind stepped away. "'Being there' has never been your strong suit, has it," she said, yanking the door open. "I don't know why I asked."

On the way home, Della took a shortcut through a wooded area just behind Rosalind's neighborhood, on a dimly lit, winding road, one of the few parts of town that hadn't seen any development. Every time she drove through, Della expected to find bulldozers idling on the shoulder and the skeletons of new houses poking up from the trees.

Tonight, as she followed the smooth curves, something dashed across the road in front of her—an animal, dark and swift and low to the ground. She braked sharply but couldn't tell what it was or where it had gone. She sat in the gloom, hands clamped around the steering wheel, and felt her heart knock against her chest.

After a few moments, Della drove on. The trees swallowed up the road behind her in the rearview mirror. She couldn't tell if she'd missed the creature. Or killed it. Or if there had been anything there at all.

❧

AT HOME IN her bright kitchen, warmed by the steam rising from a mug of fragrant tea, Della called Anne, at the shop, knowing she worked till nine on Wednesdays.

"Why does Rosalind do that?" she asked. "Look me right in the face and claim I'm missing in action?"

"Let me give you a hypothetical," Anne said. In the background Della heard water running, a burst of loud music, a shout from one of Anne's coworkers followed by hoots of laughter. The flower shop after hours must be totally different from its prim daytime personality.

"Let's say you're in bed with someone," Anne continued. "It's late, you're talking, he's listening. Maybe you're telling him about your day. And nothing happens, he doesn't move, he doesn't make a sound, but somehow you can tell he's fallen asleep. Hasn't that ever happened to you?"

"All but the part about him listening to me."

"Well, that's what you do sometimes."

"I fall asleep?"

"No, you're more subtle than that. You can be looking right at someone, but suddenly you're gone. It's not that you've stopped paying attention. You're no longer present."

"Where do I go?"

"I was hoping you'd know. I've only seen it happen a couple of times. Rosalind says she's seen it more often over the years. It drives her crazy."

So Della's family thought she was some kind of high-functioning basket case. She wanted to lay her head on the wooden table, but that would prove them right.

"Does it drive you crazy too?" Della imagined Anne in her stark green apron, a curve-bladed florist knife in her hand. In the time it took her to answer, the roar of a vacuum cleaner started up in a distant corner of the store.

"No. But I'm not your sister. And I'm not as dependent on you as Rosalind is."

Della laughed. "Dependent? Rosalind hasn't needed a thing from me since I taught her to drive. I've been eating her dust ever since."

"That's not how she sees it," said Anne.

"How does she see it?"

"Here's a radical idea: why don't you ask her?"

"She's a litigator. I can never win with her."

"Della, she doesn't want to debate you," Anne said. "She just wants to know you."

Suddenly Della's understanding of the world seemed completely mistaken. Her father was a neighbor, her mother was a conspirator, and her sister considered Della a stranger. Della pushed her fingers through her hair. "Will you tell her I'll do it?" she asked. "That I'll go see our father with her?"

"You tell her," said Anne. "She'll be thrilled. As for me, I have nine more buckets to bleach before I can get out of here tonight."

Chapter 17

"How's Room 312 doing?" The doctor was seated, studying the computer screen. Standing above him, Della could see the fresh comb marks in his blond hair.

"Expectant." The word had a sour taste.

He looked up. "What?"

"Nothing." She crossed her arms over the cold metal clipboard and clutched it to her chest. "It won't be long now."

"You okay, Della?"

"Fine."

The doctor swiveled on the wheeled metal stool and picked up the phone. "Keep me posted." Already he was clicking on the keyboard, the phone tucked between his ear and shoulder.

Della turned away from the computer station set against the wall in the wide hospital hallway. She knew the doctor's attention had moved on to another case before the words were out of his mouth. She didn't blame him; that's the way things worked in a busy hospital. Besides, there was nothing he could do for the patient in Room 312, nothing anyone could do except to ease her journey.

Ducking behind the nurses' station, Della recalled the first time a patient had asked her if he was going to die.

"Of course not!" she had replied, squeezing the wounded soldier's clammy hand. It was 95 degrees on the ward. How could he be so cold?

"Lieutenant, over here," Major Throop called from halfway down the crowded row of cots. Della hurried to her, stepping around the large glass bottles taped to the floor.

"Never lie to them, Brown," said the major in a flat, clipped voice.

"I wasn't lying to him."

"Then you were lying to yourself."

"That kid?" Della pointed across the ward, through the strands of tubing and hoses that seemed to bind the damaged men to their beds. "Look at him. He doesn't even shave yet, Major. He can't die."

"No, you look at him, Lieutenant." She dug her fingers into Della's shoulders and swiveled her around to face the patient. "Look at him like a nurse, not like the girl next door. He *can* die, and he will, probably before the night is out. Maybe there's something he wants to say before he goes. Maybe he wants to get a message to someone. If you tell him he's going to survive, you rob him of that chance."

"But if we tell him he's going to die, won't he stop fighting to stay alive?"

The major eased her grip on Della's shoulders. "I'm afraid we're nowhere near that powerful. Now go over there and tell him the truth, Brown. He probably knows anyway."

"But what should I say?"

"Tell him you talked to the doctor, and it doesn't look good. Ask him if he wants you to write a letter for him, or if he'd like to see the chaplain. Tell him it won't be long."

"I can't do that," Della had whispered.

"Yes you can. It's a tough thing, to tell someone he's about to die, but we all learn to do it. And I'm sorry, but you'll get used to it."

"I don't want to get used to it!"

"Well, you'll have to," Major Throop had snapped. "Or you'll be no use to anybody."

Now, as Della tapped information into the computer, she remembered how hard the nurses had tried to ensure that none of the expectants died alone. They stayed after their shifts and came into the hospital on their days off to sit with the young men behind the screened enclosure that marked the end of hope. Modern hospitals were much more heartless. Dying alone was common, especially among the elderly, observed only by the blank eyes of machines.

Stephanie Young, in 312, was one of the lucky ones. She had family members at her bedside: a devastated mother and a dazed, helpless brother. Both had spent the last three days hovering in the mint-green room with its dangling television and beeping monitors.

The patient was only thirty-two, but suffering had carved her face until she looked older than her weeping mother. Chemo had failed, radiation had failed, her organs had failed, one by one. Now she was in congestive heart failure and her family could only stand by, holding her cool, limp hands and listening to her drown in her own secretions. The misery was all theirs now, because Stephanie Young was already somewhere else.

With these desperately ill patients, the body was often the last to catch on, Della reflected as she suctioned the pink, frothy fluid that kept bubbling up in Stephanie's mouth. First the patient's attention seemed to be drawn elsewhere—maybe to moments in the past, to vanished loved ones, to imaginary experiences. Then the spirit departed.

Despite all the dying patients she'd tended, Della still didn't know how to describe this spirit. Soul, perhaps, or essence. Consciousness. Self. Whatever it was, it took wing, leaving only a vacant case to fill the narrow hospital bed. Finally the body—that heaving, thumping mass of flesh and fluids—heard the news, as if in some gruesome game of Telephone: Oh, we're dead. And the engine of life halted its revolutions.

That moment was close for Stephanie. She had begun the irregular Cheyne-Stokes respirations—quick, deep breaths, a long pause, then several rapid breaths—that often signaled the end of life. Della didn't want to be present when that happened; she wanted to give the family whatever dignity and privacy the cramped quarters could afford.

She had just turned to leave the room when Stephanie's mother let out a wail of grief. Della's muscles fused; she couldn't remember how to move her legs. She saw herself clearly, transfixed in the doorway, the stethoscope around her neck still rocking against her blue scrub blouse. At the same time, she saw herself—she *felt* herself—in the Twelfth Evacuation Hospital, trying to pump life into the chest of a dying five-year-old while his mother collapsed onto the floor.

Della knew little Vietnamese, and the mother's English seemed limited to her frantic cries of "Number ten! Number ten!" as she pressed her limp child into Della's arms. But Della needed no vocabulary to understand the howl of despair that rose from the crumpled woman.

The boy was beyond saving, she saw at once. He was horribly burned, the flesh of his chest and stomach charred and stinking. There was no telling how the child had gotten so brutally injured. He may have been playing when American planes spewed their rain of ruin on his village. Or helping his father make bombs to toss into a crowd of GIs. It didn't matter. Over and over, Della pressed the raw flesh of his chest, breathed into his slack, gray mouth.

She couldn't revive him. Long minutes lapsed as she puffed and pumped, her hands sliding in the slimy tissue beneath the burned crust. Finally his mother looked into her eyes and wailed. Drained, Della sank to the floor beside her. "*Xin loi*," she whispered. I'm sorry.

They sat thigh to thigh, worlds apart, as the mother's cry fell away. Della longed to reach over and comfort her, but couldn't bring herself to touch the woman's black cotton tunic with hands slick with gore. They sat there in silence, breathing raggedly, the lost child lying on the gurney above them.

Frozen in the doorway, Della knew she was in her own hospital, in her own hometown, in the middle years of her sane, safe life. She could see Dr. Lopez hurry down the bright hallway, a cell phone pressed to her ear. She could hear the man behind her sobbing, "Stephie, don't go!"

She also saw the Vietnamese woman rise and gather up her son. Della felt herself clamber to her feet and stand with hands hanging by her side as she watched the young mother walk away. Overhead she heard the growing din as a helicopter swooped low to deliver its bloody cargo of other mothers' sons.

Both things could not be happening at once, but they were, like two films running simultaneously on a single screen. Knowing which was real and which was remembered didn't help at all. She could not make it stop.

With immense effort, Della grabbed the doorframe with both hands and pulled herself out of the room. Panting, she leaned against the wall in the hallway.

John, a nurse striding by, stopped abruptly when he saw her. "Della, what's wrong?"

"I... I'm sick," she managed.

"Are you having trouble breathing?"

"No."

"What's wrong with your hands?"

Della glanced down. She was compulsively rubbing her hands on her pants, trying to wipe off the sensation of the child's raw, oozing flesh. "I don't know." She showed him her palms, red with friction.

"Stay right there." John sprinted to the nurses' station and careened back, pushing a wheeled desk chair. "Sit down. Now hold tight, I'm going to get you out of the hallway."

Short, muscular, solid as a fireplug, John wheeled her behind the high nurses' desk and squatted in front of her. His cropped black hair shone like a pelt. "Tell me what's going on, Della. Do you have pain? A fever?"

She shook her head. "I think it's... like a panic attack." The images were fading now, the terror retreating like a wave curling back into the sea. She took a shaky breath.

"Do you want to breathe into a paper bag?"

"No. It's over now. I'm okay."

"You don't look okay. You're pale and sweating."

"Wait till you're my age. You won't look so good either."

John rose. "Oh yes, let's joke it away." He picked up the telephone.

"What are you doing?"

"I'm calling a cab. You're going home."

"It's the middle of my shift."

"We'll manage without you, Della. I'll let Barbara know."

"She's not a big fan of unauthorized absences."

"I vill make it right with ze commandant," he said. "Now go."

❧

So IT WAS official: Della was losing it. Late that afternoon she sat cross-legged on her bed, dressed in jeans and her red sweater, holding a mug of tea with both hands. The sleepless nights, the strange, prowling anxieties—those she could live with. But now she'd had an honest-to-God flashback, and it was not something she could ignore. She couldn't be relied on to run through the nurse's traditional "five rights"—right patient, right drug, right dose, right method, right time—while her mind was busy replaying the greatest hits of 1969.

She tried to relax against the pillows, but the softness made her skin feel prickly. Della tossed them on the floor and leaned back on the unyielding wall. At least she was on a shrink's calendar for next week. And she'd be seeing Charlene the day after tomorrow. Della wondered if Charlene had dealt with this too. An AA adage flitted through her mind: *Don't go to the source of the pain for relief from the pain.* But Charlene was not the source of the craziness, she was someone who had lived through the craziness with Della. And to blame her letter for what it had unleashed was like blaming the thermometer for the raging fever.

Della picked up the vial of sandalwood oil from the bedside table and idly rolled it between her thumb and index finger. With her eyes closed, it was easy to envision Charlene on the day of her sudden departure, tall and awkward in her dressy cord uniform, her face puffy from tears. It was early morning, but already the atmosphere was fetid. Greasy fumes hung in the air from the bus that idled nearby to take

Charlene and the others to the airfield where they would board their freedom bird.

"This is all over for me now." Charlene had squatted on the roadside and rummaged around in her duffel bag. Her motions were frantic and jerky; there was no trace of the deft O.R. nurse. "From now on, Vietnam never happened. I never again want to see, hear, smell, or think about anything from this fucking hellhole."

Della could feel her lips trembling. "That doesn't include me, does it?"

Empty-handed, Charlene rose and looked directly into her eyes. "You most of all." She hoisted the bag and turned away.

Della watched her stride toward the bus, her footsteps a little wobbly in the regulation pumps after so many months of wearing jungle boots. Even through the protective wire mesh on the bus windows, she could see that Charlene never glanced back as the bus groaned through its gears and trundled away.

When Della stumbled into her room that evening, she found the small bottle of aromatic oil nestled on her pillow. Too spent even to untie her boots, she collapsed onto the cot. Throughout that long night, through the thunder and clash of artillery, through the furtive *skritch* of lizards scuttling up the walls, through the tumbling of her own muttered dreams, Della clutched the vial in her fist. For days afterwards her skin had smelled of sandalwood.

Surely that bitter parting wouldn't stand between them now. After all, Charlene's letter said she had tried to find Della a long time ago. And Della had tried to contact her too, back when Della was working the twelve steps and had reached the ninth one, making amends. But by then it was years after the war, and Charlene's family no longer seemed to live in Atlanta.

Charlene had left Vietnam so abruptly there was no time to exchange addresses or write down family contacts. Trying to locate one another years later was just a guessing game. Women moved, changed their last names, reinvented themselves. Sometimes they wanted to stay lost. Della had felt that way herself, when all she lived for each day was the first sting of gin in her throat. It taught her the one thing she understood about her father: the solace of being absent.

🌿

DELLA PHONED her sister.

"Rosalind Brown," she answered in a crisp voice that instantly evoked the wool-suited, high-heeled, headset-wearing creature that was Rozzie at work.

Della told her what had happened.

"Oh, Del, I'm so sorry. But this isn't your first hot flash, you know."

She smiled. "No, it certainly isn't."

"I meant flashback. You've had them before."

"When?"

"Remember that Fourth of July right after you came home, when Liz and I dragged you to the fireworks at the fairgrounds? You flinched at every explosion, and then you started to cry."

"I was probably drunk."

"No, this was different. Liz had to wrap you up in the picnic blanket and drive you home. You don't remember this?"

"Vaguely." What she recalled was afterwards. Della and Liz, alone in the house, huddled side by side in the kitchen. Della's face was pressed into her hands, tears dripping through her fingers and down her forearms, her elbows planted on the table as if she could burrow into the white painted wood. Liz had sat with her so patiently, stroking her back as Della tried to choke out an explanation. The fireworks, the explosions, the percussion in her chest—Della's every nerve was in agony from the strain of waiting for the screams of the injured, searching the smooth, sloping green of the fairground for ragged body parts. But Della could express none of that. It was all she could do to suck in short, shivery breaths between her heaving sobs.

Neither one of them said a word. But Liz had leaned over and hugged Della, fiercely. No timid pats on the back, no murmured "There, there." Just the confidence to hold her hard for long minutes, until Della's breathing quieted and she understood she was not going to shatter. It was the only time since she had returned from war that Della felt truly understood by a civilian. Now, with the phone dangling from her hand, Della wondered who could hold her together this time, if it came to that.

"Are you there?" Rosalind's voice rose. "Maybe I shouldn't have brought that up."

"No, it's okay." She pulled her knees to her chest. "Tell me what you've learned about Dad."

"Get this. He lives in a place called 'Whispering Pines.'"

"What is that, a cemetery?"

"A complex for retired people. Continuous care—you can move in when you're healthy and choose from a whole menu of assistance as you need it. The place is seriously expensive."

"So he's rich," said Della.

"Well, we know he saved a bundle on child support."

"I'm surprised there are enough people in Lockhart who can afford a place like that."

"There aren't," said Rosalind. "But there are a lot of people willing to change sheets and serve meals for the minimum wage. The retirees come from other places."

"Listen to you," said Della. "Are you representing the oppressed workers now?"

"Nope. Still a hired gun for the corporate empire. But that doesn't mean I can't look for the union label."

"Oh, Mom would be so proud. Genetics run deep."

"Let's hope not," said Rosalind.

CHAPTER 18

"Della, are you sure you're up for this?" asked Anne as they turned into the long driveway of Whispering Pines.

"I had a momentary freakout at work this morning," she grumbled from the back seat of Rosalind's Volvo. "That doesn't turn me into some kind of delicate flower."

"Still," said Anne, "I'm not sure now is the best time for this."

"The guy's in the intensive care wing." Rosalind pulled into a parking spot. "How much time do we have?"

"This place looks like a cross between a grand hotel and a funeral home," Della murmured to Anne as they examined the lobby.

Heavy wooden furniture was clustered in conversational groupings throughout the large, high-ceilinged room. Although it was after eight o'clock at night and the lobby was nearly empty, the smell of fresh coffee wafted from a silver percolator with an elegant black handle. A wooden tray held columns of white porcelain cups. In one corner, newspapers from various cities hung on dowels arranged in a rack. An elderly man in paisley pajamas and a navy silk dressing gown sat in a wingback chair, engrossed in the newspaper, his legs crossed, a leather slipper dangling from one thin foot. The only hint of the current era was the flat computer screen discreetly angled on the mahogany counter where Rosalind was talking with a staff person.

"See the silk flowers?" Anne murmured to Della, nodding her head toward a round table in the center of the room, where an enormous ceramic pot was bursting with colorful flowers.

"Where?"

"Everywhere. All the arrangements are artificial. Handmade silk, very high-end. Beautiful, and I'm not a fan of silks."

Rosalind joined them, looking grim. "Okay, Della," she said. "Mr. Brown is expecting us. Wouldn't want to keep him waiting."

"Good luck." Anne gave Rosalind's hand a quick squeeze. Della wished she had brought her own cheering squad; she hadn't thought she'd be so nervous.

The sisters didn't speak as they walked down a wide, carpeted hallway, past evenly spaced brown doors marked with shiny brass numbers. They turned a corner, crossed another hallway and pushed through swinging glass doors to the wing that housed residents who needed medical care. Here the hallway was just as broad and brightly lit, but the floor was a cheerful yellow linoleum tile, and metal handrails at waist level lined the walls.

Rosalind slowed her pace and finally stopped in front of a black wooden door. She glanced at Della and gave three sharp knocks.

They were both surprised when a man immediately pulled open the door. He was definitely not their father. He had a strong physique and thick, iron gray hair, and couldn't have been much older than Della. His blue eyes narrowed into laugh lines that spread when he smiled. "You must be Tom's daughters," he said.

"That's right," Rosalind replied. "Who are you?"

"I'm Loren Walker, his care manager." He reached into the small chest pocket of his white polo shirt and pulled out a couple of business cards.

"Did he ask you to mediate?"

"What? No. I happened to be visiting Tom when the front desk called to tell him you were here. He seemed a little … flustered. I guess you don't see him that often."

"Not since he walked out on us when we were children," Della said, and regretted it when she saw Loren's face redden. No point getting this man in the crossfire.

"Anyway, I'll be going." He stepped into the hallway and held the door for them to enter. "Tom's back in the bedroom. He asked me to answer the door. He's not very mobile these days."

In the living room, floor-to-ceiling windows overlooked a lighted courtyard. A brown leather couch faced two matching chairs. On one wall, built-in bookshelves held a few hardcovers and a sizable collection of DVDs. Adjacent to it was a galley kitchen, gleaming with stainless steel appliances. Della pictured her mother's modest apartment with its dilapidated furniture.

They walked through a dim hallway toward the lighted bedroom. Framed artwork hung on the walls, inoffensive blobs of color that looked like they had been ordered from a catalog. There were no photographs. They passed a small bathroom and a room with a closed door, perhaps a guest room. Della wondered who visited her father. For all she knew, he could have another family. Or the spare room might be for the night nurse.

Rosalind stepped into the bedroom first, and Della saw her recoil. It smelled like what it was: a sickroom. Della noted the bedside table cluttered with pill bottles, the wheeled walker in the corner, the portable toilet near the bed. She turned her attention to the sick old man who had once been her father.

Tom Brown sat up against a bank of pillows, a shrunken man stranded in the middle of a rumpled bed, clutching the blankets with speckled hands. The wavy red hair she remembered was gone, replaced by meager tufts of cotton that revealed his pale, bumpy scalp. His eyebrows had grown thin and white. His eyes looked nothing like what she remembered. They were a cloudy brown, appearing overlarge and bewildered through his smeared glasses.

Clear plastic tubes looped over his ears and crossed his stubbled cheeks, bringing oxygen to his nostrils. The canister was out of sight in the closet behind the bed, but Della could hear its respirations. Lung cancer, she thought, or maybe emphysema. From his shallow breaths and the bluish tint of his fingernails, she gathered it was fairly advanced.

He waved them into two folding chairs by the side of the bed. "So you're Della," Tom said, and the sound jolted her heart. It was almost the deep, confident voice she remembered, thinner and higher now, but still cocky. "I wouldn't have recognized you."

"I grew up." She said it mildly enough, but the thought stung: Tom Brown didn't even recognize his own daughter. Of course, she wouldn't recognize him either, but fairness was beside the point here. He had left her, and she had mourned him.

"And little Rozzie," he said, "all grown up too."

"Did you think time would stop when you stepped out of the picture?" asked Rosalind.

Della glanced at her sister in surprise. She was using her lawyer voice, tinged with steel.

"And call me Rosalind," she added.

"Well, I guess you can call me Dad."

"I don't think you've earned that title, do you, Tom?"

He grinned, and a dimple popped into one grizzled cheek. "You got me there, Rosalind. You always were right on the money, even as a tiny girl."

The man seemed to believe he could charm them. Of all the emotions jostling inside her—curiosity, grief, pity, resentment—Della realized that she and Rosalind had somehow agreed without the slightest discussion that anger would be the theme of their reunion with their father. She regretted it, but it seemed preordained, as if none of them had any choice in the matter.

"So what can I do for you girls?"

"We—we wanted to get acquainted," said Della. "To see how you are. Who you are, actually."

"I don't have a lot of breath for small talk," he said.

"Well, then, let's get down to business," said Rosalind. "What happened back then? What made you leave?"

"I hope you girls didn't come all this way just to dig up that ancient history."

"It's the only history we've got," Della said. "But if you don't want to talk about it, we won't take any more of your time." She reached for her purse.

"No, no, don't leave. But that was all so long ago."

Della blinked at the thick beige carpet, waiting for the heat of shame to fade from her face. She knew the deep loneliness of critically ill patients, and she had used it to manipulate a frail old man.

"Let me refresh your memory," said Rosalind. "You had a wife who adored you, two children who looked up to you, and a sister who doted on you. Then one day you decided to chuck it all, and you disappeared. Does that sound familiar?"

Tom closed his eyes, and his mouth sagged open. Della felt a twinge of sympathy for the man, but it came from the part of her that was a nurse, not his daughter.

"I'll tell you what happened," he said wearily. "But I don't expect you to get it."

"Fair enough." Rosalind folded her arms across her chest.

Tom seemed to energize himself at the prospect of telling a story. He sat upright in bed and tugged his tan pajama shirt into place.

"Yeah, I had all those things you mentioned, Rosalind. And I had a crummy job at a two-bit radio station, selling spots and brown-nosing sponsors. My wife was working too—not enough to really help out, just enough to make me look bad. We had house payments, car payments, you name it. Every time I turned around, another bill was due. You kids needed *everything*."

Rosalind and Della met each other's eyes. So it was going to be their fault.

"There was never a single minute when I could relax." His voice grew stronger and more aggrieved. "I could never feel like, okay, I've done my bit. There was always more I had to do. If it wasn't working, it was mowing the lawn, or fixing your bicycles, or taking Liz to the used car lot. It got to be too much for me. See, that's the part women never understand, the way having that responsibility, day in and day out, just grinds you down into dust."

"Have you asked your wife?" Rosalind said. "I think she understands it. She picked it up pretty quickly after you left her with two kids and no money."

Tom crossed his arms in an eerie echo of Rosalind's gesture. "I did what I had to do."

"Where did you go?" Della asked.

"I took back my life, and I lived it. I traveled. I met people. I did okay for myself—sold everything you could think of, appliances, cars, condoms by the gross." He began to smile, warming to his memories. "I had friends in every town. We told stories in bars and laughed till closing time. I don't think there's been a single night in my life when I had to pay for all my own drinks." He looked from one daughter to the other. "And yeah, I had a lot of women, but I learned from my mistake. Every one of them knew from the get-go that it was just for kicks."

"Didn't you get lonely?" Della asked.

"Nah. Tell you the truth, I've never been as lonely as I was living in that house with Ruth and you kids."

She was struck into silence. The father she remembered—reading to her, teaching her to swim—what happened to him?

"Did you have other children?" asked Rosalind.

"Not that I know of." His grin faded as he seemed to realize how badly he had misjudged his audience. That line must have earned him whiskeys in the past.

Della had to push herself to ask this stranger the question that had always troubled her. "But didn't you miss your children? Because I remember you. I know you loved us."

He took off his black-rimmed glasses and rubbed a hand across his eyes. The oxygen tank breathed in and out like a patient eavesdropper. "Yeah, I loved my kids. And it hurt like hell to leave them. But I had to do it, to save my own life. And I don't regret it now. I can't."

Tom slid his glasses back on and showed them his salesman's smile. "I knew your mother would manage, and look what a great job she did. It worked out better for everyone this way."

"She 'managed' because your sister helped to raise us," Rosalind said. "It never occurred to you to send any child support?"

"That's for the courts to decide. We weren't divorced."

"How could she divorce you when she couldn't find you?" Rosalind said. "What if she had wanted to remarry?"

"Your mother is a resourceful woman. She would have figured out a way." Tom gave a liquid cough and sipped some water from a glass at his bedside.

Della hitched forward in the rickety folding chair. "You know," she said, "I can understand feeling like you got trapped in the wrong life. But to sneak away like that, to leave your family wondering—forever—what happened to you … what kind of person does that?"

"I thought it was easier that way. A clean break."

"Clean? Ruth and Liz visited every morgue in the area. They hired detectives. They agonized over where to get ransom money in case you'd been kidnapped. All because you didn't have the balls to tell anyone you were leaving."

"And you could have done it so easily," Rosalind added. "A phone call after you were already gone. A letter. You could have saved us all that anguish, but you couldn't be bothered."

Della felt a weird exhilaration. She and Rosalind were speaking each other's thoughts, united in a way they hadn't been since childhood.

"We all do what we need to," said Tom, "and sometimes it's not pretty. If you two haven't learned that yet, you better get cracking. You girls aren't spring chickens anymore. Now, I'm getting a little tired, and I think you should go."

"That's it?" asked Rosalind. "After all these years, you don't even have any questions for us?"

"I do have a question. Which one is the lawyer?"

"I am."

"There's a little matter I'd like your opinion on."

Della and Rosalind didn't even have to look at one another. Without a word they rose and left the apartment. In the hallway, they began to laugh. It started with quiet snickers, but by the time they reached the lobby they were helpless with hilarity.

"Can you believe that guy?" Rosalind hooted. "What was that crack about us not being spring chickens? Was he accusing us of getting old?"

"I did what was best for everyone," Della mimicked in a nasal voice.

Rosalind continued the impersonation. "And I think the least you girls owe me is some free legal advice."

"Fucking cheap Charlie!" Della exclaimed, and only then did she notice that Anne and Loren Walker were gaping at them from the far end of the lobby, where they sat together with coffee cups raised.

"Oops," said Rosalind, and giggled again.

"Looks like it went a little better than you expected," said Anne. Loren stood up as they approached.

"No, it was horrible." Rosalind sat on the arm of Anne's chair. "I don't know what I was expecting, but he's a smug little creep. He had absolutely no interest in us. Not even basic curiosity. Thank God he's out of our lives."

Loren turned to Della. "Um, could I talk to you for a minute?" He walked a few feet away.

Della wondered if she was about to be busted for laughing too loud in this decorous place. She hoped so; that would really be funny.

He shifted his weight from one foot to the other. "This is going to sound strange, but you used a phrase a minute ago... You called your father a cheap Charlie. And I just wondered, well, I haven't heard that phrase for a while, and I wondered where you learned it."

Della saw a flush creep up Loren's throat. "Probably the same place you did," she said.

"You were in country?"

"Twelfth Evac Hospital, in Cu Chi." She felt a clutch of anxiety at mentioning it so casually to a stranger. But it seemed safe to acknowledge it to Loren; it wasn't as if she was ever coming back here.

"I was a grunt," he said. "Spent most of my tour in the Central Highlands, around Nha Trang." He rubbed the back of his neck. "That was a long time ago, huh?"

"Not long enough." She watched the muscles shift in his upraised arm.

"Are you a nurse, Mrs. uh—?"

"Della Brown," she said. "Not Mrs. anything. And yes, I am a nurse. I work at Oneida Regional, on the oncology ward."

"Do you think it would be okay if I called you sometime?"

"I'd like that. As long as you're not calling about my father."

He smiled. "I'm not actually thinking about your father right now."

On the drive home, Anne quizzed them. "I don't see what you two are so giddy about. Your father blew you off."

"And now we can blow him off," said Rosalind. "We never have to think about him again."

"We don't have to wonder about him anymore," Della added, "or miss him."

"We're finally free. We may have lost a father, but Della gained a boyfriend out of the deal."

"What do you mean, *Della* gained a boyfriend?" Anne said. "I had him first."

"Now we're definitely back in high school," Della said.

"Well, I'm going to tell everyone that the only way you can meet men is to hang out at the old people's home," said Rosalind.

"Wish I'd thought of it sooner."

"What will you tell your mother?" Anne asked Rosalind.

"The truth. That he doesn't have an ounce of regret for what he did. That he didn't ask a single question about her, or Liz, or us."

"You know, Mom told me that when she talked to him, he wanted to know all about the family," said Della.

"Mom sees what she wants to see. Just watch—she'll find a way to construe this positively, too."

"She's a very resourceful woman," Della intoned in her Tom Brown voice.

The man they had met tonight was not the father she remembered. That man was gone; perhaps he had never existed. Rosalind and Della had nothing more than genes in common with the man in Whispering Pines. He was right that they were no longer young, but they still had time to rectify old mistakes. And who knows, Della thought, fingering the business card in her pocket, maybe even time enough to make some new ones.

CHAPTER 19

DELLA HAD THE underwear all figured out. After that, she couldn't make up her mind. She could take her dressy suit, the one she wore to Abby's graduation. Or she could choose security over style and take her favorite jeans and comfy sweater. She wondered what Charlene would be wearing. She had been eyeing the closet for some time, hands stuffed into the pockets of her terrycloth bathrobe, when the phone rang.

"Hi, Mom," said Abby. "It's me."

"Hello, darlin'. How are you?" Della could tell how strange she sounded, as if her voice had been infused with honey. It was the tone she couldn't help falling into whenever she spoke to her daughter.

"I'm okay. Mom, can I come stay at the house for a few days?"

"Of course, sweetie, but why?"

"Do I need a reason?"

"No, although I'm sure you have one. But you don't have to tell me what it is." Suddenly Della knew exactly what to wear. She laid out on the bed her brown gabardine slacks and the rust-colored sweater that complemented her hair.

"I just need a break from New York," said Abby.

Della hoped it was the television she heard yammering in the background and not raucous street sounds. What kind of neighborhood did Abby live in, anyway? "You know I'm going to be gone all weekend," she said. "I won't be back until Sunday evening."

"Yeah, I know."

"Oh, I see. So visiting your dear old mom is not the object of your trip." Della pulled her canvas overnight bag from the closet shelf.

"Uh oh. Busted. I just need a little space to myself. You don't mind, do you?"

"I'll be sad to miss you. Do you think you can take time out to see your grandmother? I'll leave you the car."

"Okay. And maybe I'll still be there when you come back from your pilgrimage."

"But what about your job?"

"I quit last week, when they wouldn't let me trade shifts to go to an audition."

"I see. And what are you planning to do for work?"

"*Mom*. I'm a waitress. It'll take me sixty seconds to find a new job."

Della suppressed a sigh. She couldn't wait for the day when Abby didn't sound irritated by everything she said. Surely adolescence was supposed to end at some point. "All right, honey. Come whenever you want, stay as long as you want. Just give me a general idea of what your plans are once you figure that out."

"Well, so much for spontaneity."

"How will you get here?" Della packed her toiletry kit and a long T-shirt to sleep in.

"I'm getting a ride from a friend."

"Anyone I know?"

"No."

"Careful, now, Abby. You wouldn't want to reveal anything about your life to your mother, of all people."

"I learned from the master. So, um, what time do you leave tomorrow?"

"Don't worry," said Della. "I'll be long gone by the time you get here. I'll leave the car keys on the kitchen table."

"Are you nervous?"

"A little."

"Well, break a leg, Mom. I hope you find what you're looking for."

"Why, thank you, honey. I hope you do, too."

Della leaned her elbows on the dresser top and studied the framed photo of Abby. She knew intimately every inch of that face: the large brown eyes, sparkling with confidence; the shiny brown hair; the full lips so much like her own, already surrounded by smile lines. The fact that something as ordinary as love could create such a creature struck Della as nothing short of miraculous. She slid the photograph into her suitcase to show Charlene.

❧

Early the next morning, Della settled into her seat on the train. There was no point in fretting about what would happen in Boston, she told herself; she would just try to enjoy the next few hours of travel.

The train lurched into motion, rolling through the long dim station and into the delicate morning light. She watched the city stream past her window. The office buildings of the business district shrank into squat brick apartment buildings with rickety fire escapes clinging to the sides. Block after block of weary flats gave way to low-slung warehouses and industrial parks, then evolved into tidy suburban neighborhoods, their winter lawns brown and muddy. Soon the garden lots stretched out into dairy farms, and the train glided through the low hills of rural New York.

Della couldn't believe how relaxing it was to look out the window, letting her mind wander and her body sway with the motion of the train. The sound of the wheels on the track blended with the chatting of passengers into a soothing murmur. Could it be that Amtrak had known the answer to insomnia all along?

The subtle rocking reminded her of something she couldn't put her finger on. She thought about those long nights when she would try to rock her baby to sleep, peering deeply into Abby's large, solemn eyes. No, it was further back than that. Mac, the pilot, rocking her gently against his chest after they'd made love.

He was her first lover, so she had no way to compare. Maybe it was her youth, maybe it was the novelty of sex, maybe it was the volatile mix of passion and danger that had heightened everything she felt with Mac. There had been many men since then—too many, during those drunken years after Vietnam. Some of them, she later realized, were far more skillful than Mac. Yet none of them had made her plunge so deeply into the daze of pleasure. None had freed her from the burden of self and turned her into a nameless ache of desire.

🌿

HE HAD SOMEHOW found them a place to be alone, the quarters of some absent officer. It was midday when he came to the hooch to tell Della about this miraculous discovery, and she was asleep, having worked the night shift. But the prospect of privacy was so rare that she forced herself awake and reached for her boots, shaking them out to make sure none of the giant cockroaches known as "nurse-eaters" were hiding there.

In the latrine she ran into one of her hoochmates. Kathy was new in country, a replacement for Della's friend Joanne, who had gone home. For that reason alone, she hadn't been able to warm up to Kathy, hadn't even tried. Still, there was no one else around. So Della swore Kathy to secrecy and told her where she was going. Then she brushed her teeth and followed the pilot, logy with sleep and lust.

"How long can you stay?" Mac opened the door to the officer's bright, austere room.

"My shift begins at 1830."

"But we have this place till tomorrow. It could be our first night together. Just you and me and the stars." He pulled her down to the bed. "What about your day off?"

"What day off?"

"Remember when Captain Chilly—"

"Don't call her that."

"Okay. Remember when your pal Hillary told you to take a day for yourself, and you never did? This could be that day."

"It was your fault. You got rescued too soon, and then you didn't even want to see me. Blew my only chance for a day off."

Mac's helicopter had been forced to the ground by mechanical problems, far from the landing zone where they were supposed to pick up casualties. If enemy soldiers were anywhere in the vicinity, they would have heard the rough landing, so Mac and the other three men on his crew had limped into the jungle to watch for them. Insects had feasted on their cuts and scrapes as they waited for daylight and the chance to at least repair the radio, if not get the Huey flying again. When he finally got back to the base, Mac had sent word to Della, but he had wanted to stay with his squad mates, to do whatever it was men did to commemorate a second chance.

"I'm sorry my survival ruined your plans," he said, unbuttoning her blouse. "Let me try to make it up to you."

Since the night he had gone missing, Della had begun to notice small things about Mac that she hadn't appreciated before. The way his green eyes were lit with gold. The way he laughed with wide-open delight, as if amusement were a new feeling. The way he held his breath at first when he kissed her.

They had been kissing for a long time, their bodies pressed against one another, his hot hands traveling slowly over her skin. He had just begun to whisper in her ear when someone tapped on the door. Della leaped away from him.

"Della," a voice said. It was Kathy, sounding young and timid. "Della, are you in there?"

"What is it?"

"It's Charlene. She wants to see you ASAP."

"Okay. Tell her I'll be there as soon as I can."

"Aw hell, baby, do you have to go?" Mac nuzzled her throat.

Della felt her eyelids flutter closed. "Not yet. If it was an emergency, she would have said 'stat.' ASAP means when you're finished with what you're doing." She pulled him closer. "And I'm not finished."

Della couldn't tell how much time had passed when she first became aware of the juddering din of incoming helicopters. Mac was rocking her; the blazing gold sun hung low in the sky. "Listen," she said.

"They're Chinooks. Big guys."

"And they're flying heavy. Must be loaded with casualties."

They both froze when they heard the frantic knocking.

"Della!" Kathy was breathless. "The hospital called. It's a mass-cal. I'm heading over there now."

"I'm right behind you." She grabbed her fatigues.

"I thought you were off duty," Mac grumbled.

"Not anymore." Her shirt half-buttoned, she leaned over and kissed him before she dashed out the door.

Several times that night, as she tossed back cold coffee, Della wondered what Charlene had wanted. She kept expecting to run into her, but no doubt the operating room was as busy as the I.C.U. was.

Della wished she had taken a moment to reassure Kathy that soon she too would become accustomed to the gore and bedlam of a push—which was a pretty strange thing to reassure someone, if you thought about it. But she did not have time to think about it. There was no lull in the casualties, no break in the urgent pace. The sun had set and risen again before the helicopters ceased their bloody deliveries, and the medical staff dropped in exhaustion wherever they found a space.

Della shoved some trash aside with her boot and slumped to the floor in a corner. This was the first time she had sat down since it all began. She couldn't remember when she had last eaten, and it seemed that she had slept only a couple of hours before Mac had awakened her—could that have been just yesterday? Soon she would think of things like showers, food, sleep. But for now, it was enough just to breathe.

Major Throop slipped into the I.C.U., looking as wasted and bloodstained as the rest of the staff. When she caught sight of Della, the major trudged across the ward. Della struggled to her feet.

"Brown, have you talked with Lieutenant Johnson?"

"No, ma'am. I figured she was—" Della gestured toward the O.R.

"Della, you mean you don't know? She's leaving this morning. Her brother was killed, up at Pleiku. She's going home on emergency leave."

Her skin turned cold. "William was killed? He's only been in country a week."

The major leaned against a gurney. "It doesn't take long."

"But they promised. The Army promised he wouldn't even have to come here. How could they let him get killed?" Della knew it was crazy to argue with Major Throop, but she couldn't stop herself.

"The Army giveth and the Army taketh away." She rested her head in her hands. "Go on, Della. You don't have much time."

She rushed to their hooch and pushed open Charlene's door. Her mouth dropped at the sight. Beside the stripped metal cot stood Charlene in her travel uniform, trying with trembling hands to close her duffel bag.

"So here you are." Charlene spoke with no inflection, as if someone had punctured her voice and drained the vitality out of it.

"Oh, Charlene, I didn't know!"

"I sent Kathy to get you."

"She didn't say anything about him."

"I didn't tell her. I wanted you."

Della reached for the bag to help her close it, but Charlene swatted her away. "That was yesterday," she continued.

"Oh, God, I—I didn't realize it was an emergency."

"Did you think I would send someone to pull you away from your boyfriend if it wasn't an emergency?"

Acid and ice water had a firefight in Della's stomach. She sank to her knees on the gritty concrete floor.

"Forget it." Charlene sat on the thin, striped mattress. "My mother always said you can't rely on anyone but your family. I never believed her until now. Of course, William was relying on me. Kind of a laugh, considering."

Della put her hand on top of Charlene's.

"Don't." Charlene jerked away her hand. "Those motherfuckers murdered him, Della."

"Which ones?"

She studied Della as if trying to decide which category she belonged in. "The Viet Cong. The Army. The U.S. government. All of them. And now they can add me to their fucking body count."

"Charlene, you're still alive."

"If you say so." She picked up her duffel bag and walked out of the room without a backward glance.

Della trailed her to the waiting bus. Charlene had stood there in the shimmering heat, her uniform clean, her hands empty. She had told Della—with the pure intensity of a prayer—that she never wanted to see her again.

If Della had only taken the time to realize that Charlene needed her, she would have left Mac and run to her friend. It was a wrong she never had the opportunity to set right, because Charlene's prayer was answered. *You most of all,* Charlene had said. The words still scalded.

CHAPTER 20

THE JINGLING noise was coming from Della. Silverware, salt shaker—everything on her table trembled. She forced her legs to still themselves, and the sounds stopped. But then the jittering spread through her entire body: muscles, belly, bone. The taste of pennies rose in her mouth. She let her legs take up their rhythm again. Where on earth was Charlene?

"Anything I can get you?" the waitress asked, coming to Della's table for the second time. "Something to drink?"

"No, thanks." Della wished she would step aside. The waitress was blocking her view of the door.

"Listen, hon, are you okay?"

With hands on knees, Della quieted her legs. The water in her glass swayed, then stilled. "I'm just—waiting," she said.

"Ah." The waitress gave her a big smile. "Don't worry, he'll be along."

Della blew out a breath. She shouldn't have arrived so early. She checked her watch and was shocked to see there were still five minutes to go until their meeting time. Strangers scurried past the large streaked windows, their heads down. Somewhere a storm was building. Bare branches quivered against the white sky. Della tried to find the sun.

"Still got your head in the clouds, I see."

She jumped. "Charlene!"

"In the flesh."

Charlene stood before her, alive, elegant, real. Her face, so deeply familiar, was creased by experiences Della would never know. Her close-cropped hair was entirely silver, and silver triangles dangled from her ears.

In Charlene's expression Della saw how she herself had changed. Graying hair, lined face, the thick calves of a woman who had toiled on her feet. She felt a spasm of panic at the passing of all those years.

"I know," said Della. "I can't get used to looking like someone's mother."

"You *are* someone's mother, and so am I." Charlene pulled off her leather jacket with a jangle of metal bracelets. She slipped into the booth next to Della, ignoring the padded bench on the opposite side of the table. In that moment lived their shared history of growing up in danger: neither one of them wanted to sit with their back to the door.

"Well. Here we are." Della wished she had stood up and hugged her, but the moment had passed before she could make a move. Instead she clasped her hands in her lap. "Pretty strange, huh?"

"It is kind of surreal." Charlene smoothed her V-neck sweater. "I wore Army green so you'd recognize me."

So she too had worried about her wardrobe. The tightness in Della's chest eased. "Of course I recognized you." Touching the back of her hand, Della felt the blood leap beneath Charlene's skin.

"I've thought of you so often," Della said, her voice a little foggy.

"Same here."

"Charlene, tell me—" Words tangled up in her throat.

"Tell you what?"

"I don't know." She laughed, a soundless puff of air. "Everything. You left Vietnam, and then what?"

"Whoa. I guess we're done with small talk, huh?"

Della couldn't tell if she was offended or joking.

The waitress glided to their table with an efficient swish of sneakers. "Good afternoon, ladies." She twinkled at Della, then beamed her full attention on Charlene. "Would you care to see our wine list, ma'am? We're featuring some premium California wines this month."

"Yes, thanks," said Charlene. "No, wait. On second thought, I'd rather have a chocolate shake." She turned to Della. "What the heck. We're resurrecting our youth, right?" Della ordered coffee. They both watched the waitress disappear behind the red swinging door to the kitchen.

"They make great old-fashioned shakes here," Charlene said finally. "Remember, the kind we used to drink before we cared about calories?"

"I remember milkshakes. Are you stalling?"

"Kind of. I'm pretty nervous." She touched her fingertips to her lips.

"Yeah, me too." Della looked around the restaurant. "You know, before you got here I was thinking this place is like a dressed-up diner. My mom used to wait tables in a diner like this."

"I thought she was a cook."

"That was later. She was a waitress before that." She twisted on the slippery red seat so she could face Charlene. The air between them pulsed with questions. *Start anywhere*, she remembered Anne saying. "So, um, are you working these days?"

"I teach music."

"You mean, like piano lessons?"

"Pretty much. I teach classical piano to college students."

"That's a far cry from nursing."

"As far as I could get."

"How did you get into that? I knew you played, but I didn't know you could teach it." The waitress set down the drinks and, without stopping, swiveled to serve another table. Della recognized the years of experience in that one smooth move.

"Music was my minor in college." Charlene slid the paper wrapper off her straw. "After Vietnam I decided to go to graduate school. I got a degree in music, thanks to the good old GI Bill."

"I always knew you were smarter than me," said Della. "I never realized women could get those benefits until long after the ten-year time limit was up."

"Well, the government did its best not to let women in on that little secret," Charlene said. "And it wasn't easy to get benefits, either. Every semester I'd have to go to the veterans' affairs office to apply, and each time I'd have to jump through the same hoops: 'I never saw any girls when I was in Nam. What was your unit?' And a lot of snickering, like 'I'll show you my unit if you'll show me yours.' It was infuriating, but I wanted that money."

"You earned it," Della said.

"Every penny." Charlene tasted her shake. "Mmm. Sin in a straw. Did you ever go back to school? I remember you used to think about it."

"I'm still thinking about it. I did go to night school, after Abby began third grade. Finally finished my bachelor's degree. At least the government helped us with our house. My ex-husband was a veteran, so we got a VA loan."

"Was he in country?"

"In '67, at Long Binh. A noncombatant."

Charlene grinned. "Like us."

"A little more so than us, I think. The only blood he saw was during a bar fight."

"My husband lucked out," said Charlene. "His lottery number was 359."

"How did he feel about you being there?"

"You mean—" Charlene attempted a gruff baritone—"'I don't want to hear about any wife of mine wearing combat boots and sewing up naked men'?"

"Well, yeah."

"He's not like that. Or he wouldn't be married to me." Charlene picked up her straw wrapper and began to tie it into tiny knots. "Are you still nursing, Della?"

"Still nursing. I work on an oncology unit."

"Really? I would have thought you got enough of death and dying early on."

Della could see Charlene's operating room training in the precise paper knots, but she didn't mention it. "It's not all death and dying. But you're right, I didn't start out in oncology. When I first got back I did trauma nursing for a few years."

"Uh huh." Charlene nodded. "Adrenaline junkie. Needed that rush of being needed."

"I guess so. Except most of what they needed me to do in those days could have been done by a candystriper. After a while I switched to O.B. I was a labor and delivery room nurse for almost twenty years."

"What happened? Did you get tired of bringing new life into the world?"

"I think I might have mentioned to you on the phone…my Aunt Liz died a few years ago." Della's gaze faltered, and she found herself watching the pulse that beat at the base of Charlene's throat.

"No, you didn't tell me. I'm sorry."

"Ovarian cancer. I took care of her so she could die at home. It was one of those experiences that reminds you…well, there's more to life than meets the eye." She looked directly at Charlene, a challenge. "Remember?"

"I remember."

"I realized that helping someone die well is just as important as helping them get born well. But lots of people don't accept that. Even medical people."

"Especially medical people, if you ask me."

"So I moved over to oncology. It's not that I've made friends with death. It's just that I don't see death as the enemy."

"You know, I think that's great," said Charlene. "My husband is a surgeon, and every time he loses a patient it's a personal defeat. It's like he's convinced that no one is ever supposed to die."

"I can't believe you got out of nursing and you still ended up marrying a doctor."

Charlene smiled. "Sad, isn't it?"

"What's he like?"

"He's smart and sweet. After all these years, he still gives me flowers and silly cards. Now, don't get me wrong. I know he's not perfect. He talks too much and he still hasn't figured out where we keep the laundry hamper. But he's a good man. My sons are lucky to have a dad like that."

"Tell me about them."

"James is twenty-nine." Charlene's face softened. "He's married and works for the city. I just know that any minute now he's going to warn me to brace myself to be a grandma." She gave a little chuckle. "Now, my younger son, William—he's the wild card."

"Did you name him after your brother?" Della hoped Charlene would meet her eyes, that some kind of acknowledgment would flicker between them. But Charlene simply nodded once.

"Will's the baby of the family. He's a musician—not a nice classical musician like his mother, but a jazz musician. And good old American jazz isn't good enough for him. He plays piano in a Latin band."

"Look at you. You're so proud of him you're glowing."

"I can't help it. He's just a cool kid."

"Can he make a living playing jazz?"

"Someday, maybe. Right now he works as an office temp."

"Sounds like my daughter," Della said. "Abby's a waitress, poised to become an actress."

"That's exciting. Is there a lot of theater where you live?"

"Just summer stock. She lives in New York."

"So far, both my guys still live in Boston. But I think Will's fiancée is getting restless."

Della studied Charlene's face, her taut cheeks, the etched lines around her eyes and mouth. "It's hard to think of you as the mother of grown men."

"Your daughter's the same age you were when I knew you." It wasn't funny but they both laughed.

"What about Abby?" Charlene said. "Anyone serious in the picture?"

"I'd be the last to know. She usually doesn't mention anyone she's seeing until they're ready to break up. Sometimes not even then. I have to pump my sister Rosalind for details."

"Oh yes. Little Rosalind with the red hair."

"Auburn, please."

"How's she doing?"

"Little Rosalind is a big lawyer now. She does intellectual property rights for a fat cat corporation. We see each other a lot. And I've gotten to be close friends with her partner, Anne."

"Oh, she's—" Charlene raised her eyebrows.

"A lesbian? Yes. And completely out about it, so don't bother to be delicate."

"How about your mighty mom? I remember how she used to send you clippings of those letters to the editor she wrote, denouncing the war."

"She's retired now, so she has even more time to set the world straight."

"You know, I kept trying to find you." Charlene's voice dropped. "In the early days. But your mother wasn't in the phone book, and I couldn't remember your aunt's last name."

"My mother always has an unlisted number. She thinks it will make it harder for Big Brother to find her."

"Well, it didn't help Little Sistah much either," said Charlene. "I thought about calling every Brown in the book, but do you know how many Browns there are?"

"Too bad I don't have an exotic name, like Johnson."

She laughed. "Even I traded that one in. How come you didn't change your name when you got married?"

"I did, but I changed it back after the divorce."

Charlene savored a sip of her milkshake. "Well, at least you can't hide from the Internet."

Della looked through the restaurant's large window. Outside, time appeared to have speeded up. People in dark coats bustled past, half of them on the phone. She imagined the air shimmering with electronic signals. She wondered what in the world they could all be talking about. No one stopped to see the long shadows of trees reaching for one another. No one noticed the homeless woman standing near the corner with her excellent posture and her trembling cup.

Inside the restaurant, time was suspended, waiting for the past to catch up. Della couldn't tell if they had been there minutes or hours. It occurred to her that Charlene might have to leave before Della could bring herself to say what she needed to tell her.

She gripped the edge of the table. "When I got your letter, Charlene, it kind of knocked me off balance."

"You said that on the phone, but I wasn't sure what you meant."

"All this news about Afghanistan and Iraq and war. And then I hear from you, out of the blue. It just… unleashed everything. I've even started having nightmares again."

"What kind of nightmares?"

Was it possible Charlene didn't know? "The usual. Blood, death. Leftover body parts after a mass-cal. Remember that?"

"I'll never forget." Charlene shivered.

"Then I had a flashback at work that really scared me." Della peered down at the table top. The gray formica was lightly threaded with red, like capillaries. "I never had one before. Have you?"

"No."

"Charlene, all I wanted was to put the war behind me. I thought I could let the years pile up and bury it."

"I can imagine how well that worked," she said.

They were practically whispering. "It got me through the day."

"Sounds like the nights were a different story." Charlene pushed aside her glass. "I haven't talked about the war either, not in years. But maybe that was wrong. Maybe we should have talked about it all the time, to everyone."

"No one wanted to hear it."

"We should have made them hear it. Because we're starting it all over again in Iraq."

"I know."

"Anyway, I sure as hell want to talk about it now," said Charlene. "I want to grab all those politicians and get right up in their faces and make them understand what it is they're doing."

"Do you think that would change anything?"

"No." Charlene bit her lower lip. "It's not their kids who will go. Even if there's a draft, they'll find a way to keep their own children safe."

"Why would there be a draft?"

"There aren't enough poor, brown-skinned kids to recruit for a worldwide war like this could turn into. And you better watch your daughter, Della, because this time they'll snatch up the girls too."

Her stomach clenched. "They'll never draft women."

"Sure they will. We never got an Equal Rights Amendment, but mark my words, we'll get an equal opportunity draft if they need more soldiers."

"Honestly, Charlene, you sound like you're channeling my mother."

"It's not a conspiracy theory, it's simple demographics. Our generation didn't have enough kids to feed a big war. Take a look at us, Della. We each had only half the number of children our parents had."

"Don't blame me. I always wanted—"

"—Three children," Charlene said with her. "I remember. What happened?"

"Miscarriages."

Charlene fell silent for a moment. "Well, chalk up another one for Vietnam."

"What do you mean?" asked Della.

"I mean dioxin. Agent Orange. You must know it causes all kinds of reproductive problems."

"Yes, of course. But we weren't exposed to it. Cu Chi was defoliated way before we got there. It was mainly the guys in the bush who got sprayed."

"And who cut the uniforms off them when they were wounded? Who bathed them?"

"Jesus! I never thought of that."

"I'm sorry." Charlene rested her warm hand on Della's arm. "Don't think about it that way. There's no point. It's just that ... " She reached for her water glass. Della felt the air grow slack around her.

"Della, do you like science fiction?"

"What?"

"My boys used to watch these sci-fi movies," said Charlene. "They all had the same plot. Someone decides to bring back a creature from outer space. Everyone's excited about what the creature can do, how we can harness its powers. There's always one person who's been to the creature's planet and seen the destruction it caused. That person desperately tries to warn people, but no one will listen.

"Now that everyone's all excited about Iraq, I feel like I'm trapped inside that movie. And Della, you might be the only one I can talk to."

"That's exactly how I feel."

It was as if Charlene had broken open Della's ribcage. Della breathed fully for the first time in years. She could have wept with relief. But she had to warn Charlene, make sure she knew who she was dealing with.

"Charlene, that girl you knew? The one who was so ... " What was it Della had been? Trusting? Open-hearted? *Young*? "That girl never made it back from Vietnam."

Charlene nodded slowly. "Maybe girls like us weren't meant to survive."

"But what if that was the real me?" Della was truly whispering now.

"It wasn't." She waved a hand around them. "This is all real."

"But what if that was the best of me? What if everything I've given since then—to my child, my family, my work—what if that was just the leftovers?"

Charlene didn't reply. They both knew it could be true, almost certainly had to be true.

"Della, do you remember the golden hour?" asked Charlene.

"Of course." Every nurse knew that the treatment a patient received during the first hour after an injury could mean the difference between life and death.

"No, I mean our golden hour."

"Oh. I remember that, too." She and Charlene used to meet immediately after their shifts to talk each other down from the adrenaline buzz that gripped them after twelve hours of hectic, bloody work.

"That golden hour saved my life more than once," Della said.

"Same here," said Charlene. "It was like morphine. Made you forget all the pain and craziness."

"Sometimes we laughed like we were high, too."

"That was the best part, the laughing. You know, I've often thought if the Army had given us that golden hour after we got back from Vietnam, it would have made the rest of our lives so much easier."

"Is that why you wrote to me?" Della asked.

"I think it is," said Charlene with a pang of wonder in her voice. "I think I wrote to see if I can reclaim that golden hour with you. Because maybe then I can feel all the way healed."

"You know what? I think that's why I came here too."

Charlene reached for her jacket and pulled a suede wallet out of her pocket. "So what are your plans for this evening?" she asked.

So that was it. It was over. Della wasn't sure what had happened, and it took her a moment to find her voice. "Well, at some point I should check into my hotel."

"Better cancel that." Charlene flipped open a cell phone. "I think you'd better come back to my hooch. We've got some things to talk about."

CHAPTER 21

CHARLENE'S HOOCH turned out to be a two-story townhouse with shining wood floors and soaring ceilings. In the entryway, Della admired the intricate crown molding and wondered how Charlene kept it dusted. "You didn't tell me you were rich."

"I told you my husband was a surgeon." Charlene picked up Della's bag. "I'll put this in the guest room. Have a seat in there." She waved toward a doorway.

Della stepped into the room and loved it instantly. A large bay window overlooked the street. Built-in bookshelves lined the other three walls, filled with colorful volumes interspersed with baskets and ceramic pots in varied sizes and designs. A shapely black grand piano with a raised lid took up one end of the room, while a hunter green couch and two matching squishy chairs beckoned from in front of the window.

She touched the smooth wood of the piano and picked up a framed photograph. A younger Charlene stood in the surf, wearing cutoff jeans and an untucked white blouse. She was laughing, her head thrown back, her arm around the neck of a burly man with a big mustache and a bigger grin, who was pretending to throw her into the water.

"Is this your husband?" Della asked. Charlene came up close behind her and peered over her shoulder. Her scent had changed over the years, Della noticed. The musk of sandalwood was gone, replaced by something fresh and subtle that Della couldn't name.

"Yep, that's Arthur," said Charlene. "Wearing a baseball cap as usual, to hide his hairline. And men think we're vain."

"Will I meet him tonight?"

"He's at a medical conference in Honolulu, poor baby." Charlene reached over Della's shoulder and turned another photograph toward her. "These are my boys."

"Handsome."

"They take after their daddy."

"What are you talking about? Will looks just like you."

"A little bit, maybe, around the eyes." She nudged the photo back into place. "Della, how about a glass of wine?"

"I don't drink anymore."

"Now I know you're an imposter." Charlene stepped back and leaned on the piano, her arms crossed. "How did that happen?"

"I got drunk the day my freedom bird landed, and I stayed that way for the next few years. Missed most of the Nixon administration."

"A wise decision."

"Then the hospital I worked for started an amnesty program. Any employee could come in for help, no questions asked. I didn't want to end up killing a patient, so I came in. I've been sober ever since."

"Good for you, Della. Do you go to meetings and all that?"

"I did for the first several years, but after a while I didn't feel I needed it anymore. By then I'd been in AA longer than I'd been drinking. It's different for me than for a lot of alcoholics, I think. Of course, every alcoholic says that."

"What makes it different?"

"I never associated drinking with good times," said Della. "I associate it with ... well, you know. You were tossing them back with me."

"Then what are you drinking these days?" asked Charlene.

"Diet soda. Gallons of it."

"Coming right up. Will you mind if I imbibe?"

"Not at all."

Della stood at the window with her hands behind her back, watching a young man bounce his bicycle up the front steps of the apartment building across the street. He paused on the deep stone stoop, pushed the front door open and wheeled the bike inside. She wondered how many flights he would have to carry it. The sidewalk emptied as people hurried home to make dinner or prepare for a night out. Fog seemed to swirl in from the unseen ocean, dragging the dusk behind it.

"So." Charlene handed her a glass. "I guess we don't want to drink to old times."

"Old friends, then."

"That'll work." Charlene sat on the couch, patting the seat beside her. She slipped off her shoes and dropped them on the soft Oriental rug. "Listen, I'm sorry I didn't invite you to stay here from the beginning. I thought it would be best to see how we got along."

"That makes sense. I'm just glad you wanted to see me at all."

"I'm the one who wrote to you, remember?"

"I know. But I was worried that when it came right down to it, you might find you don't want to dredge up a lot of memories." Della gulped her soda. There was much more she wanted to say, but the familiar parched feeling scraped at her throat.

"You asked me about something at the restaurant," Charlene said, "and I want to tell you about it now. I need to get it over with."

"William," said Della.

She gave a curt nod. "When I first got home, I was in a daze. William came home a couple of days later. They gave him back to us in a gray metal casket. We could only open the top part, to see his face. Della, he looked like a babydoll, his face was so smooth and young. I know he must have died in agony. I don't see how they got him to look so peaceful."

Della wished she had something comforting to say, but there were no words for such a moment.

"I didn't cry at his funeral," Charlene went on. "It was the strangest thing. There I was in my dress uniform, standing next to my little brother's casket, and not even a sniffle. My family must have thought I was a monster."

"You were just numb," Della said.

"Stunned, I think. And kind of—not there. And you know what else? I felt cheated."

"Cheated how?"

"Coming up in those days, a black girl under Jim Crow, you'd think I'd have gotten used to it. You get locked out, slapped down, ripped off so many times in so many ways." Charlene looked beyond her, to a past Della had imagined but couldn't share. "But when it happened this time, I was shocked. I had joined the Army to keep William safe. And they took him anyway! I couldn't stop replaying it in my head: everything my recruiter had said, all the lies they told us in basic. As if I could get them to take it all back if I could pinpoint exactly where I'd been scammed."

"And after all that, you still had another year to serve," Della recalled.

Charlene nodded. "They had me working in an operating room at the VA hospital in Atlanta," she said. "That whole year it was like I wasn't human anymore, I was made of some kind of dull rubber. I did my job and that was it. My family lived in dread, waiting for another brother to get drafted. Finally at the end of '71 they changed the law so the Army couldn't take the brothers of a combat casualty. By then my hitch was up."

"So you went back to civilian life."

"I went to graduate school. And after a while I began to feel things again." Charlene smiled with one corner of her mouth. "Big mistake."

"I can imagine." Della put her drink on the coffee table, a thick slab of glass with rough sea-green edges. It seemed important somehow to set it down silently.

"Everything made me cry," Charlene said. "It was ridiculous. I'd be listening to the car radio, and I'd have to pull over to the side of the road and sob—and this would be a commercial jingle that set me off."

"Could you talk to anyone, any of your friends at school?"

"Are you kidding? Those college kids could hardly hide their contempt that my brother had been killed in Vietnam. I wasn't about to put my business out on the street. And that's when I tried to find your number. I remembered how I used to wake you up to talk in the middle of the night and you never got mad. It began to seem like you were the only person I *could* talk to. It made me feel so frantic, Della. I knew you were out there but I couldn't reach you."

Della touched Charlene's wrist briefly. "When the war ended," Charlene said quietly, "everyone tried to forget about it as fast as they could, and so did I. But I couldn't do it. I went to the local vet center, but they didn't have anything for women, and the guys there couldn't care less about a woman's problems."

"Our brothers in arms," said Della. "I had the same experience."

"Well, I'll bet none of them had been wounded," Charlene said, "or they would have felt differently about nurses."

"Maybe." But Della thought they must at least have had friends who were wounded. Although who knows, maybe men don't tell each other about those times when they lean on the strength of women.

"When I met Arthur, he was finally someone I could talk to," said Charlene. "He didn't understand, exactly, because he hadn't been there. But he knew how to listen."

"It's funny how rare that is."

"That's for sure." Charlene took in a long, shaky breath and let it out slowly. She sank back against the firm green cushions and let her eyes close for a second. Then she smiled. "Hey, I'm getting hungry. Are you ready for some dinner?" Her voice sounded lighter, brighter.

"I don't want to put you to any trouble."

"It's less trouble than sitting here starving. Come on."

Charlene's kitchen was the opposite of cozy: there was not a soft surface to be found. The floor was slate, the appliances brushed stainless steel, the cabinets made of a sleek, reddish wood with slim matching handles. The long window behind the sink was uncurtained. Yet Della felt sheltered there.

"I made a salad earlier today," said Charlene, "and it'll only take a couple of minutes to whip up some pasta. Are you still a vegetarian?" She filled a heavy pot with water, set it on the burner, shook in some salt. She moved with purpose, as though it was a relief to perform these familiar domestic actions. "You're the only person I've ever heard of who made it through Vietnam without eating any protein."

"I ate lots of peanut butter and pizza."

"Not to mention all the insect life that got into our food." Charlene handed her a salad bowl from the refrigerator.

"Well, that first week in Vietnam cured me of meat-eating for good," said Della.

"Then I guess there are a lot of cows and chickens out there who should be very grateful to Robert McNamara."

They dined at the metal table and talked about everyday things: children, work, families. Della told Charlene about finding her father and losing him again. "Hey, has your dad recovered from all his war wounds?" Della asked.

"What?"

"Don't you remember how we told all the patients that our fathers had gotten the same kind of injury back in World War II? 'Of course girls will still like you. My dad lost his legs, too, and it didn't stop my mom.'"

"Oh, Lord, I'd forgotten all about that." Charlene laughed. "My poor daddy. I must have amputated all his limbs and his nose too in those stories."

"At least it reassured the guys that they might still have a social life."

"Which reminds me," said Charlene. "Why aren't you dating?"

"You married women never understand." Della reached for another dollop of spaghetti sauce. "It's a desert out there."

"Even in my gilded cage, I've heard the rumor that there's a shortage of good men."

"It's a fact. But I haven't given up hope. Not completely."

"Don't you miss sex?"

"Sure. But it's more than that." Della kept her eyes on the rattan placemat. "What I miss most is the touching. Being held. My skin gets lonely."

"Not your heart?"

"Well, you used to be a nurse. You know it's all connected."

After dinner Charlene put on the kettle. Della picked up a teacup and examined it. Thin white porcelain, dotted with rows of dimples so delicate she could see the pink of her finger through them. Hard to believe such a thing could stand up to human lips, much less boiling water. Could this be Charlene's everyday crockery, or had she brought out the wedding china for their reunion? Neither seemed likely. Della set down the cup carefully, longing for a sturdy mug from her own kitchen.

Charlene poured in the tea with no particular gentleness. It smelled like tender young plants and the souring snows of winter. Della was surprised to see that the tea was not a pale green but a deep, rich red. Charlene set the steaming cups, napkins, and a plate of ginger snaps onto a black wooden tray, and led the way back into the piano room.

"Tell me about this flashback you had," she said, reaching for a cup. "What did it feel like?"

"Awful. Like living in two worlds at once. I was at work, and at the same time I was back there. It was all completely realistic—sights, sounds, smells, everything. You know it can't really be happening, but it sure feels like it is." Della looked at her closely. "You've never had anything like that?"

"Not exactly," Charlene said slowly. "I do have these images in my head, but I've learned to live with them. It took me a long time, though."

"How did you learn that?"

"I had some help, including a good therapist. I had someone at home who would listen. Mostly I played the piano. It's like a form of meditation for me." Charlene crossed her long legs. "The other thing is, I had kind of a marker."

"A marker?"

"My brother William. He was always younger than I was, obviously. Then he was younger than the kids I went to graduate school with. Soon he was younger than the music students I taught. And before long he was younger than my own children. I kept looking back, and William kept getting smaller and smaller. It reminded me of how far I had traveled."

"I thought I had left it all behind too," Della said, "but apparently not."

"I keep being surprised by how things can surface in midlife. Our kids are grown, our lives are fairly settled—could be it's time to deal with this."

She was right. Without letting herself stop to think, Della blurted, "I have to tell you something, Charlene. One of the things I regret most in my life is letting you down." But that was too easy. She pushed herself to name her offense. "When you learned about William and you sent for me, but I didn't come."

Charlene frowned. A deep vertical line appeared between her brows. "Yes. That hurt."

She waited for Charlene to say more. When she didn't, Della folded one leg under herself and faced Charlene on the couch. She had been craving to tell Charlene this for so long. Why was it such an effort to form the words? Della swallowed some tea and felt the heat race down her limbs.

"Charlene, I'm so sorry. I know how much it hurt you, because the last thing you said to me was that you never wanted to see me again."

Charlene closed her eyes. "You can't imagine how many times I've wished I could go back and erase that." She brushed a hand over her eyes. "Lord, I hope you haven't carted that around all these years."

Della felt her face redden. The curse of being white, Rosalind called it.

"Oh, Della, that wasn't real. I was still in shock. Besides, you didn't know why I wanted you. You were—" Charlene shrugged—

"embracing life. If you could find some comfort in that hellhole, more power to you."

"Yes, but I had 'embraced life' a few times before that, and you never called for me. I should have known it was important," said Della. "You were having the worst moment of your life, and I was off with some man whose name I can't even remember."

"You were there for me through a lot of bad moments that year."

"But I blew the most important one."

"Look, Della, let yourself off the hook. I did, a long time ago. Oh, I hated you at first, I admit it. But it wasn't *you*." She cast her eyes around the room and settled on the coffee table. "I took a tray, and I piled it high with all the things that were awful about that war, and I made you carry it. So maybe I should be apologizing to you."

"I don't think so."

"You made it back to the hooch before I left," Charlene said. "You were exhausted, covered in blood, but you made it. That meant something to me. If I'd had to climb on that bus without anyone there … " She trailed off.

"But you didn't even say goodbye." Della hated the way her voice trembled.

"I didn't need any goodbyes," said Charlene. "I needed a witness."

"To what?"

"I don't know. Maybe to the fact that I was there at all. That I made any kind of a difference."

"Yeah. We all needed a witness for that one."

"All right, then." Charlene smiled at Della, her eyes glistening. "Thanks for being my witness. And I accept your apology."

Her eyes welled up in response. Della reached over to set her tea cup on the glass coffee table, but the edge had turned shimmery and she let go too soon. The white cup hit the rug with a soft *thomp*. Red splattered everywhere. The earth skidded sideways.

"Della!" Charlene was squatting on the floor, blotting the rug with a stack of napkins.

How did she get down there?

"What is it?" Charlene said. "You're white as a ghost."

"That sound. The cup." Della's heart walloped against her chest. Blood pounded in her ears.

"The cup's fine." She held it up. "These things are stronger than they look."

"The stain," she said.

Charlene glanced at the sodden, pinkish napkins in her hand. "Do you have any idea how often my kids have spilled on this rug? Don't worry about it."

"The sound," Della tried again. "When the cup fell. It sounded like the bucket."

"What buck—" Charlene sat back on her heels. "Oh Jesus, the bucket. I haven't thought of that in a thousand years."

"That's what I keep dreaming about."

Now that Charlene understood her, Della was calm. She could breathe again. "A white cup full of blood. It spills and shatters and makes a sound like the bucket."

"That's your recurring nightmare?"

"Yes."

"Mine takes place in a restaurant," Charlene said, her voice a husky whisper. "It's dark in there, lit by a red bulb. There's the smell of *nuac mom*. I walk up to the buffet table and pick up the lid on one of the serving dishes. It's filled with body parts. Hands, knees, eyeballs. All swimming in a soup of blood. There's a big ladle to serve it up. I look down the long buffet table and see an endless line of silver serving dishes."

"Oh, Charlene. That's horrifying." Della hugged herself tightly.

"I've never even told my husband."

"He doesn't know you have nightmares?"

"Oh, he's well aware of that. But I don't tell him the details. Not this one, anyway. I don't want to … expose him to it. But it's safe to tell you anything." She gave Della a bleak smile. "You're already infected."

"Roger that."

She rose slowly. "Let me get rid of this mess."

Della let her head drop back against the couch. Soon Charlene returned with a glass of water for her and a refill of wine for herself.

"I wonder if you'll keep having that dream about the cup now," Charlene said. "Of course there's plenty more where that came from."

To Della it seemed there was no shortage of raw materials. And they were manufacturing a fresh batch of nightmares for a new generation. The kids who went to Iraq would have no way to see the family resemblance between their war and hers. It could take them another thirty years to realize that history would keep replaying the same old songs until someone tore up the music.

"Maybe we'll both stop having nightmares now that things are different," Della said.

"Because we have someone we can tell?"

"And because I finally got a chance to make it right between us."

"If only they were all so easy," said Charlene. "Most of the people I'd like to apologize to are dead."

"Like who?"

"I sure didn't protect William like I was supposed to. And with the patients, I always had the feeling that maybe if I'd tried harder, if I'd been a little less tired or a little more skilled..."

"Exactly."

"There's this one guy I can't stop thinking about," Charlene murmured. "Do you have one like that?"

"A few."

"Mine was a sergeant," Charlene said. "Blond, green eyes, baby-soft hair, around twenty-five years old. He was from Birmingham. The Jeep he was driving had run over a mine. He had been chewed up by shrapnel; his legs were a stew of crushed bone and mashed tissue. I started an IV for fluids. Then I poured irrigation solution over his wounds to see what the hell was going on. There was so much blood and filth it was hard to tell."

"It's amazing we had so few cases of sepsis," Della said, "with the amount of dirt and shrapnel in those wounds."

Charlene's eyes were distant; she had one hand pressed to her throat. "I was popping Kelly clamps on every pumping vessel I could find, but we couldn't control the bleeding. We must have pumped seventy units of blood into this guy, but it just kept pouring out. My uniform was soaked with it. My boots were squishing. He kept looking up at me, with his eyes so wide and terrified, saying, 'Don't let me die, ma'am, please don't let me die.' And of course, I let him die."

"His body was a sieve," Della said. "No one could have saved him."

"I know that."

"Knowing it doesn't help, though, does it?"

Charlene shook her head. "It wasn't until the next day that I realized how strange it sounded to hear a white man from Alabama keep calling me 'ma'am.'" She was quiet for several seconds, her brown eyes large and unblinking. "I can still taste it, you know," she said. "The blood. There was so much of it, even the air tasted like metal."

"My thing is burned flesh," said Della.

"Then there's burned hair."

"That's another good one."

"Della, I always say I don't want to talk about this stuff. And it's true, I don't. But in a way—God, it's such a relief. Do you know what I mean?"

"Absolutely."

"Tell me about yours," Charlene said. "The ones you can't let go of."

"Well, one of them is the guy who got you demoted," said Della. "Remember him?"

"Sweet Jesus, that poor child."

"There's another one who looked a little like Rosalind," Della continued. "Red hair and freckles. He was a double amp, with practically nothing left of his thighs. The night I got him, he was screaming and cursing and crying, disrupting the whole ward. I didn't blame him—here was a kid who had just lost half his body. And if I could have spent some time with him, maybe I could have helped him calm down. But we were so busy that night, I couldn't stay more than a few minutes with any patient. So I gave him Seconal instead of my attention. And by the next night, he was dead."

"But not because you sedated him."

"No, of course not. He had multiple complications. But I keep thinking: those hours I stole from him—for my own convenience— were the last few hours of his life."

They sat cross-legged on the couch, their knees touching. Della felt as if they were resuming a recent conversation.

"After William's funeral, I looked into going back to Vietnam," Charlene said. "I couldn't fit into the World. But I would have had to sign up for another year in country. The Army didn't want to send me back with only a few weeks left on my tour."

"I felt the same way when I got home," Della said, "like I couldn't connect with anyone. I felt that way during my last few weeks in country, too. You were gone, Micky was gone, Mary Grace was gone, Joanne was gone. Then Mac went home. Most of the guys we were tight with had either DEROSed or died. After you left, I just kind of faded away."

"How'd you manage that?"

"I stopped hanging out with people," said Della. "Stopped going to parties and carousing in the O club."

"I know you didn't stop drinking."

"I bought my booze by the bottle and did my drinking alone. Eventually people stopped inviting me to do things. No one dropped by my room to talk. It was fine with me, it was what I wanted. But it also made me feel—" Della hesitated, searching for the right words. "Gone. Like no one could even see me. I became invisible after you left, Charlene, and in a way I've been invisible ever since."

"What do you mean, invisible?"

"Last week I had a patient," Della said, "a woman in her forties. Three of her friends and her ten-year-old daughter sat around her bed. They were bent over, working on a piece of quilting that was spread out on the bed. All I could see was the top of their heads and their silver needles flashing in the light. The daughter was concentrating so hard her little head bobbed with each stitch."

"What was wrong with the mother?" asked Charlene.

"End-stage breast cancer."

"I don't understand. Why were her friends making a quilt?"

"To memorialize her, you know, like the AIDS quilt. They were sewing all sorts of things into it: colorful laces from her running shoes, patches from her favorite shirt, a tiny toy monkey."

"That's a little cold," said Charlene, "working on it right in front of her."

"She wanted them to. She had asked her friends to teach her daughter how to sew, so she could be part of the project."

"Lord." Charlene sucked in her breath. "Talk about facing facts."

"By now that little girl is motherless. The woman's friends are probably making food for the funeral. Someone else is in that hospital bed. And I'm here, alive and healthy. But you want to know something kind of sick? In a way, I envy that woman."

"Why in the world?"

"Because she was known," said Della. "Her friends knew exactly how to represent her. And it made me wonder: who knows me that way?"

"Well, it if was up to me I'd sew in a crossword puzzle, a hemostat, and a can of beer."

"That's what I mean. People look at me and they see a lot of surface things. They see a mother, a daughter, a sister, an ex-wife. They see a nurse. But they don't see me. I've been in hiding too long."

Charlene took both her hands. "I see you, Della. I see you right now. And you *shine*."

Della looked into Charlene's eyes. She knew how famished her own expression must be but she couldn't stop, not quite yet. Finally she squeezed Charlene's hands and let them go. "Play something for me."

"Really? Classical isn't everyone's cup of tea."

"As far as I'm concerned, 'classical' means Martha Reeves and the Vandellas. I just want to hear you play."

Charlene pulled out the piano bench and sat very erect, hands hovering over the keyboard. After a moment she seemed to relax against some comfortable surface, although there was nothing behind her but air. She lowered her hands.

The music began simply but soon beat like blood inside Della's skin. The most extraordinary sounds saturated the room. Della felt herself pressed against the couch by centrifugal forces. She couldn't believe such richness could be created merely by Charlene's long dark fingers darting among the keys.

Charlene played on, her head bent back as if she were following a musical score inked on the sky. The rest of the world faded away. Car doors slamming on the street outside, a distant siren, the troubled past and the ominous future—all of it disappeared. Nothing existed except this moment and the mournful, uplifting music.

Something inside Della gave way, and she was flooded with a lightness that could only be gratitude. An image flashed with perfect clarity behind her closed eyelids: her own red blood, freshly donated, flowing through a plastic tube into the arm of a wounded soldier. He was one of the fortunate ones who would recover, who would go home to live his own remarkable life. Della would never know what happened to him, but she knew that her blood had surged through him, just as Charlene's music was now surging through her.

Neither woman spoke after the music ended. "That was beautiful," Della said finally. "What was it called?"

"It's Beethoven's Sonata Number 8 in C Minor, Opus 13. It's called the *Pathetique*. I played the second section, the adagio."

"How does it feel, to be able to make magic like that?"

"Well, let's see." Charlene's eyes were half-closed. "When I first begin to learn a piece, there's this incredible moment of joy. I read the sheet music, I hear it in my head, and I know I'm about to play something gorgeous. But then, the instant my fingers touch the keys—it's ruined. All I can produce is a clunky, stumbling mess. I can play the part for the left hand or the right. But when I try to play the two parts together, my hands fight with each other. It takes hours of practice until they no longer compete for my attention."

"Sounds like a workout for the corpus callosum," Della said. "You know, that pathway that connects the hemispheres of the brain?"

"Nursing school was a long time ago."

"Go on."

"That's pretty much where I stay for a good while," said Charlene. "Practicing, plodding through the piece, over and over. It's such tedium, I can barely remember the joy. But if I practice enough, suddenly my hands stop warring. Each note plays the next note for me. Each chord cues the next chord. And I find the lovely piece of music that was there all along."

"You said playing the piano was like meditation."

"You can get into a state where you move beyond the level of conscious awareness. I don't mean you're tripping or anything. But you're not consciously saying, 'Okay feet, now press those pedals in time with the hands.' Every part of you is working together—hands, eyes, ears, brain, breath, body. It's like the music is playing you."

"It must be thrilling."

"Yes, and … deeply satisfying. The feeling of the keys on your fingertips. The action of the hammers on the strings, the effect of your foot on the pedals. Everything about the piano feeds some deep human need. Or at least that's how it feels to me." Charlene gave a quick smile. "I hope I'm not sounding too touchy-feely."

"No. I love it." Della looked at her own square, competent hands. "Do you think I could learn to do that?"

"Play the piano?"

"Or maybe the flute." An instrument she could hold, a sound as intimate as breath. "Do you think I could learn, at my age?"

"Of course. You know, science, math, music—it's all related. At our age, it just takes a little longer to absorb, that's all."

Late that night they sprawled on the large bed in the guest room. The walls were an inky blue; the floor was covered with a woven straw mat that had felt surprisingly pleasant to Della's bare feet. On the wall across from the bed hung three large photographs of an underwater scene. The pictures were crowded with tropical fish of exotic hues and shapes—a busy neighborhood under the sea. One bright orange fish stared directly into the camera, its black eyes wide as if taken by surprise, its small mouth a perfect circle. Della felt like an ocean dweller herself, floating and weightless, as she lay on her back under smooth blue sheets.

"Remember how beautiful the night sky was?" Charlene asked drowsily. She lay on her side next to Della, on top of the covers.

"The stars were incredible." Della threaded her fingers behind her head. "Even the firefights were pretty, with those red and green tracer bullets."

"Guess you can find beauty just about anywhere, if you're hungry enough for it," said Charlene. "Della, have you ever run into one of our patients?"

"No, have you?"

"Not that I know of. But I've always wanted to. I have this fantasy that someday, on the subway or in the grocery store or just walking down the street, I'll pass some gray-haired man with a limp and he'll stop and say, 'Hey—you were my nurse!'"

"So he could thank you?" asked Della.

"No, just so I could see for myself that one of them really did make it. That he's got kids who maybe wouldn't be here if we hadn't been there."

"I bet we could track down some of those guys," Della said. "Ben's division has reunions every few years. Maybe the Twenty-Fifth Infantry does too."

"I know we could catch up with some of the nurses," said Charlene. "There's a whole world of women veterans on the Internet. Websites, listservs, all kinds of ways to connect. I discovered it when I was trying to find you."

"Really?" Della's eyes flew open. "Have you found anyone we used to know?"

"Major Throop, of all people."

"Are you sure?"

"Major Ada Throop, retired, Army Nurse Corps. How many of those could there be?"

"I can't believe it. Have you spoken with her?"

"I've been waiting for you. I thought we could email her together, and see if we can contact some of the other nurses. Would you want to?"

"Hell, yes. I'd love it."

Charlene pushed herself upright. "First thing tomorrow, we'll fire up the computer. But for now, my bed is calling. I feel like a washcloth—wrung out. But in a good way."

"How can it feel good to be wrung out?" asked Della.

"Like you've taken something from me that I didn't want and didn't even know I had. You know—emptied, but full." Charlene pressed her lips together. "Am I babbling?"

"I can't tell. I'm too wrung out."

She smiled. "Come get me if you can't sleep."

"Charlene," Della said, stopping her in the doorway. "You don't think it's a little '*pathetique*' that I'm still messed up after all these years?"

"We're both messed up. I'd be scared of anyone who wasn't messed up by what we saw."

"Well, you seem to be hiding it much better."

Charlene sighed. "You do important work. You've raised a child. You've stayed close to your family. You're even friends with your ex, for God's sake. What exactly do you think you should have done better?"

Not let so many of them die. Kept hold of you. Loved my husband as much as my child. Learned to forget.

"It's late," Della said.

"Very." Still she hesitated. "Della, you know those patients we can't let go of? Maybe it's good we carry them around. Maybe it's like a memorial. I try to believe that."

"I'll try too."

Charlene smiled, her eyes soft with sleepiness. "Goodnight, Brown."

"Goodnight, Johnson."

Charlene closed the door and padded down the long hallway. Far away, Della heard water running. For a moment she hated this well-built house, the airy rooms and sturdy walls. She wished Charlene's bed was just inches away, separated by a plywood partition that would deliver all the intimate messages of their nighttime stirrings. As Della sank into sleep, she thought she smelled a gentle whiff of sandalwood.

CHAPTER 22

ON THE MORNING of her mother's death, Della washed the dishes. The dishwasher gaped empty as she sponged the meager cups and saucers of their hurried meal.

Ruthless, she thought. That would be her world from now on. Funny how expecting an event did nothing to prepare you for it.

The kitchen clock pressed out six silver disks of sound. Daylight was still just a hint on the horizon. Rosalind, Anne, and Abby had scattered after breakfast, leaving their chairs awry. There was nothing for any of them to do; Ruth was gone, and no one could call her back. Yet a swell of urgency pushed them all to move faster, faster.

Della jolted awake to the sound of a telephone. It was just a dream, she told herself, rubbing her face. Of course it was: she'd never owned a dishwasher. But the disaster she had conjured was real enough. Why else would the summons of a telephone rip through the peaceful morning of Charlene's house?

Della struggled to sit up. Her bones sagged with doom; the air was heavy with it. When Charlene knocked on her door, Della didn't even flinch.

"For you." In the glow from the hallway, Charlene's face looked as strained as her voice. Stepping into the guest room, she turned on the bright overhead light. Della squinted and reached for the black telephone.

She steeled herself to hear Rosalind utter the inevitable words: "It's Mom." So her mouth opened soundlessly when she held the phone to her ear and found her mother's voice, familiar and gentle.

"Della, dear," said Ruth. "It's Abby."

Anguish twisted through her. She couldn't draw breath. Della hunched over the phone, clutching it with both hands. Charlene sat beside her and pressed a hand on her back.

"It was a car accident, Della. She's alive, but you'd better come home."

"How bad is it?" Her voice was thin and wavery.

"It's serious. I don't know the details."

"Where is she?"

"At Oneida, in the emergency room. Rosalind and Anne are with her. I'm going over as soon as they move her to a room."

"Is she conscious? Is she breathing on her own?"

"I don't know, dear. Rosalind will call you as soon as they know anything."

"Tell Abby I'm coming." Della lunged out of bed, sending the phone clattering to the floor.

Charlene scooped it up. "What's happening?"

"Abby was in an accident." She looked at Charlene, perched on the edge of the bed in silky, forest green pajamas. Della glanced down at herself in her long blue T-shirt, her knees trembling. She felt the room closing in on her, the murky walls, the stifling underwater images. She caught sight of the neon orange fish in the photograph, with its bulging eyes and gasping mouth, and it hit her: the fish was not merely surprised to see a human visitor, it was in fatal shock. As the photographer glided away to find the next shot, the fish must have begun its slow ascent to the sunlight, all its brilliant color draining away until it floated on the surface, just another lump of gray flesh. Della pushed her fists against her eyes.

"How's she doing?" Charlene's voice was steady and calming.

"It's bad. I don't know how bad." Della grabbed her overnight bag and shook clean clothes onto the bed.

The phone rang in Charlene's hand. They locked eyes for a moment as Charlene passed it over.

"Della, did Mom call you?" Rosalind shouted over the din of a crowded room.

She must have been calling from the family waiting area of the hospital. Della had been in that large, dingy room dozens of times, but always as a nurse, there to shepherd a family toward its fate.

"Yes." She leaned against the blue wall. "How's Abby?"

"The doctor said Abby has some cracked ribs and a collapsed lung. She also fractured her … I can't remember what they called it, but it's her thigh bone."

"A broken femur. Jesus." Della glanced at Charlene, but no alarm registered in her face. She must have forgotten that long-bone fractures could be fatal if fat emboli escaped the bone and rode the bloodstream to the lungs.

"Is that serious?" asked Rosalind.

"It can be. What about internal injuries?"

"I'm not sure. They're still checking."

"Rosalind, can she speak?" Charlene slipped out of the room. Della wanted to follow her, but holding herself upright seemed to be the most she could manage.

"Well, not right now," said Rosalind. "She's all drugged up."

"Has she spoken?"

"Yes. They let me in there for a minute and she talked to me."

"What did she say? Exactly?"

"She said, 'Mom's going to kill me. I totally fucked up.'"

"Oh, thank God." Della gave a choking laugh. "If she's scared of me, then her brain's still intact. When did they say they'd transfer her out of the E.R.?"

"Soon."

"Who's her doctor?"

"Um … Goldberg, I think?"

"Okay, she's very good." Della clutched her head. "Oh my God, Rosalind."

"I know."

"Is Ben there?"

"I called him. He's on his way."

"Tell Abby I'll be there soon. Tell her she's not in trouble."

"She's pretty out of it, Della."

"Talk to her, Rozzie. She can hear."

In the bathroom Della glimpsed her stricken expression in the mirror. She wondered if this moment was "before" or "after."

She was dressed and trying to zip her overnight bag with shaking hands when Charlene came back into the room, murmuring into her cell phone. She wore slim black pants and her soft leather jacket.

"Can you take me to the airport, Charlene? I've got to get on a plane. I don't care who they have to bump."

Charlene snapped the phone shut. "I just booked you a seat on the next flight. We'll have to hurry. Leave your bag here to save time at security."

Boston was a brick and glass blur as Charlene's car raced toward the airport. The early morning light was feeble, as if it could easily collapse back into nighttime. "It's like a dream," Della said.

"I know. When your kids are in danger, it always feels unreal." They hurtled through the narrow streets. Charlene's slim hands on the wheel looked relaxed and competent.

"No, I mean it's like the dream I was having just before the phone rang. Only in the dream my mother was dead."

"No one is dead," Charlene said firmly.

Signs for the airport swooped past the car windows. Della crossed her arms over her chest. "God, I feel so … breakable."

"But you won't break. Don't forget how strong you are, Della. Practically indestructible." Charlene pulled to a stop in front of the terminal. "Abby's going to be okay, and so are you."

Della unlatched the seat belt and turned toward her. "Charlene, come with me."

Charlene faced her directly, a full, unwavering look. "I can't. You know that."

"I know."

"But I'll be here when you call," said Charlene. "That's what's different."

During the flight, Della kept her face turned to the small window. The thick plastic was covered with tiny scratches, as if someone had polished it with sandpaper. But Della was not trying to see the view, she was mesmerized by her own horrifying images: Abby shrieking as her ragged femur ripped through the skin; Abby lying shattered and alone in the mangled car.

What was all that crap Della had been spouting to Charlene last night? 'Death's not the enemy. I'm not afraid of death.' What bullshit. Death was the enemy, and Della was nauseated with terror.

If it was her time to die, fine, no problem. But if death came for her daughter—well, there was no way to finish that sentence. Della recalled Ruth, describing the death of her own mother. "A peaceful passage," she always said, "like a setting sun." But Della's grandmother had been elderly and ill. Abby was young and vital, and for her the sun would fall howling out of the sky.

Della couldn't let herself think like that. Here she was, trapped on this slow-moving plane, helpless as a mother, useless as a nurse. If she couldn't control her desperation she would go mad, she would split out of her skin or bash her head through the blurry window.

She forced herself to watch a drop of condensation fight its way up the windowpane. She remembered Charlene expounding during that long flight to Vietnam.

"I'm a healer," that younger, more fiery Charlene had declared. "I'm not here for the war effort, I'm here for the guys. I've got no problem with anyone in Vietnam. No one in Vietnam is telling me where I can live and where I can't. No one in Vietnam is aiming fire hoses at me. No one in Vietnam is planting bombs in churches to help little black girls get to Jesus."

That speech had deeply impressed Della, first because she was so totally without political opinions herself, and second because she had never heard anyone but Ruth sound so riled. Much later she wondered if Charlene had felt differently once she realized that people in Vietnam were in fact trying to kill her, not because of the color of her skin but the color of her uniform.

Charlene's parents would never have let her volunteer for Vietnam if they'd known that. Della thought maybe Charlene's idea was the best: let's draft all the young women. Let them see it firsthand—not the crisp troops parading with their thrilling precision, but the stinking reality of war, the shit and pus and putrid flesh of it. Maybe it would take a nation of women warriors to raise a generation that craved peace.

When Della had treated Vietnamese children at the Twelfth Evac, the patients' families would camp out in the hospital, feeding and caring for their children. Of course, the American families did not have that option. Only once could she recall an American parent visiting his child. The father was a lieutenant colonel stationed in country, and he had roared like something no longer human at the sight of his brain-damaged son, permanently clenched into a fetal position.

How had that man survived the sight? How would Della bear to see her daughter in pain, her eyes sunken, each breath an ache? With a physical pang she remembered cradling Abby, the sweet smell of her, the perfect weight, the soft rounded bundle of trust.

She had mourned that baby for years as Abby grew into a chubby child and lanky teenager. Odd, Della had forgotten all about that: how much she had missed baby Abby even while she adored the growing girl. She wondered if every mother felt the same loss. Maybe that was the natural arc of motherhood: you had to surrender the baby, release the child, set free the young woman until your beloved daughter grew into what she had been all along—a stranger. Someone permanently and infinitely different from yourself.

🍃

At the hospital, Della flew out of the cab and through the familiar wood-paneled lobby. Today she was not a nurse, not an employee, just another parent gulping back panic. Dashing past the lumbering elevator, she took the hard rubber stairs two at a time and emerged breathless on the third floor.

The trauma unit bloomed like a daisy around the nurses' station in the center. Each petal was a small room holding a narrow bed and an array of monitoring equipment; each room was enclosed by a glass wall that faced the nurses' station. Della rushed into Abby's room and had to fight the compulsion to fling herself onto the bed and cover Abby's ravaged body with her own.

Abby lay motionless, a bandage taped to one pale cheek, her long hair strewn across the light green sheets. Clear plastic tubes ferried oxygen from the sighing tank into her flaring nostrils. Protective apparatus surrounded Abby's damaged leg; an oxygen saturation monitor lit up her fingertip. Over the years, Della had seen many family members recoil at the sight of their loved ones tethered to so much machinery. But to her, this was the technology of hope.

She studied the numbers on the electronic monitor that hung over the bed. Abby's blood pressure was a little low, but her heart and pulse rates looked good. Even her saturation rate was a decent 92 percent, meaning that blood and other vital fluids were flowing properly through the body's systems. Della let out a long breath.

In the far corner of the room, Rosalind watched her silently. She sat on a plastic chair on the other side of the bed, a thick legal document that bristled with sticky notes balanced on her knees. Della gave her a quick look of gratitude, then bent over the bed.

A strip of tape secured Abby's IV lines on the back of her hand. Della hoped the nurses hadn't needed to probe; she hoped they had filled a latex glove with warm water, as she did for her patients, and laid it on Abby's skin to help the vein rise. Very gently, she touched Abby's warm cheek. The skin was so soft, so delicate. How had her little girl survived that holocaust of shredded metal and flying glass? Della's legs turned rubbery. In an instant Rosalind was beside her.

"Della, do you want some water?"

"No, I'm okay. It's just a hard thing to look at. Abby can be so tough, you forget how fragile the flesh is."

"She's young and resilient, Della. This will be a story she'll scare her kids with."

"Well, she's scared her mom with it, that's for sure." She turned to her sister. "Do you know anything?"

Rosalind slipped the sheaf of papers into her leather briefcase. "Not much more than I did this morning. They've scheduled surgery on her leg for this afternoon. The doctor is supposed to come by to talk to you."

Della thought of the scars, the months of sliding screws and sideplates. Ben had been worried about the wrong things. There would be no nude scenes for Abby.

"How did it happen?"

"Apparently she was on the road early this morning," said Rosalind, "maybe seven o'clock. At an intersection, a drunk driver smashed into her passenger side."

"What street, where?"

"You know that twisty road behind my house, the one that goes through the woods?"

"The one with hardly any streetlights," Della said. "There's only one intersection on that stretch."

"That's where it happened. A medevac helicopter picked her up. She was lucid enough to have them call me."

"But who called 911? The drunk driver?"

"No, there was a surveyor team working nearby. I guess they're planning to build something on that land."

"What was Abby doing there, at that hour?" Della's brain wasn't working right. Each piece of information took too long to sink in.

"She's seeing someone," said Rosalind. "He lives in that apartment complex off Sanders Road."

"Abby has a boyfriend in Sterling? Why didn't she tell me?"

"Della, she never tells you that stuff. You're her mother. Anyway, I gather it's pretty new."

"Well, thank God for those surveyors. And thank God you could be here." Della looked more closely at Rosalind's drawn face. "You must have been here for hours."

"Anne and I drove here as soon as we got the call. Once Abby was asleep, I left Anne with her and went to pick up Mom. I stopped at your house to get some things you might need." She opened the tall, narrow cabinet next to the bed and handed Della a plastic bag.

Inside Della found her address book, a toothbrush, a pen, the crossword puzzle torn from today's Sunday *New York Times*, and her favorite red sweater. She pulled out the sweater with a quizzical look.

Rosalind shrugged. "I thought it might comfort you."

"That is so sweet. Thanks, Rozzie." Della pushed her arms into the familiar sweater, folding back its stretched, fraying cuffs. "This does help. I can't believe you had the presence of mind to think of all this." She returned the bag to Rosalind. "Where's Ben?"

"He's in the cafeteria, with Anne and your mom."

"Has he seen Abby yet?" Della found herself wishing Anne was in the room with them, bringing her solid, serene presence.

"Yes. She woke a little bit when he was here. She even spoke. She said, 'Daddy, fix your hair.'" Rosalind chuckled. "He did look wild. His hair was sticking out in every direction and his sweatshirt was on backwards. I guess we got him out of bed. Come to think of it, I wonder why she called me instead of her dad."

"Ben tends to panic when it comes to his little girl," Della said. "I guess she knows that about him."

"He is kind of a wreck."

"No wonder." Della stared down at Abby. *If anything happens*, she thought, and clutched the cool metal safety bars that bordered the bed. Who would she be if she were not a mother?

Rosalind came up behind her and wrapped her arms around Della's waist. Della felt her shoulders stiffen.

"Della, breathe. It's going be okay." Rosalind spoke with a quiet authority that surprised her. She supposed this must be how the rest of the world perceived her little sister: strong and capable.

Della closed her eyes and leaned back against her taller, younger sister. After a moment she smiled—at her own resistance, at the comfort that washed through her, at the tingling behind her eyelids. "Maybe she'll be all right," Della murmured. "Maybe it's just a million-dollar wound."

"I don't think it's that bad," Rosalind said, "but if it is, get ready to sue your insurance company."

They stood in silence, watching Abby breathe. Della wished their own strength and health could somehow seep into her.

"In a minute I'll go get Abby's nurse," Della said. "She can tell me everything I need to know." Della touched her daughter's hand again. "Why do you think Abby was leaving her boyfriend's place so early? Did they have a fight?"

"She didn't say."

Della realized this would be only the first in an endless chain of unanswered questions, if anything happened. But nothing was going to happen. She could see for herself: Abby was stable, resting comfortably. Yes, her leg would ache, the cracked ribs would cause misery with each cough, and soon much of her torso would turn into a painful tattoo of mottled purple and green. But the moments of mortal danger were over. Most likely.

She glanced at Rosalind. "Do you want to get something to eat? I'd like some time with Abby." Rosalind gathered her things and edged past Della out the door.

Della slid the chair closer to the narrow bed and sat on the edge. "Mama's here," she said softly. "You're going to be all right, honey. You're safe, you're in the hospital, you're already healing." She stroked the soft skin on the underside of Abby's forearm. Baby skin, not yet toughened by life.

"Mom and Dad are here with you," she continued in a low voice. "The accident wasn't your fault at all, Abby. The other driver was drunk. You just rest now." Della pulled up the lightweight green blanket. "You're going to be fine."

Abby slept, her face unguarded. Listening to her even breathing, Della grew aware of the familiar refrain of medical care: the regular beep of monitors, the hum of fluorescent lights, the electrical purr of smoothly operating equipment, the background chorus of voices and pages in the hallway. She wished she could talk to someone who was as fluent as she was in the cryptic language of hospitals.

Della looked up at the transparent bag that held Abby's IV fluid. The idea of using plastic bags instead of clumsy glass bottles was developed in Vietnam. Now it was standard practice. She studied the small utilitarian room, and her inspection widened to encompass the entire trauma unit. Della hadn't worked in trauma for decades, so it took her a few seconds to place that nagging sense of recognition.

It wasn't déjà vu. The trauma unit was intensely familiar because she knew its ancestor. This model of twenty-first-century care was based directly on lessons learned in Vietnam.

The medevac helicopter that saved Abby's life, the techniques they must have used on her to prevent the complications of trauma, the screening tests for coagulation rates—Della's comrades had pioneered all of these advances in that green and poisoned country. Working on the battlefield, in operating rooms, on medical evacuation flights, during mass casualty emergencies, they invented new science out of desperation.

Della felt her cramped chest expand with relief. Abby would make it. She would pull through because of the medical heritage brought home from Vietnam. But even with her heart swollen by a mother's monstrous love, Della knew no medical breakthroughs could ever be reason enough for the things she had seen. So many thousands could not have died to preserve one person, even if that one meant more to her than all the others combined. No one could live in a world with such brutal arithmetic.

Della had offered herself to war, and it had burnt her to the bone. Now, somewhere deep inside, she sensed that sacrifice finally reaching its destination.

Look at her, Charlene, she declared silently. *Abby is what you've always wanted to see: someone who wouldn't be here if we hadn't been there.*

All the sons she couldn't save—Della felt them now, felt their forgiveness, their generosity toward the future that was lost to them. The loneliness that had sheathed her like skin fell away, leaving her tender and trembling.

No longer was Della alone with her sleeping daughter. The room was filled with women in Army green and Red Cross blue, women in sweat-stained fatigues and bloody scrubs. The women who had died in country from disease or disaster, in enemy fire or at the hands of their countrymen. The women who had come home from Vietnam bearing their own invisible deaths from Agent Orange. The women who had absorbed in one year a lifetime's lessons in grief.

Della's sisters reached through history to save a young woman they would never know, a daughter of war and peace and the purgatory in between.

ACKNOWLEDGMENTS

OVER THE YEARS it took me to write this book, many people have helped me in a variety of ways. Let me thank some of them here.

For reading the novel at several stages of its evolution and sharing your insights, thanks to Tonya Davis, Lynn Jenkins English, Barbara Esstman, Shane Murphy Goldsmith, Pat Holt, Diane Johnson, and Robin Parks. And to Janet Coleman, who in all these years never said, "Are you *ever* going to finish this book?"

A special thank you to Ann Kelsey and Marilyn Knapp Litt, who provided a wealth of information and resources about the war in Vietnam and the women who served there. For sharing her vast knowledge of all things medical and military, as well as her recurring nightmares after two tours in Vietnam, I am grateful to the late Chris Banigan. For their generosity in sharing memories and details about their service in Vietnam, many thanks to the women of In Country Women. I hope I've done you justice.

Jennifer Anderson shared her nursing education with me, Dr. Rebecca Zuurbier provided medical fact-checking (any remaining errors are solely my own), the firm of Nixon Peabody translated legalese, and Annie Karl Halvorsen helped me understand what it feels like to play the piano. Susan Hester and Sandy Douglass turned the launch of Shade Mountain Press into a celebration. Many thanks to you all.

For their help in renaming a major character, thanks to Marjorie Fine, Marvin Randolph, and Michael Alan Weinberg.

Immense gratitude to Rosalie Morales Kearns, a fantastic editor and publisher (not to mention writer), and Robin Parks, whose powerful short story collection was published by Shade Mountain Press shortly before mine. I've had so much fun undertaking this publishing adventure with you.

ABOUT THE AUTHOR

Lynn Kanter is the author of the novels *The Mayor of Heaven* (1997) and *On Lill Street* (1992), both published by Third Side Press. Her short fiction has appeared in the anthologies *Lost Orchard* (SUNY Press), *Breaking Up Is Hard to Do*, and *The Time of Our Lives: Women Write on Sex after 40* (both Crossing Press), and the literary journal *Verbsap*. Her nonfiction has appeared in *Referential Magazine* and the anthologies *Coming Out of Cancer* (Seal Press), *Testimonies* (Alyson Publications), and *Confronting Cancer, Constructing Change* (Third Side Press). She was a founding member of Virago Video, a women's video production company, and wrote the award-winning documentary *Fighting for the Obvious*.

Lynn grew up on the South Side of Chicago, and in her teen years lived in Ohio, Florida, and New York state before moving back to Chicago. She graduated from Kirkland College in upstate New York. She is a lifelong activist for feminist and other progressive causes, and has the T-shirts to prove it.

Since 1992 Lynn has worked as a writer for the Center for Community Change, a national social justice organization. She lives with her wife in Washington, DC.